Undiscovered
Country

Undiscovered Country

LIN ENGER

Little, Brown and Company
New York   Boston   London

Little, Brown and Company
Hachette Book Group USA
237 Park Avenue, New York, NY 10017
Visit our Web site at www.HachetteBookGroupUSA.com

First Edition: July 2008   JUL 1 1 2008

The characters and events in this book are fictitious. Any similarity to real persons, living or dead, is coincidental and not intended by the author.

The excerpt from "Birches" on page 178 is from Robert Frost's *Mountain Interval*, Henry Holt and Company, 1916.

Library of Congress Cataloging-in-Publication Data

Enger, Lin.
    Undiscovered country : a novel / Lin Enger. — 1st ed.
        p. cm.
    ISBN-10: 0-316-00694-7
    ISBN-13: 978-0-316-00694-1
    1. Fathers and sons — Fiction.   2. Family secrets — Fiction.   3. Forgiveness — Fiction.
4. Revenge — Fiction.   5. Minnesota — Fiction.   6. Domestic fiction.   I. Title.
    PS3555.N422U54 2008
    813'.54 — dc22   2007030138

10 9 8 7 6 5 4 3 2 1

RRD-IN

Designed by Paula Russell Szafranski

Printed in the United States of America

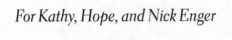

For Kathy, Hope, and Nick Enger

The undiscover'd country, from whose bourn

No traveler returns, —

—HAMLET

Undiscovered Country

As I write this, I'm sitting in the kitchen of the small house where we've lived now for a decade. Evening is closing in, and off to the south the Santa Rosas are beginning to glow a brownish gold. It's my favorite time of day out here — the green of the Joshua trees, the buttermilk stucco, the orange-tile roofs, the ceramic turquoise birdbath in our backyard, everything supercharged, even the faded red of my old Land Cruiser. At my feet Sonny's big black nose rests in a puddle of drool. Every so often he grunts and sighs in his sleep. He's probably swimming in the gold-specked waters of Tahquitz Creek where I used to take him before arthritis set into his shoulders and hips. Or maybe he's chasing down the wood-chucks that burrowed underneath our elm trees back in Battle-point where he spent his first spring.

Sometimes I like to pretend the small town I grew up in exists only in my head and that I have the power to invent a new history for it, my life thus turning out differently than it has — Dad still alive, still mayor, and Mom alive too, content and well adjusted.

It's pleasant to dream that I've made a life for myself back there, teaching English at the community college, as I do here. I imagine my little brother, Magnus, about to finish up at Battlepoint High School instead of the big one out here in this desert valley. It's comforting to think of us surrounded by people who've known us since we were born.

In fact, I don't even want to go back for a visit.

Magnus feels differently. He was only eight when we left, less than half my age at the time, and there's so much he seems not to remember about those years and that place. Battlepoint, I tell him, is the seat of one of the least-populated counties in Minnesota and exceptional only for Crow Lake, whose shoreline it crowds, and for the vast forest of pines surrounding it. The sun rises from the trees and drops back into them. During winter, there are sixteen hours of darkness. In summer, seventeen hours of light.

You remember, don't you? I ask him.

My brother watches me through his black-frame glasses and flicks a wing of blond hair out of his face. He's skeptical. It's a game we play sometimes, one that makes me nervous. *Tell me more*, his eyes say.

And so I explain again how the annual snowfall there is sixty inches, and how by mid-December the lake ice is thick enough to hold the trucks and cars that traffic back and forth between the access in town and the ragtag village of fish houses on the two-mile bar. I offer him tales of deer hunting. I describe the cold shock of jumping off the dock in mid-April, just days after the ice has gone out of the lake. I try to make him understand the peculiar heat of the northern sun in July and how it causes the earth to sweat beneath your feet. Sometimes these little stories and geography lessons are enough for Magnus. Other times, late at night, the two of us sitting up over strong black coffee, our voices sounding haunted and hollow in the dark, they're not.

No, he'll say then, tell me about us. By which he means, *Our family: explain to me what happened to it.* And he'll lean forward and drum the table with his sturdy fingers, reminding me of Dad.

Moments like this I have little choice but to give him more of what he wants, a fuller accounting, to put forward the narrative to which he belongs. The problem is, whenever I try to spin it out for him like that, explain to him what happened, how we ended up out here and why there's no good reason to go back, I find myself sanitizing things and leaving others out completely. Lying to him. You have to understand, I'm more of a father to Magnus than a brother — and isn't it only right for parents to try to protect their children?

Yes, I tell myself, just as it's right in due course to level with them. And that, finally, is what I mean to do.

I

IN THE WOODS

1

This first part, I have to warn you, is ugly, and for too long now I've been carrying it alone, going to sleep on it at night and then waking in the dark, my T-shirt soaked through, the images and sounds playing out in my head, even as I tell myself it's just a dream, there's nothing I can do, it's over and done.

Imagine it with me:

Gray dusk, mid-November, the north woods of Minnesota. You're up in a tree, a red maple whose leaves have all dropped, and all around you the late-autumn woods are stirring in preparation for sleep — squirrels barking in descant, a pair of ground sparrows wrestling in the moist, dead leaves, an owl sliding past and fastening itself to the upper branch of a dead spruce thirty feet away. There's still a chance the deer you've been waiting for will show itself, but that's unlikely now and it doesn't matter, because in the silence you've discovered your eyes and your ears and, best of all, your own company, on which someday you'll have to rely.

In other words, you're learning to trust yourself.

I was perched that day cross-legged on a small wooden platform eight or so feet off the ground, my lever-action .30-30 resting in my lap. My hands were so cold and numb that I couldn't persuade them to pluck my watch from the bottom of my ammo pocket where it lay among a dozen unspent brass cartridges. With effort I maneuvered my fingers through zippers and wool and wedged them into my armpits to thaw. They felt like little frozen breakfast sausages, like nothing that belonged to me. When I could move them again, I fished out my watch by its broken band. Five twenty-two, it said. Just a few minutes more of legal shooting time, and then I'd be climbing down from my perch and making my way across the quarter-mile ridge to the old hairy white pine where my dad was sitting, and together the two of us would hike to the car, parked out of sight in the high brown ditchgrass.

For as long as I could remember I had been Dad's pal, his shadow, his right-hand man. I fished and hunted with him. I worked alongside him on his fix-up projects — installing wooden booths in his supper club, the Valhalla, sanding the floors of the ex-governor's old lake-home the year we bought it and moved in there, constructing a sauna in its attic. I hammered, painted, mea-sured, pried and stapled. I tore things down and built them up. There was never a time when I was embarrassed to be seen with my dad, never any real awkwardness between us — though if there had been, I guess it wouldn't matter now. If only I could just close my eyes and will myself back to that day, climb into that tree, grab hold of my collar and yank myself to my feet, say, *Go, man, go now — hurry,* and then watch that skinny young kid that was me vault out of his deer stand and race through the woods to save his dad, whom he loved. Whom I loved. The problem is, I didn't know he needed saving. And anyway, I'm stuck with how it actually happened, the breeze stiffening out of the northeast, chilling my back and carrying with it the smell of winter coming.

As I watched the sun's pink top falling beneath the treeline, I imagined how good it was going to feel getting thawed out. I imagined Dad and myself in the old hunting car, a giant twenty-year-old Mercury, saw him listen, pleased, to the little revs he produced with his foot, saw him reach into his pocket and throw me a candy bar before spreading his fat grizzly-bear hand in front of the vent to check for heat.

At five thirty I dropped my watch back into my ammo pocket. Then, with my thumb poised to eject the cartridges from my rifle, I heard the single report. Even considering the heavy growth of trees between us, it should have been louder, but that doesn't explain the immediate feeling I had that something was wrong. I thought of Mom at home with Magnus, pictured her at the kitchen window, lovely but taut-faced, the last of the sun chroming her platinum hair.

Guns, she'd always say during hunting season, shaking her head. Years ago she had allowed Dad to teach her how to use his rifle — she'd even gone out into the woods with him a few times. But apparently that was an indulgence from early in the marriage.

I slid to the edge of my flat wooden perch, flipped over on my belly and scrambled down the crude ladder of boards we'd nailed to the maple's trunk. From four or five feet up I jumped, and my knees jammed my chest on impact. I ran. Against all training and good sense, I ran with a loaded rifle through the woods, knowing I should wait for the second shot, the kill shot, before moving, knowing I should stop and unload. I sprinted along the top of the ridge, ducking the shaggy branches of the white pines, stumbling through clumps of red willow and then down the steep slope into the marsh where I crashed through cattails and high-stepped the ice-crusted muck. At the other side, on the edge of a five-acre cluster of white pine and birch, I paused. My heart was going hard, pushing blood out to my fingertips, which tingled, warm. Dad's stand was only forty yards ahead, nailed seven feet up in a dying white pine, but I couldn't see it or him. The sun had gone under by now, and a dirty blue darkness was rising from the forest floor.

Dad! I called, and then moved forward again. I felt my heart beating in my neck and tried to quicken my pace, but then I tripped on a tree root, a long naked thing my eyes picked up only as it hooked my booted toe.

Okay, I said out loud. I got back on my feet, relieved my gun hadn't discharged, and tried to calm myself, slow my breathing. And it was then, just after I'd unloaded my rifle, that I saw him. For a moment I thought he was hiding from me back there behind the rotting trunk of the tipped-over birch tree, waiting to leap up and scare me. But next I saw his orange hunting cap ten feet away, hooked on the branch of a wild caragana, and then I saw his right eye staring past me into the woods — and then I saw where the top of his head should have been.

From the eyebrows up, he was simply gone, poof, blown away. Yet in spite of his ruined head, in spite of the way his right leg was tucked back under him at an angle he never could have managed, I felt certain that he was going to sit up and laugh, reassure me, *It's all right, Jesse, everything's okay,* because according to him everything always was.

2

I don't know how long I stood there. I don't remember if I bent down to check for a pulse or if I laid my bare hand on his leather-gloved one that rested so peacefully on his chest, above his heart. I do know this: I can close my eyes and see him distinctly, in color. He was on his side, head resting on his right arm, which was stretched out straight and pointing toward the base of the tree from which he'd fallen. His rifle lay next to him, the ugly mouth of the barrel on his shoulder. The hood of his old khaki hunting coat had flopped open on the ground beneath him, and sticking out of the inner pocket of his blaze-orange vest, which had been unzipped and lay open, was a Baby Ruth candy bar. One leg was bent gracelessly beneath him, and his right eye stared past me into the trees, through the trees, actually, and into the deepening night, and through it too, far beyond anything. You can't imagine the distance I saw in that blue eye. The other one had slipped back into his head, and all that showed of it was a bit of white in a bloody corner.

How could you do this to us? I thought.

In high-velocity rifle wounds — especially those in which the barrel of the gun, when discharged, is close to the head or touching it — the gas produced by combustion follows the bullet into the cranium, which then explodes under pressure. I've made a point of learning the physics of this, of being able to explain to myself why there was so much damage, why there was no forehead remaining, no head whatsoever above the ears and eyebrows, only a ragged lip of bone and flesh surrounding a bowl that held a profane, incomprehensible matter, red, black and pink.

Like I said, I don't remember what I did when I found him, but what happened next I remember too well: running north down the darkening gravel road through the first-arriving slant of snowflakes, toward the Hansen farm a mile away, this instead of reaching into Dad's pocket for the keys to the Mercury and driving into town for help, which would have made more sense. I remember the scraping, burning pain in my lungs and the fire number at the end of the Hansen driveway, one zero zero three, saying that out loud to myself, then pausing on the rotten planks of their front step and sucking air. You'd think I would have crashed in, yelling for a phone, but instead I waited a little while, commanding my breathing to slow. Then I knocked, firmly but not too hard. Immediately I heard movement inside. The muscles in my calves and thighs convulsed. A light snapped on, then Jake Hansen was squinting and shaking his head, his nose an inch behind the glass.

It's Jesse Matson, I said. I need to make a phone call.

He shoved the door open, his green eyes watching me sideways, buck teeth clamped nervously on his bottom lip. He was two years younger than I was, small for his age, a mouthy kid. Tonight, though, he was quiet, his narrow head tilted to one side, as if he'd never laid eyes on me but knew I'd come here for the purpose of doing him harm.

I need your phone, I repeated.

Why? Jake asked.

I couldn't bring myself to tell him why. Maybe it was the humility of a death belonging to me. Maybe I'd begun to doubt my wits. In any case, I stared at Jake and he stared back, his face as pale and bland as a dinner plate.

Something's wrong, I said finally, pointing toward the woods, toward Dad.

Jake lifted an arm, not just a hand but the whole arm, as if it were a two-by-four, and aimed it toward a long vertical door next to the refrigerator. I walked over and swung it open, finding there on a small shelf above the hanging broom a black rotary phone. I inserted my finger into the nine hole, spun the dial clockwise and watched it spin back around. Then I dialed one, twice, quickly.

A woman came on the line, her soft voice asking if I needed help. It was no use sending an ambulance, I told her. He was already dead. I explained to her where I was and recited the Hansens' fire number: one zero zero three. For a moment she was silent. When she started speaking again, her voice was even quieter.

You need to stay put, and everything will be all right, okay? I want you to sit there — you're sitting down, aren't you? — and just listen to me. We're going to talk for a while, you and I. Okay? I want you to tell me about yourself.

Her whisper brought to mind a gingham apron and tortoise-shell glasses, a stout, flour-dusted woman in a church basement.

Didn't you hear me? I said.

Shhh, please. It's going to be all right. I'm not going anywhere, and you aren't either. Tell me now, what year in school are you?

Jake appeared with a blue plastic tumbler full of water, holding it out to me, and I hung up on the woman's whispering voice and accepted the glass, which felt cool in my fingers. I sat down at the table. Jake sat down too and set about watching me, his ears protruding from his skull like two small satellite dishes.

How, I wonder at times, does he remember that night? I hope he's satisfied with how he handled himself. For years I've been meaning to find his phone number and give him a call, apologize, tell him thanks, but somehow I never get around to it.

I drank the water and watched pink splotches spread on Jake Hansen's face and neck. Neither of us spoke. I felt beaten up, numb. I tried to block the stream of images crowding my mind, my little brother's face, smashed and crumpled with grief, and Mom's too, flattened into nothing.

Who's going to tell them? I thought.

Wafers of snow tapped against the kitchen window.

I couldn't help but remember a photograph we had. I still have it, in fact. It's of all of us, taken during a camping trip to Lake Winnipeg. The print quality is poor, ghost images and blurred lines. We're looking into the camera, our faces buoyant and glistening. At Mom's request, the woman from the next tent had snapped it after her family and ours had combined our resources for a picnic — hamburgers and bratwurst grilled over a woodfire. Afterward we'd played volleyball on the beach, and I remember Dad grunting and laughing, throwing his heavy body around, clumsy and fast at the same time. Mom was sleek, nimble — she leaped and dove and swatted that striped beachball like a kid. She was still doing summer-stock theater then, still clinging, probably, to her dream of moving to Minneapolis and finding better roles and big-city acclamation.

Now, though, sitting in the Hansens' kitchen, what I recalled about the photograph was the protective way Dad held on to us, arms all-encompassing, as if there were nothing in the world that could pull us away from him.

Or him from us.

Dr. Milius was the first to arrive, coming quietly into the kitchen, sitting down across the table from me and putting a warm hand on one of my knotted fists. Though he said nothing, his steadiness leaked into me like a small electrical charge. A short man with a yellowing white beard that reached to his chest, he was the doctor who had delivered me seventeen years before, given me penicillin shots in the butt for ear infections and physical exams for cross-country. *Turn your head. Cough.* I didn't think of him as flesh and blood, but as some kind of gnome who existed solely for our benefit and that of the town. That night, of course, he was there in his role as county coroner, not as medical doctor.

Do you think you can lead us back out there, Jesse? he asked, finally. Help us find him?

He got up and came around to where I sat, and I jammed my ear against his heart, which was beating slow and steady, like the bass drum in a funeral march. The material substance of him and his vaguely sour scent reminded me of Dad.

You're in shock, he said. But you'll get through this. I promise.

I will?

He took me by the shoulders, held me at arm's length and looked into my eyes.

Minutes later when the sirens came, I followed him to the door where I saw snow falling like ticker tape. Then Battlepoint Hospital's rattletrap ambulance came rolling up the driveway, the sheriff's black Jeep right behind it — and all around the perimeter of the farm a red storm of lights, flashing and beating against the pines.

Sheriff Stone gave me a pair of gloves — his own, I think, large black leather ones — and insisted that I wear them. I'll crank the heater, he said as he put me in the backseat of the Jeep with Dr. Milius. Get you warmed up.

He was wearing his red-fox-fur hat, which for some reason struck me as ludicrous. I think I laughed. Then he gunned the engine and brought us surging out of the Hansens' yard, and it occurred to me that Mom wasn't here and should be.

Sheriff Stone had tried to find her, of course, but as it happened she was in the maternity ward of the hospital that night. She'd dropped Magnus off at a friend's and was sitting through labor with a young neighbor of ours, LuAnn Parker, whose trucker husband was broken-down someplace in Texas. At about one in the morning, when Mom finally got the news, her heart slipped into a bad rhythm, alternately stalling and leaping in her chest.

Magnus and I didn't see her until late the next morning at the hospital, where they'd kept her overnight after stabilizing her heart. She didn't look good at all, and that's saying a lot. Mom was in her middle thirties and still gorgeous. There was a luster and delicacy about her, a perfect arrangement of perfect parts, as if any little thing might throw it off. But that morning she was worn-out, her skin stretched across her nose and cheeks, her lake-blue eyes bulging. Magnus ran to her, climbed up on the bed and curled against her. I moved forward and touched her shoulder, which felt like a child's, birdlike and vulnerable. For a while we stayed like that, the three of us, silent, hardly breathing. Then she shifted herself around to comfort my brother as he cried. He was a big boy for eight years old, square-faced and barrel-chested like Dad, a small Viking in black plastic glasses. His quiet sobs shook the whole bed.

As I watched Mom take his head in her hands and let her small fingers roam through his stiff hair, I was suddenly angry, my stomach burning with it. I wanted to be there on the bed *with* them. I wanted her hands on *my* head too, her fingers in *my* hair. But she made no move to draw me in, and so I stood there feeling huge and awkward, my body out of scale with theirs. Then she looked up at me, and I couldn't help myself.

You should've been the one to find him, not me, I said to her. It's not fair. You wouldn't be lying there, looking at me like that.

Her eyes darted toward Magnus, whose head was tucked into the crook of her neck.

We'll talk later, she whispered.

You don't have a clue. You don't get it.

Magnus lifted his head, and Mom pulled him back close. She said, Bring up a chair, Jesse. Right here, and sit down.

I forced myself to breathe. My hands felt clammy and my lungs tight. Magnus was peering at me, blinking through the lenses of his glasses, which were fogged like a windshield, his thin lips clamped in a firm line. I took a chair from the other side of the room and brought it next to the bed.

Breathe, I told myself.

Why did you get so sick? Magnus said to Mom. What happened to your heart? What made it start going funny like that?

Things like that just happen sometimes, sweetie. But they gave me some pills, and I'll be okay now. No need to worry.

In fact, I'd already spoken with Dr. Milius — or he'd spoken with me, pulling me aside and telling me that Mom had experienced a cardiac arrhythmia. It shouldn't threaten her health, he said, eyes blinking, serious. That is, with proper treatment. We need to stay on top of it.

The doctor on call had used a procedure called cardioversion to even out her rhythm, and this morning Dr. Milius had prescribed digoxin to regulate her heart rate, and Halcion to make sure she got the sleep she needed.

I've got to make sure she takes care of herself, he told me.

I felt like saying, *It's about time.* I doubted if he knew how little Mom slept or how for the last few years she'd isolated herself in her room for a day or two every month, door closed and shades drawn, old rock tunes thumping from the radio as she gathered herself for another go at the world. Dr. Milius had delivered her children, immunized us against disease, and doctored our sore throats and coughs. What more was he supposed to do? Not even Dad had been able to save her from her periodic funks, though I wondered sometimes how hard he had tried. His habit, whenever Mom retreated, was to put on a determined cheerfulness and wait her out.

Listen, she said, pushing herself up straight in bed. From now on, it's going to be our job to take care of each other, and that's what we'll do. Her voice was small and tenuous, her lips chapped and white, skull hollowed out at the temples. The tone of her voice was thin and lacked conviction — as if she were auditioning for a part halfheartedly.

Breathe.

Don't worry, Magnus said then. I think they made a mistake. I'm pretty sure of it. I think Dad's going to be okay.

The rage flared in my stomach again — at my brother for thinking what he'd just said and at myself for half believing him, but mostly at Dad for leaving. I willed him to come back, to walk into the room right now. In my head I made a picture of myself pounding his chest and face, and saw him dropping to his knees in pain on the yellow tile floor.

Say, Mom said. She reached out to the bed stand for the glass of water there and handed it to Magnus. This is getting warm. Could you run down the hall and fill it up at that cold fountain for me? The silver one across from the nurse's desk?

My little brother took the glass and left. Watching him go, I felt my stomach rise, anticipating some confidence from Mom, or at least an acknowledgment of what I'd seen. But she only looked at me dead-eyed and opened up her arms. For a few moments I let her hold me, but then I had to push myself free so that I could speak. The words wouldn't stay in my mouth.

You wouldn't believe what he looked like, I said. How could he do that to me? Didn't he know I'd be the one to find him? Didn't he think of that?

Mom cut me off, her hands darting to my face, the tips of her fingers pressing against my mouth.

Mom, I can see him, right in here, I said, knocking my forehead with my fist. I'll never be able to get rid of it.

She covered her eyes with her hands and shook her head, stranding me there on my chair, alone. A minute later, when Magnus came back with the water, my uncle was right behind him, boots clapping neat little double beats on the floor. Clay had always reminded me of a gunfighter out of a Western movie, his long mane prematurely gray, black mustache untrimmed and drooping. He always seemed more certain of himself than his situation warranted, but today he was a mess. His mouth jumped into a smile, then flattened out. I'd never seen him look so solemn, so confused, not even at his wife's funeral a couple of years before.

He bent down and hugged me with one arm, a sinewy shoulder pressing into my neck. I smelled the cologne he always wore too much of, musky and sharp. He stepped to the side of Mom's bed, picked up one of her pale hands and held it.

She pulled her hand away and slipped it beneath a fold in the green bedspread.

Clay took a chair from the side of the room and pulled it up next to me. He rubbed his eyes with the heels of his hands and propped an ankle on one knee. He had on the silver-toed boots he wore when he was playing bass in whatever mediocre rock-and-roll band he happened to be in at the time. Mom rearranged herself against her pillow and drew Magnus closer to her, wrapped an arm around his chest.

You know how much I loved him, Clay said. My big brother! I mean, how many times was he there for me? He glanced in my direction, eyes muddy and red-rimmed, as if they'd gone wandering on their own last night through smoke and fire and only just now returned. He looked back at Mom. Listen, he said. I was thinking. Maybe I could help out at the Valhalla for a while. Do the books, make out the schedule, whatever. After work I could go over and spend the evening — if my band's not playing. Stick around till it's time to lock up. Keep things on an even keel.

Mom shook her head, eyes closed. That's good of you, Clay, but I already called Rich and Marly and told them we're closing up till after Christmas. I called Ernie at the bank too. It's just too much to think about right now. The restaurant'll have to wait.

I want to help, Genevieve. Any way I can. I hope you know that.

She rested the side of her face against Magnus's coarse blond hair and nodded.

Clay's smile flashed again and disappeared. By the time he left a few minutes later, taking Magnus with him, anger twisted inside me like a blade, carving out a hollow nausea. I willed myself not to get sick.

We don't need his help, I said.

You're sure of that? Mom asked.

He's probably *glad* Dad's dead.

Jesse. Listen to yourself.

Think about it.

I will *not* think about it. Please, don't be crazy.

She raised a hand against me, her palm flat like a traffic cop's, and I got up and walked out of the room. What complicated things for Mom was the fact that she had dated Clay in high school, this of course before she had fallen for Dad, who was fond of pointing out that he'd rescued her from his little brother.

Don't be smug, Mom liked to say. If I'd married Clay, maybe he'd be the mayor in the family. Or, with his looks, governor.

It was a good-humored shot, and Dad never seemed to take offense. In fact, this part of family history was a source of amusement — even for Clay, who sent Mom nonanniversary cards and joked about prenup deal breakers. Until now, there had been no reason to give it any thought.

In the hospital chapel, with its pine-paneled walls and dozen folding chairs, I tried to sort out the chaos in my head. If there were anything like fairness in the world, Dad would be the one still living, and my uncle would be gone. The younger of the two by three years, Clay had already racked up a lifetime of bad luck and bad karma. He hadn't married until he was past thirty, and before that he'd had a long series of girlfriends and a longer one of jobs. When I was young, I'd get up in the morning sometimes and find him asleep on our living room couch, kicked out or evicted. Having him around wasn't terrible, but I did resent the attention he required. Suppertime conversations always focused on him — his narrated adventures of life on the road with a weekend bar band, his latest jilting — and then Dad would head back to the restaurant while Clay stayed on, taking advantage of Mom's ear and enduring her lectures. She treated him like a son and seemed to believe his long run of hard luck made him deserving of our sympathy. I wasn't sure I agreed.

Things didn't change much when Clay got married to Marnie Primrose and moved with her into the lakeside farm where she'd grown up. They fought like spoiled teenagers, and every time she locked him out, he came and stayed with us. Two years of that, then Marnie died of cancer.

I need to point out that all this while, as Clay's fortunes mostly fell, Dad's rose. He leveraged his way into a dead restaurant and made it the best in town. He purchased and resuscitated the ex-governor's summer home, a rock-and-timber two-story rich in mice and nightmare plumbing. And then on top of it all, he got himself elected mayor. I never really considered whether Clay was bitter over his brother's success, because the two always seemed to get along fine.

During the final year of Dad's life, however, things between them got rocky. What happened was that Dad tied his reelection for mayor to a plan that would use the unprecedented budget surplus to put up thirty or so inexpensive houses, which would then be sold with no down payment to low-income families. He wanted to make things better for the influx of Latino workers who'd been recruited by the town's new turkey-processing plant. So far, so good. The trouble was, his proposal had the new homes going up on the present site of the trailer park — Little Mexico, people called it — where most of the new turkey-plant workers lived, and where Clay was employed as manager, a job that, ironically, Dad had pulled strings to get for him.

I remember the night he announced his proposal to the town council. Clay had gotten wind of what was going on, and he was there in the meeting room on the second floor of city hall, sitting at the back, stroking his mustache. Dad laid things out with his usual rhetorical flair, peering over the top of the plastic half-glasses he'd bought at the drugstore after first getting elected. A debate ensued between Dad and those who wanted to use the surplus for other things — a straight-out rebate or a new community center, for instance. I think Dad was surprised by the resistance he ran into. In any case, when the meeting was over he and I walked to the rear of the building, stepped into the old service elevator and rode down to the alley, where we found Clay waiting for us in the dark, leaning against the driver's door of the Mercury. An unpleasant smile split the bottom of his face.

You're looking pleased with yourself, he said.

Not on purpose. Dad shook his head.

Nobody elected you king, Harold. That's something you want to remember.

The pale yellow floodlight above us threw into high relief the permanent half-marble lump on Clay's forehead, the result of an accident years ago when the ancient bus of the band he was in at the time had lost a wheel and plowed into a freeway sign at seventy miles per hour. It was the only flaw in his handsome face. He lifted a boot and kicked at the dirt, shifted himself against the door of our car. Hard as he tried to be imposing, next to Dad's girth, my uncle looked scrawny and underfed.

You give any thought yet to what'll happen to *me* if you get your development? Look, Harold, I need this job. Can't you see? For the first time in my life, things are going all right. I've been there two years.

Dad reached into his pocket and pulled out his car keys.

There's always some way to keep me down, isn't there, Clay said.

Hey, who got you the job in the first place? Dad countered. He reached up and laid a hand on Clay's shoulder. Then he gave me a look, and I went around to the passenger side and popped the door.

Come on over to the restaurant in the morning, I heard Dad say. I'll pour the coffee.

By the time I was settled in the passenger seat, Clay had stepped away from the car and stood flat-footed on the dirt lot, arms hanging at his sides. Dad climbed in behind the wheel, the weight of him rocking the old boat on its springs. He put the key in the ignition and fired the engine and gunned it a couple of times. When it fell back to a smooth idle, he cranked down the window and slung an elbow over the side.

Genevieve told me she had a chance to hear this new band you're putting together. Over at the Galaxy. Said you sounded real good.

Yeah? Clay's shoulders straightened a little. I think this might be it. I really do. We're into original stuff, not just covers. Who knows?

That's great, Dad said.

He threw the transmission into reverse, backed into the alley and jammed the shift lever into drive, the rear end clanking. He spun the wheel, and the big front end came around, headlights sweeping over his brother, who hauled one long arm up from where it was hanging and managed an awkward wave good-bye.

3

I put on my hooded gray sweatshirt and nylon running pants, my navy watch cap, my running shoes and finally my buckskin gloves, and then I headed south toward downtown. The sky was low and damp, the temperature hovering around the freezing mark — not all that cold, but I could feel ice crystals ticking against my face as I ran. That afternoon Dr. Milius had come to the hospital to explain that his preliminary findings suggested suicide. Official cause of death, however, would be determined by the state coroner in St. Paul, where Dad's body had already been sent.

At the Valhalla I let myself in with my key and stood for a few minutes next to the glass case that housed Dad's Viking battle-ax. The smells of the place were familiar to me, and I found them comforting now — the heavily oiled wood, the candle smoke scented with vanilla, the odor of fry grease. I stepped into the dining room. He'd finished everything in dark-stained oak: the high-backed booths, the tables and chairs, the paneled walls and ceiling.

A medieval Viking hall had been the motif he was trying for. He used to say, *People want to get away, Jesse, they want to feel like they've been somewhere,* and in fact I think many of his customers did feel that way. I remember women unbuttoning the tops of their blouses and touching their throats, slipping their feet from their shoes. Men rolling up their sleeves and flexing the muscles of their forearms. And me, watching from the kitchen or my dish cart and thinking, *Dream on.*

It was a relief to be out of the house. I'd had all the reality I could take for a while — all the crying, all the dull stares. I simply couldn't hang around any longer watching Mom's perfect face come apart. Worse, I felt drained, sucked dry by Magnus, who all day had been watching me as if there were something I was holding back, some revelation that would save us from the broken world we'd stumbled into.

I moved into the lobby and stood just far enough from the window to avoid being seen. Headlights of cars swept over me as they turned from Second onto Main. The yellow caution light flashed at the intersection. Then, like the fragment of a lovely dream, Christine Montez came walking down the sidewalk with her cousin Theresa. I stepped back, out of the light. Christine said something I couldn't make out, then paused to admire herself in the window. She leaned close, turning to examine the line of her jaw, fingering a small blemish there. Not for the first time, she reminded me of a painting that hung above the desk in Dad's basement office at home, of an olive-skinned, barefoot Madonna, her hair dark and loose, arms bare to the elbows, ringed fingers slender, provocative, baby Jesus in her lap, his cheeks and limbs carnally plump. Even as a child I'd been drawn to that painting. It triggered feelings — pleasant and disturbing both — that I didn't understand, and whenever I sneaked downstairs to stare at it, I worried that someone might find me out.

The year before, Christine and I had been photo-lab partners during a journalism unit in English class, and for a single week, an hour each day, we worked silently beneath the dim red darkroom lamp — making contact sheets, navigating the enlarger, and bathing our prints in the chemical baths where the latent images emerged and clarified as if summoned by our whims. On the last day I surprised myself by touching her. She was at the enlarger, fine-tuning the focus on a negative of her baby sister, when I moved close and put my fingers on the small of her waist. She didn't flinch or speak but simply turned to face me. All I had to do was lean forward.

A simple kiss is all it was. It didn't lead to another or even to conversation, but for weeks afterward we searched each other's eyes in the hallways and classrooms at school, waiting — or at least I was — for the word or phrase that would conjure that moment in the darkroom. I didn't know what my next move should be. Something, some fear, paralyzed me. Maybe it was how she looked, the black targets of her eyes, her mouthwatering lips, her compact body. I couldn't imagine that somebody as ordinary-looking as I was could be a match for her. Or maybe it was our separate places in the community — there wasn't a lot of intermingling between the white kids and the ones who lived in Little Mexico. More than anything, though, I think I was scared on account of her dad, who was doing time in prison for nearly killing a man. My friend Charlie Blue's mother, Diane, had been there in the bowling alley when it happened, and the way she described it, Daniel Montez had overheard Rudy Foss telling a Mexican joke to a couple of his pals and gone after all three of them. Rudy, son of Councilman Bull Foss, was the one who hadn't gotten away.

In any case, I kept my distance, and Christine did too.

Come on, I heard her say now. Movie starts in two minutes.

Through the plate-glass window I watched as she took a final assessment, caught one last angle of her face in the glass. Then she was gone. Three blocks away the electronic bells of Pastor Lundberg's church started tolling.

My usual route was back and forth through the residential streets of town, but tonight for some reason I retraced my steps north to our street, Lake, and followed it east all the way out past the swimming beach on Battlepoint, the long spit of land for which the town was named. I'd been running since eighth grade and loved the soaring sensation I got when I reached a point beyond tired and something else kicked in. Not only that, I liked the break from human contact.

Tonight that's what I needed.

For more than a mile Lake Street ran parallel to the Burlington Northern line, and just past town's edge was a double bridge, where both the road and the rail tracks passed over Boy River. The channel wasn't wide, probably twenty yards, but in that place the flow had cut a deep cleft in the edge of a glacial moraine. In spring when the water ran high, kids jumped in on dares. More than one had miscalculated and died on the rocks below.

I was halfway across when I noticed Dwayne Primrose on the tracks to my right, moving with that unforgettable stride of his, puppet legs swinging, each step covering an amazing distance, arms pressed flat to his sides. He had on his denim coat with the dirty sheepskin collar and his signature mittens, pink and hand-knit — children's mittens, outsized. He was about thirty-five and

lived in a tiny apartment on the second floor of the Valhalla building. At the risk of putting too sharp a point on it, I'll add here that
he was the town dimwit. Socially handicapped might be a better
way to put it. Possibly just pure of heart. He was the brother of
Clay's dead wife, Marnie, and Clay watched out for him — helped
him with his shopping, chauffeured him around town, made certain he had enough food in his refrigerator. I'd seen him on these
tracks many times. This was the route he followed to the house
where Clay lived, the house Primrose himself had grown up in
and that his sister, Marnie, had inherited from their parents, and
Clay from her when she died.

I waved as I ran by him but didn't realize he'd seen me until I'd
gone another dozen strides and heard him call out, Jesse! in that
high-pitched, atonal voice of his. I turned and came jogging back.
He'd crossed over and was stepping down off the tracks, moving
in his unhurried way through dead weeds and grass to the edge of
the road. We met on its gravel shoulder.

Hey, I said.

His lips were puckering and unpuckering, as they often did.
Just wondering, he said. Did you know a cornet's the same length
as a trumpet?

Primrose had been a trumpet player in high school, as I was
now, and so we had that in common.

No, I told him. It's shorter.

It only looks that way. They're the same. But the cornet's got
two or three bends in the tubing before it reaches the valves, and
the trumpet's only got one. That makes the cornet *look* shorter.
He spoke in an odd mechanical drone, as if he'd put everything to
memory and practiced it before a mirror.

I started to run in place, lifting my knees high. I better go, I said. It's getting cold.

Mine's a cornet. Yours is a trumpet. And they're both the same length, even if it doesn't look like it. If they weren't, they wouldn't be in the same key.

He reached out and took my shoulder in the tips of his fingers, a gentle yet firm grip, then pushed his face close to mine and whispered, What happened, Jesse? You were there.

His eyes were moist — confused, I thought — and I smelled onions on his breath. I lifted my knees higher and tried to back away, but he held on to my shoulder.

There's going to be a ruling, I told him. The state coroner's the one that decides.

I'm sorry, Primrose said. I'm sorry. His lips twitched and steam left his nose in two white lines. I shrugged out of his grip and backed away, then turned and headed west, back toward town. Glancing over my shoulder, I saw him standing in place, his narrow body leaning like a frail tree in the wind.

I wasn't tired yet, or ready to go home, so I ran back again on Lake, right on past our house to the other edge of town, then north past Little Mexico and the turkey plant. At the intersection of County 20, I angled by the junkyard, where the bent, crushed and twisted cars were stacked higher than the wooden fence built to hide them. Off to my right, the whole time, lay Crow Lake. It wasn't a cold night but felt so because of the dampness. Clouds hung like tattered bedsheets among the treetops. I moved without strain — no need to connive my legs into keeping pace. I ran light and smooth, a low buzzing heat prickling against the inside layer of my clothes.

Before I'd even thought of turning back I came to the place where the hardtop ended and the road narrowed to a gravel trail, a change I registered through the soles of my shoes. Trees rose up on both sides of me, but I could see where they thinned out ahead, and then soon, off to my right, the wrought-iron gate at the entrance to Sawmill Cemetery. I glanced at the stones: high ones and small ones, crosses, obelisks. I ran on past and kept going, still not tired. I could have run all night — there was no labor in my breathing, the air going in and out of my lungs, my limbs comfortably warm, my feet lifting and touching, my arms pumping in a cadence that was close to perfect. I started to experiment, closing my eyes and running blind for five, ten strides, my sense of direction absolute. Then fifteen, twenty strides, blind, unaware of the ground beneath my feet, free of the earth, and able — for a few moments, anyway — to look back with a tenderness that was almost painful on everything I'd left behind.

By ten that night Mom was in her own bed, propped against the headboard and staring at the TV, which I'd lugged into her room and planted on the dresser. Forty-five minutes ago I'd given her the Halcion Dr. Milius had prescribed, two of the little powder-blue tablets instead of the one he had indicated, and now I watched the surface of her eyes glaze over. She started blinking, eyelids fleshy and slow, then tried to smile but managed only a twitch at the corner of her mouth. Another couple of minutes and she nodded gravely and tipped over like a bag of flour on a pantry shelf. Half an hour later, after spiking Magnus's cocoa with a half tablet of the Halcion, I was on my way over to my friend Charlie's house.

I would have walked except the temperature was dropping and I couldn't bear the thought of letting any of the cold inside me, knowing now what it meant. I drove the Mercury, fishtailing down Lake Street, thumping through pillowdrifts and holding my breath to keep from frosting up the windshield. Charlie lived four blocks east of us, next to the city park, in a small rambler attached to the bait shop that his dad had operated until a few years ago, when for no apparent reason he'd hanged himself from a branch of the giant elm in his backyard. Now his widow ran the place. Diane.

She was the one who came to the door — in fact she opened it before I'd lifted a hand to knock. She waved me inside, standing back and watching me cautiously, as if trying to gauge how I'd changed. Then she grabbed me and hugged me hard, squeezed me in her skinny arms and cried, her tears hot on my neck.

I'll just let you boys talk, she said, stepping back. I'm up early, you know.

Charlie had appeared out of his bedroom, and she laid a hand on his shoulder, looked from him to me, and shook her head. He led me through the breezeway and out into the bait shop, where he plugged in the five-gallon coffeemaker that his mom kept filled at all times. He lit a cigarette, then offered me one from his pack. For once, I accepted.

His eyes gleamed, and I thought he might cry. Instead, he laid his cigarette on the side of a minnow tank and danced toward me in a boxer's shuffle. He jabbed me in the chest with a left hand — hard enough to rock me back on my heels.

Remember? he asked, and jabbed at me again.

I stepped back, throwing a combination in return, but didn't have any heart for it. After his dad died, he and I had gone on a boxing spree. Every day after school, his house or mine. He'd come after me like a maniac, fists like pistons, all over me at once, and there was nothing for me to do but to fend him off until finally I'd get mad and fight back. It seemed to help him, take his mind off things. Tonight, though, I couldn't find any impulse in that direction, any energy for a fight. He dismissed it all with a wave and slumped down in one of the ladder-back chairs they kept for the old-timers who liked to come in and tell stories. I pulled up a chair too, and we sat there next to the smelly fish tanks and smoked cigarettes and drank coffee.

It's too weird, he said. I saw your dad as this guy that had it all together.

He was.

Hell, yes, Charlie said.

I mean, you can't fake a whole life, can you? I asked.

Charlie leaned back and drew down hard, the end of his cigarette glowing bright. He blew a line of smoke rings, *puh, puh, puh.*

I told him what it was like finding Dad in the woods, what the bullet had done to his head, how I'd gone running for help. I told him about Mom's heart and explained that we'd decided to shut down the Valhalla until after Christmas. Charlie studied me hard, his tongue flashing out from time to time to moisten the scar at the corner of his mouth where he'd been snagged by his dad's fishhook when he was six. They'd been casting Dardevles off their dock for northerns when one of his dad's big treble hooks had caught Charlie and pulled right on through, leaving a one-inch tear. The scar had whitened over the years, though in cold weather it flared up bright red and swelled.

But *you* didn't see it coming either, right? I asked. I mean, with your dad.

Hey, I was thirteen, what did I know about anything? Uh-uh.

Zip. It was unbelievable. It was like the worst plot from the worst novel from the schlockiest hack-writer you can imagine.

Charlie had become a big reader after his dad died. When he wasn't in school or helping his mother, he sequestered himself in his room, smoking, his head in a book. Of the two of us, he's the one you would have expected to become the English teacher. Not me.

But *Mom*, he said, talk about tormenting yourself. Ever since then, it's all this shit we should've noticed but didn't. Like he had a major case of depression and we were idiots for not doing anything about it. Maybe she's right. We've got to find some excuse for him, don't we? For what he did to us?

I guess. Otherwise how can you forgive him?

Charlie laughed. You're a funny guy, Jesse.

What else are you going to do? I asked.

You wanna know?

I nodded.

Hold it against him forever is what I'm gonna do. Every night, you know what I tell him in my heart? Burn. In. Hell.

I always liked your dad, I said.

Me too, said Charlie. The son of a bitch.

We talked most of the night, and to Charlie's credit he didn't try to tell me things would get better. Mostly, he listened. Yet there was something about him that bothered me that night. It was the way his lips kept slipping into the tiniest smile and the scar puckered at the corner of his mouth. *Now you know what it's like*, he seemed to be telling me. *Now we're the same, you and me.*

At about five o'clock, time for his mom to come out and open the shop for morning business, I stood up from my chair, put on

my blanket-lined canvas hunting coat and leaned across the minnow tank to set my coffee mug on the counter. That's when I felt
something crinkle at my right side, up against my ribs. I reached
into the pocket of my coat and came up with a Baby Ruth candy
bar, which I held up beneath the buzzing fluorescent bulbs suspended above the minnow tanks.

Hungry? Charlie asked.

Dad loved these, I said.

I had no memory, and still don't, of bending down and slipping the candy bar from Dad's pocket as he lay on the floor of the
woods — but that's surely what I must have done. Carefully now I
tucked it back into my pocket and told Charlie I had to go home.

I don't want to be gone when Mom wakes up, I said. The last
thing she needs is another scare.

Outside, there was no morning in the trees yet. It was absolute
dark and aching cold, with a north wind hard off the water. The
lake wanted to freeze up solid but wasn't able to, riled as it was,
clanking and chiming. I drove with my left hand on the wheel,
my right in my coat pocket. With my fingertips I brushed at the
smooth wrapper of the candy bar.

I went on past our place and made a loop through downtown,
then retraced my route east past Charlie's to the public beach on
Battlepoint. I parked in the gravel lot and sat for a while, watching
the extravagant water and listening to the ice. On summer nights
Dad and I had often come here after a day of shingling or sanding
floors or painting, especially during those first years in the Lake
Street house when he and I had pretty much restored it from the
ground up. Sometimes we didn't even bother to change into our
swimsuits — we'd just climb into the Mercury, drive out to the beach
and plunge right in wearing our dusty, sweaty clothes. Dad always

hit the water first. He'd kick off his shoes and run down across the sand in that rolling gait of his, bearlike, rocking back and forth, then splash in up to his thighs and launch himself in a whale flop.

This morning, though, the lake wasn't inviting. It looked angry, bent on killing somebody. I let the engine idle and sat for maybe fifteen minutes watching the waves and, not far above them, the windblown, ragged clouds. I was tired, beat, absolutely wasted — two nights without sleep and not at all sure it would come even now.

I was trying to decide whether to stay a little longer and eat the Baby Ruth bar or go on home to bed, when I saw him in the black water. He was thirty yards out, at the far reach of my headlights, chest-deep, arms afloat on either side of him, hands rising and falling on the waves and the plates of ice. He was still wearing his blaze-orange vest. The hood of his hunting coat flapping about his head — now, as I remember it — brings to mind a monk in flight from some secret order. He tottered straight for me into the glare, lurching as he entered the shallows, one leg splayed to the side. At the front of the Mercury he reached out and touched the chrome hood ornament with the tips of his bloated fingers, tentatively, as if he expected an electric shock. I popped open the door and stepped from the car. I could smell the sharp cordite stink of gunpowder and also the beeswax he used on his hunting boots.

What are you doing? I asked.

The sound of my voice straightened his shoulders. Then the canvas hood of his coat blew free, and I saw in the headlights that his face was like a burned-out building, blackened at the windows and caved in on itself. His right eye was a luminous blue grape, red-veined, bewildered. It blinked at me suspiciously. The other had disappeared somewhere behind its empty socket. Odd as it might seem, I wasn't surprised or frightened. He was my dad, after all, and I'd spent part of every day of my life with him. And because he'd left so unexpectedly, it seemed fitting that he should come back to explain himself. I was angry, though. Furious. I wanted to scream in his face. I wanted to shoot him, kill him again. Who did he think he was, ripping my life apart and stomping on it?

He spoke then, and there was no mistaking the sound of his voice, which had never been suitable for the man he was. It was a voice that made you wonder if he'd stuck something up his nose when he was a kid, a bean or a little pink pencil eraser, and forgotten it in there. My anger melted, against my will.

I'm lost, Dad said. Can you help me? He looked me up and down, as though he'd seen me someplace but couldn't remember when or where. His face held a concentrated darkness: heavy, dense, compact.

My impulse was to jump back into the car and drive off, but I couldn't move. My legs felt heavy, as if they were filled with sand.

You're so beautiful, he said. Then he started coughing, lake water rattling in his lungs. When I stepped forward and pounded his back, I was surprised at how solid his flesh was. I let my hand linger on his shoulder, which was soaked through and ice-cold. He finally straightened himself and scrutinized my face, his grape-blue eye blinking and glimmering as if things were beginning to clarify for him. He looked all around: at his old green hunting car, at the clouds above us dragging their misty tails, at the wild lake and the shattered ice tumbling ashore.

Everything... God in heaven, everything's so lovely! His voice was breathless. His lips trembled.

Again I had the urge to get away, to put distance between us, but Dad reached out and took my elbow. The strength in his fingers was uncanny — my arm went numb at his touch.

I didn't shoot myself, he said. You have to believe me.

He tried to laugh but it broke off in his throat. He let go of me and made fists with both hands and brought them up beneath his chin. A spasm or seizure took hold of him, twisting his face to one side, and when it left he spoke again, his eye fixed on me in horror, as if *I* were the ghost. His fingers covered both sides of his face, jowl to cheekbone.

I was sitting there on my stand, listening to the wind, he said. I was thinking about climbing down and going home, and that's when I felt him there behind me. I swiveled around on my butt, and he put the end of the barrel on my forehead, right here. I can still feel it. It's so cold. So cold. All he said to me was, *Sorry, Harold* — nothing else, and then he sent me away. I didn't want to leave, Jesse. I loved it here, I loved my life.

Like a balloon on a string, the image of my uncle's face bobbed up in front of me. I said, Clay? Clay?

Every good thing I had was a knife in his heart, Dad said. And now look at me. I wasn't ready for this, Jesse. I wasn't ready. None of us were.

Dad turned and peered off to the east, where a break in the clouds revealed the moon, three-quarters full and nearly down. It rested gingerly on the pointed tops of the pine trees.

I have to leave, he said.

To go where? I asked him.

He opened his mouth, covered his face with his hands and shuddered. From between his fingers his remaining eye glimmered at me like a bright blue ring.

Listen, Jesse! You can't allow this to stand. You can't let him do this, do you hear me? There's no one else, just you.

The words cracked and scraped from his throat.

And don't tell your mother, he whispered. Not about this, not about him. Do you understand? It wouldn't be safe.

I nodded to show I was listening.

Dad lifted an arm and pointed past me, toward something on the beach.

I turned and saw a deer, fifty yards off. A doe, mature and well formed, probably four or five years old. As I watched, she stepped lightly toward the water and lowered her head to drink. Then a wave tumbled in, ice laden, and she jumped back and spun around, white tail flicking, and disappeared up the shoreline into the trees.

I turned back to Dad but he was gone.

Behind the wheel of the Mercury once more, I peered out across the water but couldn't see him — there was nothing but waves and ice, the scudding clouds.

What was happening to me? My head felt like the bowling ball Dad had once dropped — for no reason other than to see what would happen — from his bedroom window onto the sidewalk. It didn't bounce at all but just hit the concrete and stayed there, absorbing the impact within itself. I'd gone forty-eight hours now without sleep. Maybe I wasn't crazy at all. Maybe I was only tired.

Except I knew he'd been here. I *knew* I'd seen him — as clearly as I could see myself now in the rearview mirror. And I believed what he'd said to me was true. Which raised a hell of a problem. What was I supposed to *do*? What did he *expect* me to do? Take my .30-30 and go out to Clay's place and blow him away? Shoot him like he'd shot Dad? I tried to imagine that: knocking on the door of his house, then setting the end of the barrel against his forehead the moment he opened up, and just pulling the trigger. Or hiding in the lilac hedge and picking him off when he came out to get the mail or walk down to the barn. I needed to go and talk to Sheriff Stone, of course — but what would I tell him? That my *dad* had paid me a visit? How long would it take that piece of information to get back to my uncle? No, I'd have to play it smart somehow, come at things from the side, from behind, roundabout.

The deep ache in my brain was like nothing I'd ever felt before. It made me want to drive the Mercury straight into the water — back off and take a running start, then just motor right in and let the icy water flood the interior. And then my lungs. What we want and what we do are different things, though, separated by conscience or fear, and so instead, I started the engine, shifted into reverse and eased the Mercury back, away from the lake, then drove on home, where I sat in the driveway for ten or fifteen minutes — maybe an hour, I don't know — trying to absorb the fact that my life was over, that through no fault of mine I had lost my dad and then been handed the burden of that loss — to carry, redress, expiate, or avenge. Which?

I had no idea.

Now, a decade later, sitting at this sun-drenched table, I still don't know how to convey the enormity of that moment, the challenge of simply getting up out of the car and walking to the house. It was like an insurmountable physical ordeal had been laid before me, as if I'd been given a large stone, the size of a man's fist, say, and ordered to swallow it. And I knew I'd have to do it somehow, get my mouth and throat around it, reduce my existence to a black, airless, choking nightmare that would end only when the stone passed through, changing me — for the worse, maybe, but changing me nonetheless. I got up out of the car and moved toward the house, still me, but older.

Inside, listening through Mom's door, I heard the radio beside her bed going softly, some seventies band, Led Zeppelin, I think. Lots of guitar, a screeching voice. I pushed the door open and peered inside. Light from the streetlamp showed me she was dressed and lying on top of the bedspread, her hands folded on her stomach. I cleared my throat. She didn't say anything. The air felt warm and dense.

Mom, can we talk? I asked. My eyeballs were dry and throbbing in their sockets, my hands and feet numb.

She took a breath and rolled onto her side, away from me. I remembered Dad's words, the last thing he had said — *And don't tell your mother, it wouldn't be safe.* I wondered what he'd meant. What had she done? How was she culpable? Or maybe she was innocent, and Dad was trying to protect her.

We haven't talked yet, I said, meaning, *We haven't talked about Dad.*

She groaned as though I'd asked her to endure some torture for a cause she didn't believe in. She said, I'm too tired, Jesse. Please, I have to sleep. You have no idea.

No idea about what?

How used up I am.

Outside, a whistle blew, and the six o'clock eastbound rumbled in. The tracks were close by — they ran practically right out our front door — and several times a day the weight and movement of the trains rattled the dishes in our cupboards, tilted the pictures on our walls.

He didn't leave a note, Mom. I don't think he meant to go. I don't think he meant to leave us.

She made a production of heaving herself around on the bed to look at me, her face smudged and bleary, like a child's drawing that's been half erased.

He's gone, though, isn't he, she said, then flipped herself over, away from me and toward the wall.

For probably a minute I waited there in the dark, sending her a silent message: *You can't ignore me like this.*

But she could and she did. And since I was too exhausted to fight, I went to my room, sat down on my bed and laid myself out on it without undressing. In a vague, unfocused way, I thought about Clay, remembering for some reason his wedding reception, which had been held in the basement of the American Legion. The band he was in at the time had played that night, and Clay spent most of the evening struggling with his guitar, up there on stage in a black tux, shirt collar open, tie swinging from his neck as he stomped and swayed — his new wife, Marnie, at a front table watching him, her white dress pushed up around her thighs.

I turned my thoughts to Dad, imagined him stumbling around town, having a look at the places he'd spent his time — the Valhalla, say, or the council room at city hall, or the little nine-hole golf course with its narrow, pine-crowded fairways that he could never seem to thread with his drives. I wondered if he'd come back home, here to the house, and wasn't sure if I liked the idea or not. Being near him — or near his ghost, or whatever it was he'd become — had been like standing too close to the edge of a cliff or waterfall. That sharp tingling at the root of your belly, the breathless jump in your lungs.

In my second grade classroom we had a pair of white mice, little pink-eyed things that ran maniacally on a squeaky exercise wheel.

Kids who scored a hundred percent on spelling tests or volunteered to wash the chalkboards were allowed to take the mice out of their cage and stroke their small bodies, probe them for the tiny drumroll of their hearts. The novelty didn't last beyond the first weeks of the year, but the mice stayed on, and I grew to despise them, to hate the tinny scrape of their wheel as I tried to read or scratch out my arithmetic problems. The smell of their cage sickened me.

Then one afternoon, late in the fall, I found myself alone in the classroom. School was out, and my classmates had all fled. Mrs. Cresswell was down the hall, in the bathroom or at a meeting. I walked to the back of the room and stood next to the mouse cage and watched them. For once they were quiet, staring up at me, their tails pointing straight out behind them. Without planning to or even thinking, I grabbed them out of their cage, wrapped them quickly in the wool scarf that Mom insisted I wear to school and pushed them into the small zippered pocket on the outside of my backpack. By the time I got home that afternoon they were dead, their bodies jammed together, the sharp nose of one indenting the soft belly of the other.

Mrs. Cresswell pressed hard for the guilty one to confess and even sent a letter home to our parents, but I never admitted to the crime, not to anybody. The fact is, I'm good at keeping things to myself. Whatever little piece of grit there is that needs hiding, I can usually find a fold in which to tuck it away and patiently leave it there to pearl up or fester. It's a strength or a flaw, depending on the situation.

My point is this: I don't know how much I would have told Mom if she'd given me the slightest encouragement to talk that morning. I may well have kept my own counsel, obedient to

Dad's warning. Or I might have stayed quiet out of fear for Mom's health — I didn't want her heart falling out of its rhythm again. But there's another possibility too, one I don't like to consider — that even if she'd prodded and poked and tempted me with small confessions and secrets, I would have resisted out of pure selfishness. Dad, after all, had appeared to *me*, not her, and I wasn't immune to the small thrill of that distinction.

4

In small towns, as in families, ambition can be a dangerous thing.

Dad's proposal to raze Little Mexico and replace it with low-income housing may have been progressive and may have been generous, but it was also controversial, and aside from putting his brother's job in peril, it pulled into the mayoral race a tough opponent: Cole Brighton, the wealthy, well-liked owner of the trailer park and president of the chamber of commerce. Brighton argued that mobile homes offered the most sensible choice for Battle-point's low-income workers: inexpensive, transitional housing for a population that was sure to wax and wane with the vicissitudes of the turkey business. He also noted whenever possible that the mayor was deficient in the family-loyalty department — a point, you have to admit, that had some merit.

What made the situation difficult at home was the fact that Mom agreed with Brighton. I remember the sound of my parents arguing in the night, mostly Dad's voice, a whisper so sharp it cut through the walls. I saw the looks she gave him, which he seemed to ignore. I saw the changes in the geometry of her bones and in the way she chewed her food and opened doors and pushed the mower through our bumpy lawn and gazed out the window, nights, when there was a moon or a glow from the aurora borealis. I saw the dark lavender pouches beneath her eyes and knew she was sleeping even less than she normally did. She didn't think it was right that Clay should lose his job and was also afraid that Dad's political ambitions might hurt the Valhalla. She'd never been thrilled about the restaurant — she may have seen it as the wall her own dreams had run up against — but she certainly didn't want to compromise the family's well-being. In fact, business *had* fallen off a bit, and we'd gotten angry phone calls at home from people who lacked the nerve to give their names.

Who does he think it was that elected him? a woman asked me at about seven one morning. The people in those trailer houses?

On a Friday night in October, though, something happened to convince me there was nothing to worry about, that Dad hadn't fallen out of favor with the townspeople — or at least not with most of them. It was the last home football game of the season, a couple of weeks before the election, the temperature warm for late October, no wind, perfect lip weather for a trumpet player. I was blowing my brains out in the pep band, football games being my chance to leave everything behind, exercise my power, fill the cool field with my silver sounds. The fact is, I saw the game as an adjunct to my own performance.

As usual, Dwayne Primrose was there, sitting in the bleachers a few feet away from me, just across the painted red line that separated the band from the rest of the crowd. According to the band director, Mr. Skogen, Primrose was the best trumpet player Battlepoint had ever had. It was one of the town's mysteries, how somebody like Dwayne could possess a talent like that.

Those chops — he could've blown a high C on a tuba, Skogen said once, shaking his head.

Dwayne's habit at football games was to lean close to the bell of my horn, his long face resting on a hand, elbow propped on a skinny knee, and watch and listen to the trumpet section for signs of embouchure trouble, breathing problems, missed sharps and flats. He might tap me on the shoulder and tell me to slide my mouthpiece higher on my lips, or flap his elbows like a pair of wings, which meant *Lift your arms, open the air supply.*

At halftime we worked our way through four or five jazz-rock numbers meant to keep the crowd up or at least on hand until the teams came back for the second half. One piece had a wild, cascading trumpet score, and Skogen usually saved it for last, as he did tonight, glancing up first toward the school to see if the team was on its way back yet. He lifted his arms, and the ivory baton twitched like a cat's whisker. I raised my instrument. Skogen went up on his toes to start the count, and I gulped my belly full of air, then nailed the first note, a G above the staff. At the same instant, I caught sight of Dad climbing out of the Mercury, which he'd parked on the other side of the field. I watched him work his way around the sidelines, handing something out as he went, his right arm reaching out to people, returning and reaching out again. He was distributing the stack of flyers he'd printed at his own expense. Two weeks to go, and he wasn't wasting any chances, smiling, pumping hands, sticking flyers in people's faces, clapping men on the back.

We finished the number just as Dad, twenty yards upfield,

approached old Floyd Jasper, the barber, who liked to watch games from his chaise lounge. As Dad bent over him, the stack of flyers popped free somehow and scattered like a flock of doves. The wind caught them up and broadcast them downfield, some flapping along the ground and others sailing on a mild current toward the goalposts.

Dad charged after them and Floyd did too, launching out of his chaise lounge and lunging forward, stiff-backed and bandy-legged. Then Dwayne Primrose joined in, clambering down from the bleachers, his feet like a pair of wooden blocks apivot on stick legs. Soon, half the crowd was on the field, men and women of all ages, children too, heads bobbing as they went, ducking and rising as they snapped flyers off the turf and snatched them out of the air. I saw Dad stop and look around at all these people he loved, drop his arms to his sides, open his mouth and laugh.

All was going to be well, I thought.

Skogen lifted his baton. Time for the fight song. The crowd hushed, and everyone looked up toward the school. I looked too and saw the football team charging toward us, silent, like a pack of wolves. I raised up my horn, took a breath, and played that thing by heart, blasting it out with everything I had.

A few weeks later Dad and I walked side by side into the woods with our rifles, barrels angled away from each other. The clouds were low and gray, stuffed with snow, and I imagined the pointed tops of the pines ripping them open and spilling out flakes like down. I remember listening to the coins jingling in his pocket.

He was normally loose-jointed and loose-tongued in the woods, but that afternoon he was silent as we moved among the hardening shadows of the spruce and birch, the red maples and white pines. A few days earlier he'd squeaked by in his bid for reelection, and already the city council had begun to move forward on his development plan, initiating the buyout process and soliciting bids from contractors. Yet Dad seemed anything but euphoric.

You know what? he said to me on the night he won. There's nothing like a victory to make you feel your age.

At Stringer Creek we crossed at the same bend where we always crossed, the place where years earlier Dad had discovered an antique, possibly ancient battle-ax wedged in tightly between two rocks. It was of Old World, Norse design, fashioned from iron, and for a short time it thrust Dad into the center of an anthropological controversy: whether the Vikings had made forays deep into the continent centuries before the French and English. Dad became a believer, naturally. But he also learned that few experts gave credence to the scattering of artifacts that had turned up over the years — a rune stone, several mooring stones, firesteels, spears — and ended up channeling his newfound interest into the renovation of the supper club he'd bought on Main Street. He put the ax on display in a glass case in the lobby.

I wonder sometimes if it's real, he said now, sitting down on a tree stump after crossing the creek.

I was struck by how tired he sounded, and it still hurts to remember how his eyes looked that day, the way the low-riding sun lit up the specks of honey in his blue irises. Even his wandering eye, the left one, nearly came to rest on me for a moment.

I didn't think you had any doubts, I said.

He stood up then and surprised me with a bear hug. I hugged him back, an experience something like hugging a large tree, if you can imagine that, your arms not even close to circling the thing, your small self made to feel smaller and more ephemeral in doing it.

When I let go and stepped back, he said to me, Jesse, I love you. You've got to know that.

You too, I said, bushwhacked by feelings I couldn't understand. To arrest the burning prickles in my eyes, I looked down at my boots and bit the inside of my mouth. Then I turned away and headed for my tree stand.

I often imagine the last view he had of me. The back of my head, blaze-orange stocking cap and blond hair curling out from under it. The back of my orange goose-down vest. The back of my skinny legs, looking not quite as sticklike in the lined canvas pants he'd bought for me out of a catalog, worried as he was that I might get cold up there in that tree, winter coming on, waiting for a shot.

5

We had the memorial Mass on Wednesday, four days after he died. It was a splendid ceremony, with incense, intermittent kneeling and solemn chants, Father Dittmer looking regal in a white surplice laden with gold brocade. All of this seemed strange to me, since I'd never attended Mass with Dad.

I should explain here that we were a two-faith family, Lutheran and Catholic, just as Battlepoint was a two-faith town, more or less. When I was born, my parents negotiated a deal that allowed Mom to raise us in the Lutheran church if she agreed to let him stay put where he was most comfortable. I won't explain here why Dad, the son of a Lutheran deacon, had converted to Catholicism — it's not important now. I will say that the arrangement he had with Mom must have been satisfactory, at least to him. He always seemed happy at dinner Sundays, summarizing Father Dittmer's homilies, then probing us for bits and pieces of the Protestant theology we picked up from Pastor Lundberg's haphazard sermons.

Anyway, there was no casket that day, because the body was still at the state coroner's office.

Sitting in the front pew, Mom and Magnus on one side, Clay on the other, I felt the pressure of innumerable eyes against my back. I tried to focus on what Father Dittmer was saying, on the heavy chords of the organ, but every time my arm or shoulder touched Clay's, a chill passed through me, and I had an urge to turn to him, grab hold of his face like a rotting melon that needs pitching, and search his eyes. I couldn't tell whether he was grieving or gloating.

With the passing of a couple days, my visit with Dad by the lake had started to seem less like a moment I'd lived and more like the polished little piece of a dream. I was paralyzed by the horror of what I'd been through, by the absurdity of my situation, one second overwhelmed with self-revulsion — I had to be crazy! — and the next, plotting in my head how to arrange for the gas stove in Clay's kitchen to blow up, how to sabotage the brakes on his car, how to slip rat poison into his food. I couldn't stop thinking about a Fourth of July we'd spent at Clay and Marnie's. They had an old barn out there full of cats, and though Clay was allergic to cat dander, he put up with his wife's pets as long as they kept their distance from the house. On that rainy day, though, one of them wandered up and rubbed against the screen door. Clay got up and fetched a rifle from the basement, went outside and shot the cat in his front yard. Watching from a window, I saw it leap six feet straight into the air and come down in a bloody mess on its head.

Having grown up around guns and hunting, the experience of seeing an animal killed didn't bother me — but Clay had always made a habit of telling people he didn't like hunting, that he didn't have the heart for it, that he'd rather let someone else harvest his meat for him.

I glanced from the statue of the Madonna to the life-size bronze crucifix and then to the large stained-glass window above us, where Abraham lifted his knife above Isaac, their figures pallid before an overcast sky. Although newly built, St. Leo's was a dark church, with high slanted ceilings, a cool stone floor and the smell about it of earth and water. As Father Dittmer finished a prayer, the sun came blasting through the clouds, igniting the stained glass. Isaac's robe shone like polished gold, and scarlet tears coursed down through his father's beard. The knife's blade glinted silver. And then a door slammed at the back of the church.

I turned and saw Dwayne Primrose standing in the center aisle, gaping over his shoulder at the noise he'd made. He had on the pants he always wore, work greens three inches too short, and a pair of blunt-toed shoes. Beneath a tattered overcoat he wore his usual green workshirt, which he'd forgotten to button, and beneath that a soiled white T-shirt that showed the unpadded rack of his ribs. On his narrow skull rode the earphones of the portable CD player that Clay had bought for him. It must have been turned to maximum volume because I could hear a high trumpet solo twisting like neon wire through the air. For a few moments Primrose stood there pursing and unpursing his lips. He was stunned, the center of attention. Then he shuddered and retreated to the door, lifted a hand to push his way through, dropped it and turned around again, his lean face contorted. I waited for someone to help him, for an usher to step in, but Primrose seemed to occupy a country of his own, beyond reach.

Finally Clay got up from beside me and moved down the aisle and guided the poor man into the nearest open pew. He slung an arm around Primrose's thin back and patted his shoulder. I remember how they looked, the two of them, bent forward in the pew, nothing but the crowns of their heads showing, Clay's well-combed gray pelt and, beside it, Primrose's bald top, a gleaming circle.

I'd often heard Dad say that his brother befriended Dwayne Primrose for a single reason, to make up for the way he'd treated the man's sister during the few years he was married to her. Dad was probably right. But guilt, I suppose, is the inspiration for much of the good we see in the world, and anyway, I doubt if Primrose was overly scrupulous about Clay's motives.

Afterward in the basement the churchwomen served deviled eggs and tiny sandwiches made of rye bread, Cheez Whiz and olives. They set out paper cups of Jell-O in several flavors: lime, cherry, lemon and orange. It seemed like most of the town was there. Dr. Milius. Pastor Lundberg and his wife. My English teacher, Mr. Bascom. Mr. Skogen, the band director. My class-mates from school. Magnus's classmates. Off in a corner, sitting at their own table, was a contingent from Little Mexico, includ-ing Christine Montez, with her tiny mother and her baby sister. Christine didn't come over to offer her condolences, though sev-eral times I saw her staring across the room at me.

Mostly what I remember is trying to use my body as a buf-fer between the town and my mom, who sat hunched between Magnus and Pastor Lundberg, her mouth stuck in a devastated grin, her chrome blond hair radiant beneath the gaudy fluores-cent lights. And I remember Clay working the room for us, shak-ing hands, accepting professions of sympathy, moving about with gravity and resolve. He looked tired, I thought, heavier somehow.

When the crowd had started to thin, Charlie brought me a cup of coffee and a sandwich — I hadn't eaten anything — and asked if I wanted to go for a drive. We went out along the lake road in the four-by-four his mom used for hauling fish houses across the ice. At the public beach on Battlepoint, where I'd seen Dad, we sat for a while, watching the moon rise bone-white out of the trees and paint itself large on the new skin of ice. At one point a pack of dogs half a dozen strong passed silent across the glare, stealthy and low-slung. We cracked the windows to let the smoke from Charlie's cigarette escape and intermittently ran the engine to keep ourselves warm.

You know what Jack Runion said to us? Charlie asked. The undertaker?

What?

He turned to me and blew a smoke ring that grew until I could see his whole face inside of it.

He said it to Mom, actually. He said we might want to think about having him cremated, because of how he looked. You know, what the rope did, squeezing his neck like that.

What did you do?

Had him cremated. We took his ashes out in a boat one morning when there wasn't any wind and sprinkled them around in different spots. The two-mile bar, Heron Bay, places Dad liked to fish. Now, though, I think she regrets it. She's always saying, Who are they going to bury *me* next to when it's my turn? She says, If I don't find a new husband, I'll have to go into the ground all by myself.

Or have herself cremated, I offered.

It's weird, though. I mean the ashes, ending up everywhere, just blowing around. Any spot of dust that drifts by — it could be him. Like he's still here somehow. You know what I mean?

I think I do, I said. You want to hear something?

Depends on what it is.

Charlie narrowed his eyes at me, and I stopped myself, but only for a moment. I guess my talent for keeping a secret goes only so far.

He came back to see me, I said.

Who did?

My dad. After I left your place, I didn't feel like going home. It happened right here.

Your dad, Charlie said, releasing smoke from his lungs.

Yeah. He came up out of the lake.

I pointed toward the spot where I'd first caught sight of him in the ice-laden water.

Your dad. He just up and walked out of the lake. Charlie's eyes in the pale moonlight looked angry, and I should have stopped right there but for some reason couldn't.

Well, I said. Yeah.

Charlie tilted his head back and laughed. You're nuts, man. But hey, the same thing used to happen to me. I'd think I'd see my dad sometimes, down on the dock or in his chair in the living room, places I was used to seeing him. It happened quite a bit there for a while. Then it stopped.

But I *did* see him. I'm not kidding.

My friend's smile faded. He looked out toward the frozen lake and took a long drag off his cigarette.

We talked, I said. He spoke to me.

Charlie looked at me sideways. He said, Who do you think you are, anyway? Hamlet?

We'd read the play in English class the year before, and Charlie had loved it. Afterward, on his own, he'd read *Othello, King Lear,* all the tragedies, and described their plots to me. At the time I couldn't have been less interested, but now, at once, I saw what I'd missed. How could I have been so dull? *Hamlet* had everything in it. Everything.

Charlie laughed again. Next thing, Jesse, you'll be telling me your old man was murdered and your uncle's the one that did it. Is that how it was? Is that what he told you? Is your dad out there roaming the earth at night? In torment? Give me a break, man. Shit happens, and there doesn't have to be an explanation. The world's out of joint, for sure, but don't start thinking you're at the center of it. The tragedy doesn't revolve around *you*. Come on, snap out of it.

I remembered one of the discussions we'd had in class about Hamlet and Claudius, and saying, Why doesn't he just kill him and get it over with? I hadn't been able to imagine the dynamics at work — the moral questions he faced, the political dilemmas, the dangers to himself. I couldn't wiggle out of my own skin, none of it made any sense to me. But now, crazy as it seemed, I was right where *he'd* been — and recognizing that gave me a little charge of confidence. I took a breath, and it tasted clean, closed my eyes and saw, suddenly, what I looked like from the outside — or at least wanted to look like — my eyes clear, my face set hard, my hands strong and steady-looking.

You'll get over it, Charlie said now. Or *this* part of it. Trust me, I know what I'm talking about. Hey, man, are you listening?

Yeah, I told him.

Don't go there. Don't be an idiot.

I shrugged.

Come on.

Okay, I said.

That's more like it. Good. He knocked my shoulder with a fist, then leaned forward and started the engine.

At home I found Clay in the living room with Mom. They were sitting in the pair of Queen Annes that framed the fireplace. She was slouched, shoulders and elbows curled around her heart, her face clenched in a knot. His long fingers were spired in front of his mouth, and his legs were crossed at the knees, the toe of one red-stockinged foot keeping pace with the ticking of the grand-father clock in the corner. On the coffee table in front of them sat a couple of big metal drawers from the green filing cabinet in Dad's basement office.

He's going to have a look at the books, Mom said.

Clay offered me a smile that was weighted to one side of his mouth, as if to say, *Everything's under control, nothing to worry about.* He'd always loved giving us advice on the restaurant, mak-ing sure to mention his business education, by which he meant the course or two he'd taken at a storefront technical school dur-ing his year of bartending in Fargo.

Well, he said. He stood up and hoisted one of the file drawers, then nodded at Mom and offered me a solemn wink before walk-ing to the door, where he wiggled into his cowboy boots.

It's going to be all right, he said to us, leaving. You'll see.

Yes, we will, I thought.

Outside, his Austin Healy cranked and fired and whined off down Lake Street. For me, the tiny car he drove — the only one of its kind in the county and always breaking down — defined my uncle, his need for attention, his seeming inability to make any-thing in his life work.

Mom and I watched each other for a few moments, then she

reached out and pulled the chain on the floor lamp beside her chair, flooding herself in yellow-gold light. With a small movement of her shoulders, she invited me to sit down, which I did. The chair Clay had vacated was cold and moist. I felt hollowed out, scraped clean. There was so much to say — pretty much everything that mattered — and none of it could be spoken. The confidence I'd felt just minutes ago with Charlie was gone.

Mom touched her fingertips to her forehead. I just thought of something, she said. We need to run over to the Valhalla.

Now? Why?

It's Wednesday night. The wine. I didn't call to cancel the order.

Every other Wednesday at ten thirty a truck from Minneapolis dropped Dad's biweekly wine order in the alley behind the Valhalla. A dozen or so cases of reds and whites, mostly inexpensive table wines. A case or two of champagne. Some sherry and some port. Dad always drove over after watching the ten o'clock news and hauled the cases into the basement. Sometimes I helped.

Mom and I made quick work of it, stacking the unneeded wine in a neat pile of boxes in the kitchen. After we'd set down the last case, she surprised me, tearing it open and lifting a bottle by its slender neck. She searched a dozen drawers before locating a corkscrew, then said, Come on, we have to talk. She grabbed a wineglass from one of the cupboards and led me through the dining room to the open stairway at the building's far side.

There was a small section of overflow seating on the second floor, and Mom chose a table by a window that looked out on Main, more or less deserted already. Standing close behind us, guarding the stairwell balustrade, was the life-size wooden Viking that Dad had bought from Demetrius Moon, mailman turned sculptor, who worked out of a renovated dairy barn on Dogfish Bay. Beowulf, we called the wooden man. Actually, Charlie had given him the name, and it stuck. Tonight his presence made me nervous, and I shifted my chair around to keep an eye on him.

Mom opened the bottle and filled her glass. She said, I've got *this* coming at least, wouldn't you say?

I'd rarely seen her take anything stronger than coffee, but now, showing me the length of her smooth white neck, she took a liberal swallow of the wine. As she set down the glass, light from the streetlamp washed the lines and shadows from her face, making her look young, innocent, like a girl who knew things she had no business knowing.

It's a mess, she said, and her hand fluttered toward Beowulf, the stairwell. There's a balloon payment coming in April that we can't meet, and till then there's the regular mortgage, the utilities, lots of things. Clay pretty much laid it out for me. It's a matter of owing money, quite a lot of it, and not taking any in.

Then we better reopen, I said.

There's nothing to reopen *with*. No operating budget. That roof work we had done in October? We paid for it out of that. Clay says he can't see how we could've met payroll in December, even if your dad was still here.

You're taking Clay's word for it?

He's been talking to Ernie at the bank.

With the heel of a hand Mom rubbed her eyes, one and then the other, leaving mascara smudges, raccoonlike. Outside, a sparkle of snow drifted through the cone of light from the streetlamp. A mammoth yellow pickup truck, old and dented, crawled down Main Street — Christine Montez, in the truck she drove to school each day. I saw Mom open one wrist and check her pulse against her watch. It was something she'd done continually since coming home from the hospital.

Look, Jesse, he didn't just leave, he dug a hole for us first.

My neck and ears started to burn, and my impulse was to slam the table and yell. I forced myself to take a breath and blow it out.

Sounds like you think he left on purpose. There hasn't been a ruling yet, Mom.

Yes, well, believe what you want.

It wouldn't have been Dad's way, you should know that.

You think you knew him better than I did?

No.

Good, because you didn't. And you never knew his dad, either, and what happened there.

I met Grandpa.

Yes, when he was old and dying. It's not the same.

What was so terrible about him? I asked. All I could remember was a white-haired man with a huge bony jaw and deep pits for eyes. All I'd ever heard was how strict he was, about religion and most everything else. Dad rarely spoke of him.

Mom sighed. She looked past me, her face slack, exhausted. She said, He was hard-core, but you know that. He took to heart God's call to perfection. Literally, I mean. Everything your dad did, and your uncle, from the time they were small — if it didn't meet with his approval, it was a sign of moral failure. A sin. Little things.

Like what? I asked.

Like taking lunch money for school and buying candy with it. Like sneaking a cigarette. Like getting a speeding ticket — that was a capital offense. Your grandpa drove him fifteen miles out into the woods and made him walk back home.

Dad told me he had it coming.

Mom laughed. That's the thing, Jesse. He went along with it all, put up with it. He absorbed the guilt, he took it on. He never confronted the fact that his dad didn't *like* him, that he was more interested in God — or maybe the church — than he was in his own sons.

He confronted it, I said. He *left* Grandpa's church.

After he grew up, sure. After he went into the service. And really, that was just another way to avoid things; he didn't have to see his dad on Sundays anymore. Now Clay, at least he stood up to the old man, got right in his face. He might've gotten beat for it — and believe me, he did, more than once — but at least he didn't live his life under the radar, like your dad did.

So that explains it? I asked. Dad never felt accepted by his father, and so he killed himself? That makes it pretty simple.

Mom covered her face in her hands, shook her head. I don't know, she said. However it happened, though, he's gone, right? And we're left holding the bag.

I thought of how Dad had looked as he came out of the lake, ravaged face and bloated hands, head half gone. There was no way, I saw now, that he could have shown himself to Mom — she wouldn't have been able to see him. I glanced sideways toward Beowulf, then around the room at the heavy oak chairs and tables Dad had been so proud of. To get them, he and I had driven to a little town in upper Michigan, to a restaurant that a bank was after. I can still remember the couple who owned it — the man sported two prosthetic legs and his wife had a bad tic in her face. We bought them out, took nearly everything they had, not just the furniture, but the sensible white plates and bowls, the chrome-plated flatware and a pair of stainless steel ovens. We hauled it all back in a rented semitrailer.

We can sell out, I said. Have an auction. The building, every-thing. We could move to California.

That's where Mom had lived until she was in high school, and where her parents had retired. Once, before they died, we'd all gone out to visit them. I'd been ten or eleven then, Magnus a baby.

Mom shook her head.

Why not? I asked.

I'm not disagreeing. Of course we'll sell. I mean, unless we find a way to get started again. But old buildings don't bring anything in this town, everybody wants to be out on the strip. And the furniture and appliances, all of it's twice used, practi-cally worthless. Besides, like Clay says, who wants a bunch of dark Viking stuff?

Clay? What does *he* know about anything?

Mom lifted her glass and drained it. She closed her eyes, the color of her lids a tired purple. Her weakness disgusted me.

What about life insurance? I asked.

She sighed and looked up at the ceiling. Do you know what a suicide clause is? Look, there's just too much to try and figure out, too much to do, and you know what? I don't feel like doing it. I don't feel like meeting with the Realtor or going in to talk with Ernie about money. I don't feel like talking to the insurance guy. I don't want to have to think about where we're going to live or what sort of job I should try to find. I don't feel like going out and start-ing the car and driving home. Or washing my hair. Or brushing my teeth. I don't feel like putting one foot in front of the other.

A sound interrupted us then, a low clear note from a trumpet — in this case, though, a cornet. It held steady for a few measures, then rose two octaves through a major scale before fading in a slight vibrato to silence — Dwayne Primrose, in his tiny apartment on the other side of the wall. His music was part of the Valhalla's atmosphere. Whenever he started in, people would pause in their conversations and glance at those around them as if acknowledging a shared secret.

He practiced for just a little while tonight, a melody I'd heard but couldn't place, melancholy yet resolute, and it brought tears to my eyes. For some reason, I remembered what it was like as a child, playing on the cold living room floor of our rented house, Mom and Dad lying on the couch together, watching me — and the peace I'd felt in the presence of the love they had for each other. I couldn't remember the last time I'd had that feeling.

When Primrose was done, Mom and I sat for a time as she finished her wine. I thought she was going to stand up and tell me it was time to go home, but instead she sighed and refilled her glass. I thought about Dad's warning: *Don't tell your mother, it wouldn't be safe.* I hadn't allowed myself to consider at any length what he may have meant by that. The possible scenarios were too disturbing. I'd already absorbed as much heartache as I could hold — or as much as I thought I could.

Let me ask you something, I said to Mom.

All right. She looked at me, her eyes red and starting to lose their focus.

All this horseshit about Clay — what's going on? I asked. Are you just going to let him come in and take over where Dad left off?

I don't know what you're saying, Jesse. And don't use that kind of language.

Just tell me.

There's nothing *going on*.

Then tell him to get lost, I don't want him around.

I can't do that. He wants to help. He needs to help. We're the only family he's got. More to the point, he's the only family *we've* got. It's really not that complicated.

Oh, I'd say it's complicated, Mom. I mean, how does he *feel* about you? Have you given any thought to that? You went out together in high school.

They'd been in the same class. Mom had moved to Battlepoint when she was a junior and hadn't met Dad until her senior year, when he got out of the army and moved back to town.

Of course we went out. You've always known that.

Did he like you?

I suppose he did, she said. But it was only a matter of a month or two. And when I met your dad, that was that.

She poured herself more wine. Her mouth was starting to move with awkward deliberation around her words, and her lips were crimson, fuller than usual. She frowned, began to rock herself forward and back.

Clay can't do us any good, Mom, you need to see that.

Don't be harsh, Jesse. Things haven't been easy for him. He and Marnie had what — a couple years together? And God knows, they weren't much of a match. Not to mention his musical career.

I laughed. Musical career? Is that what you said?

And now he'll be losing the trailer-park job, which is the last thing he needs. Your dad had it wrong there, I have to say.

Dad saved Clay's ass a hundred times, and you know it, Mom.

She closed her eyes and drained off her third glass of wine, raising it high and getting every drop. She said, With your dad everything was easy, he had this confidence. About us, I mean. Himself too. From the moment I met him, it was like he knew I'd want him and I did. Clay was different. He seemed to understand that what he felt for me might never come back to him — and yet he felt it anyway. Do you see? There's something endearing about that. You can't help but feel grateful. And guilty too — God, you wouldn't believe the guilt, Jesse. Mom squeezed her eyes closed in a long blink, then she planted her hands on the tabletop, pushed herself to her feet and stood up straight, squaring her shoulders. I have to go to the bathroom, she said. I'll be right back.

Dad helped him too much, I said. Way too much. He should've let Clay make it on his own.

She nodded, then moved toward the stairwell, her steps slow and calculated.

In fact, the only thing standing between Clay and self-obliteration — as far as I could tell — had been Dad, and if Mom couldn't see that, she was blind. I remembered a Saturday morning not long before Marnie died of cancer. Dad and I were sanding the maple floors in our living room when Clay came tearing through the front door, his breathing frayed and tattered, hair flopped down over his forehead.

If somebody comes looking, I'm not here, he said, and crossed to the stairway that led to the second floor. He hadn't even started climbing before a man burst into the house without knocking, his face swollen and red, eyes shining like diamond studs. He stood for a moment, silent, then magically transported himself across the bare sawdusty floor. Clay fought him off and escaped into the kitchen, the other guy holding tight to the ridiculously stretched cloth of Clay's orange shirt. I must have followed them, because I can still see the man swinging at Clay's head, missing outright and striking his fist on the sharp edge of a kitchen cabinet. Then stumbling to one knee and shaking out his hand.

I remember thinking, *What am I doing here?*

Then the man was back on his feet and moving forward. I watched Clay pluck from a kitchen drawer one of Mom's black-handled carvers and hold it up, eyes glimmering at the long blade that Dad kept sharp with a rubbing stone. The knife moved like a snake's head. The other man took a step backward and swept the rack of cook pans behind him, grabbing the handle of an iron griddle. For a moment the two men were still, as if caught in a wedge of intensified gravity. Then came a flurry of arms and heads, a pivoting shoulder and pumping elbow, a chaos into which Dad interposed himself. The knife went spinning on the maple floor, the man flew backward into a kitchen chair and Dad lifted Clay by the collar and appointed him butt-first into the stainless steel kitchen sink. Amazingly, nobody was hurt, no blood drawn.

I was thirteen then and knew instinctively why the man had come after my uncle. I knew by the way Clay tucked his long hair behind his ears just so and by the sour clamp of his wife's mouth whenever she looked at him. Dad asked me not to say anything about what had happened — to Mom, to Clay's wife, to anybody. What would be the point, he asked, in giving them more evidence for what they already knew? Though Dad had often complained about his little brother, he also protected him fiercely.

Mom came back up the stairs and meandered toward me using chair backs for support, her face tense with concentration. She sat down and blinked at me.

What you have to realize, Jesse — what you need to remember — is how much I loved your dad. He couldn't have been a better husband. Think of it: He never left the house without telling me where he was going and when he'd be back. It might have been down to the corner to put a letter in the box, but he'd tell me.

She was nodding as she spoke, her eyes lifting away and misting over, as if she could see through to some shimmering, unblemished world.

I said, What about the days I came home from school and you'd be hiding in your room — I mean, if things were so good? What *happened* to you, anyway? What happened to you and Dad?

The muscles around Mom's mouth twitched and tightened. You think it's my fault, don't you? she said. You're going to blame *me* for it. You and everybody else.

You're different now, Mom. I remember what it used to be like, being with you. The way you always sang in the morning before I left for school. The song from that stupid musical — Everything's Up to Date in Kansas City?

Mom drew back in her chair, and her head fell to one side. Her eyes were bleary, but they tightened on me nonetheless. Stupid? she asked.

I didn't mean you, Mom. Or your singing. I *loved* your singing. I meant the song.

Did you think it was stupid when I sang it on stage that summer in Opportunity? I think you were five or six then. I bet you don't even remember.

I do remember. And you were great. You were great.

In fact, I'd been stunned by how wonderful she was — a head full of shockingly dark curls, a ruffled dress, quick movements I vaguely recognized and a voice far bigger and more confident than it sounded at home. This was my mother? I remember looking up at Dad's face, which was proud and shining. But there was something else there too. He seemed to be studying her, trying to decide who Mom was, the person on stage or the woman we lived with.

The critic from the newspaper — *he* thought I was pretty good, she said to me, nodding.

Because you were, Mom. But it hasn't been all sweet and good. Things changed. I'm not sure when, but they did.

What do you want me to tell you, Jesse? That I'm a miserable person? That I made your *father* miserable?

No. Just don't act like everything's been perfect. If you want to make up a story for Magnus, fine, but don't try that with me. You've got to grow up and look at things straight on now, figure out what we're going to do, how you're going to get us through all this. And I mean *you*, not you and Clay. Leave him the hell out of it.

Her face went lax and her lips sagged. When she blinked, her lashes disturbed the stray hairs that had fallen across her eyes. I'd never seen her drunk before. But then she twisted her neck, cranked it suddenly and forced herself to sit up straight. She leveled her gaze at me. Her eyes were poison. You don't think much of me, do you? she said. But you might be surprised.

A wrinkle curled her lip. For a few moments she watched me, waiting, and when I didn't say anything else she leaned forward and put a finger in my face. And I won't be talked to like that again, she said.

What she did next couldn't have astonished me more than it did. Yet even as it happened it felt like something I'd seen before and was only remembering, as I'm doing now. She got up from the table and walked up to Beowulf, where he stood guard over the balustrade. He was six and a half feet tall, with a bearded face and a coat of mail, each link etched in the wood, his broadsword sanded to high gleam, its tip resting on the floor, his fists veined and heavy-knuckled where they gripped the sword's haft. Mom placed her hands on his wooden hips like a dance partner, then threw herself against his chest. The wooden railing behind him was three feet high, just short of his waist, and when he tipped backward against it, the weight of his torso and shoulders carried him over the top, headfirst into the stairwell, his big sandaled feet disappearing last. There was a crack like a rifle shot, then a quick series of floor-jarring thumps.

I joined Mom at the balustrade, and together we looked down at the long stiff body, feet resting on the bottom step, shoulders on the floor. The varnished pine head had snapped off clean, and now it rocked back and forth, its nose wagging at us, its narrow lips slightly parted, as if exhaling. Mom turned my way and held her face at a certain angle, aware, I'm sure, that I was seeing her differently than I ever had before.

She didn't say a word.

Before going on, I need to step back and say that while I was growing up, Mom was good to me in every way — she was a good mother. She fed me at all the right times and kept me in clean clothes. She read to me at night, acting out the stories in high dramatic fashion, hiding under the bed, for example, and growling like a troll for *The Three Billy Goats Gruff.* She also kept us afloat, working as a cashier at the Battlepoint Bank during the years before Dad made a success of the Valhalla. I've mentioned the dreams she had for herself, but I need to add that she never lobbied much for them. Her way, when she wanted something, was to create a quiet scene, sound a silent alarm. I remember once she wanted to visit a friend in Minneapolis who had just gotten divorced. This was a year or so after Magnus was born, and apparently Dad thought the trip was impractical. He didn't want her to go, though I'm not sure why. It seems like a small enough thing. But on the morning she would have left, and while Dad showered, Mom kissed me good-bye and pedaled away on her old black three-speed bicycle in a heavy rain, her backpack tied on top of the bike's rear fender. I watched her through the living room window.

Twenty minutes later we caught up to her a mile or two south of town, head down and fighting the wind. I remember how she slouched in the passenger seat on the way home, crying as if her life had ended — and Dad, staring ahead through the beating wiper blades.

In the weeks that followed our conversation in the Valhalla, I would have to reconsider who my mother was and what she was capable of doing — or overlooking. There were depths and darknesses in her that I couldn't fathom. For now, though, it was enough to know that I couldn't count on her as an ally. And that was all right, because watching her send Beowulf into the stairwell had galvanized something in me. After days of being oppressed by a drowning weariness, I felt, suddenly, a hard anger, a hammered-steel blade in my chest. It was time for me to seize control. I needed to build a snare for my uncle — devise some trick that would force him to show his hand. I was done being pushed around, done waiting for the next thing to happen, for the second boot to fall, for Clay to step in and take my father's place.

6

Magnus and I left the house at about six. The sky was clear and the stars as sharp as holes punched in tin. I'd spent a sleepless, scheming night and now found myself tagging along after my brother through the cold, predawn dark. Before going to bed I'd found a note on my pillow. *Dear Jesse*, it said, *I've got my papers tomorrow. Can you help?* A neighbor had been taking his route for him, but now with the memorial Mass behind us, apparently we were supposed to get over it and move on.

The course he followed made little sense to me — sometimes we crossed and recrossed a street within a single block. He poked along, pointing at things proprietarily, a fat gray cat asleep in a picture window, a clothesline hung with a pair of ice-caked boxers and a frozen bra, a half-smoked cigar standing vertically on its squashed ash on the top step of a pink rambler.

Suddenly Magnus turned to me and asked, Were his eyes open, Jesse?

No, I said. They weren't open.

Chloe said if your eyes are open, your soul can't leave your body. So you can't get up to heaven.

Chloe was a classmate of Magnus's who lived down the street.

That's ridiculous, and you know it. When did you see her? At the funeral?

He nodded, clamping his mouth like he still does when he's trying to hold something back. He opened a porch door, which squeaked on its rusty pull spring, tossed a rolled newspaper inside and eased the door shut again.

But Dad's eyes were closed, right? he asked. He was looking at me hard enough to burn calories.

You heard me.

Magnus walked on ahead, speeding his pace, almost running, and I had to trot to keep up with him. At the end of the block he turned around and said, Did he have his orange hunting cap on?

Yes, he did.

Chloe said it probably got blown off his head. That it was probably full of brains.

I remembered having the same thought when I saw it dangling on the branch of the caragana bush, and now I wondered when or if that cap would be returned to us. And his other things too. His clothes and his deer rifle, the change in his pocket, his rifle shells, his ring of keys.

Tell Chloe to shut up, I said to Magnus. Tell her that from me. Tell her if she keeps talking like that, I'll come over to her house with a bag of rotten fish heads and dump them in her swimming pool.

Chloe's dad, according to Chloe, traveled the world buying and selling zoo animals, and though I wasn't sure she was telling the truth, her dad was making money somehow — nobody else in Battlepoint had a swimming pool in their backyard.

Magnus blinked at me behind his glasses. Where'll you get a bag of fish heads? he asked.

Charlie's mom.

He was quiet for another block before he spoke again.

Did he do it, Jesse?

What do you mean, I asked, knowing full well.

I mean, did he *do* it?

Of course not. It was an accident, like Mom said.

Mom never said that. Mom never said anything.

Well, that's what it was.

How do you know? Did you see it happen?

No.

Then you don't know.

I know Dad, I said.

Are you sure?

I took his shoulders in my hands, looked as deeply into his eyes as he'd let me, and saw there, in large part, what my role in life was going to be for the next decade or so, until he grew up. I saw it with clarity — and I was not mistaken.

Yes, I said. I'm sure. I'm sure.

My brother stepped forward into my arms then, and his body felt breakable and small. I hung on to him for all I was worth.

An hour later the sun was just starting to show through the trees when I found Sheriff Stone cleaning his revolver in the tiny law-enforcement annex behind the courthouse. A plan had started coming together in my mind, a trap of sorts, but in the meantime I had to know as much as I could — at the very least, whether homicide was being considered a possibility.

He didn't seem surprised to see me, or happy either, but he gave me a cup of coffee from a tarnished pot, a maple long john from a bakery box, and sat me down on a cracked leather sofa. His office looked like the inside of a hunter's shack: a rack of guns on one wall, a bunk along another, a small fridge with a microwave oven stacked on top in one corner. In the center of the floor sat a large wooden desk on which his revolver lay open on a red cloth. The place smelled of gun oil and cigarette smoke. Sheriff Stone had gone through a recent divorce, and it was common knowledge that he was using his office as a temporary home. Also, people said he drank. Earlier that year the county board had made a move against him, tried to strip him of his job, but Dad had lobbied on his behalf. As mayor, Dad didn't have any say in county matters, but still, he threw his weight around a little, and the move failed. I was hoping Sheriff Stone had the good sense, or self-respect, to feel that he owed me.

You think I know something that'll settle your mind? he asked, sitting down behind his desk.

I want to talk about the investigation, I said.

He picked up the revolver, spun its cylinder and clicked it shut, then opened a drawer and put it away. He folded the red cloth and shoved it into the back pocket of his pants.

Investigation, he said, and laughed. There's not all that much to investigate. Not a lot of trails, so to speak.

But you have to prove it was his rifle, don't you? I heard my voice as a straight line, no fluttering, and was proud of myself for it.

No. The state coroner will try to make that determination. But the thing is, he won't be able to tell.

Why not?

Look, Jesse, you're backing me into a corner here. I really don't want to have to say.

You can tell me. Please.

Sheriff Stone rubbed both hands over the top of his bald head, as if searching for bumps and flaws. He chewed on his upper lip with his bottom teeth. You have to realize, he said. With a contact wound like that, the damage is so extensive there's no evidence to speak of. They'll be able to say it was a high-powered rifle, but that's about it, because there's no chance of finding the projectile. It probably ended up in the next township somewhere. And no bullet to test means no proof it was your dad's rifle. Or anyone else's.

Was there a shell in the chamber? I asked.

No. Nothing in the magazine either. The rifle was empty. Of course it's a semiautomatic, as you know.

What Sheriff Stone meant was, if Dad had turned the weapon on himself, the rifle's mechanism would automatically have ejected the empty cartridge.

What about casings? I asked.

He held up three fingers. Federals, he said. Your dad's brand, right?

How did you know?

Dick Morey at the hardware store.

How hard did you look? Are you sure you found everything?

You don't think I'm serious about this?

I didn't say that.

Here's the deal, Jesse. I take it real serious.

It's just that with the snow—

He lifted a hand to shut me up. He said, Eddie Vinter and me, we scoured that ground. Sifted through every square inch in a forty-foot radius around the tree. Found the three casings, and that's all she wrote. We took our sweet time.

All right, I said.

You probably know this, but every rifle leaves its own mark on the primer of a spent cartridge. Kind of like fingerprints. At the state coroner's office, they'll be checking that out to see if there's a match between the cartridges we found and your dad's rifle.

It might not mean much if there is, I said. A couple weeks ago he took a few shots from that stand, at a target we set up. Sighting it in. So the cartridges you found are probably going to match. If one of them doesn't, we better pay attention.

Sheriff Stone nodded. Glad you told me, I'll pass it along. But listen up here. You oughta know why Dr. Milius said what he did the other day. You know what I'm talking about, right? Suicide?

Yes, I said.

Because a contact wound like your dad suffered? It always points in that one direction.

A sharp heat flared in my gut. I said, That stand is low, no more than six, seven feet off the ground. A guy could've reached up and put the end of the barrel right on him.

You think your dad would let somebody do that?

What if he came up on him from behind? Surprised him.

Anything's possible, I guess.

There was nobody else there to see. There's a ridge between his stand and the one I was sitting in. Can't you see how it might've been?

Sheriff Stone watched me, his gray eyes steady. He was rubbing the top of his bare head again. He said, If there's something I should know, you'd better just come out with it.

There was nothing I could say — was there? — to a man whose

training and experience had taught him to see everything in terms of material evidence. If I told him what was on my mind, the first thing he'd do is call Dr. Milius or somebody else and make sure I had my head checked.

Listen, he said. I'll be talking to everybody who lives out there, every soul within a mile of that spot. I'll ask them if they saw anything out of the ordinary that night. Anything at all. I'll be thorough, cross every *t*. Also, there's always a chance the coroner will come up with something we missed. It happens.

He looked away then, to the small window facing east — I could tell he wanted this to be over. I looked too, and saw two little boys in the vacant lot across the street trying to prompt a rangy dog into pulling them on their sled. A rope had been knotted around its neck, and though the boys waved their arms and threw handfuls of snow at it, the dog refused to move, but stood there spraddle-legged, head down. Through the window came the faint sound of its bark.

Tell me the truth, I said to him. You knew my dad. Do you really think he'd do that?

Sheriff Stone took his time answering, and when he spoke, he looked me straight in the eye. He said, It's not my job to figure out what people would or wouldn't do, Jesse. My job is to figure out what — given the facts we can *point* at — happened.

Sheriff Stone's assessment of the situation seemed logical enough, I had to admit, but knowing what I knew about him, I doubted whether he and Eddie Vinter had been as diligent as he claimed they had. And so I elected to exercise some diligence of my own.

It was a school day, but I wasn't at school. Mom had told us we couldn't go back until we'd each had a talk with Pastor

Lundberg — her way of addressing issues she wasn't able or willing to address herself. She'd scheduled us for the next morning. I spent a few hours cleaning the house, the bathrooms, floors, the kitchen, everything Mom wanted done, and when she left with Magnus to go shopping for groceries at three thirty that afternoon, I had my chance. It took me about half an hour of searching the basement, but finally, behind the folded-up Ping-Pong table and stuck between two piles of boxes, I found it: Dad's old metal detector.

As I drove north out of town, the sun was pinkish red and watery-looking, a sore bleeding down into the tops of the pines. I pulled over at the right spot and parked the Mercury as close to the ditch as possible, the tires riding up against the ridge left by the plow. A ten-minute walk through knee-high drifts brought me to the place where he'd been lying. The tipped-over birch tree was half hidden now. I started beneath the stand, waving the sensing disc back and forth an inch or two off the surface of the snow. I wasn't sure what Sheriff Stone had meant when he said he'd scoured and sifted, but there was no way I was going to take his word for it.

When I was little, Dad and I had spent a couple summers hunting treasure at the town beach and the public park on Lake Street. We found junk mostly, bottle caps and pop-tops off beer cans, a few old coins. Nothing valuable. Once in a while a piece of junk jewelry. As hobbies go, hunting treasure is a lot like fishing. What you get is almost always less that what you hoped for, and the thrills are too widely spaced to keep most people going for long.

Steadily I shuffled along, circling the tree's base and ducking beneath its lower limbs. I was about ten feet south of the tree when the machine croaked twice, a low metallic chirp. I fell to my knees and started digging, plunging my hands through the snow, raking my fingers through the leaves beneath it, and then clawing down into the twigs and grass. What I found was an eighteen-penny spike, rusty and bent. My impulse was to toss it away, but then I remembered the day several years before when Dad and I had built the stand, and how my hammer had glanced off a spike and struck my thumb. I'd cried in spite of myself, the pain so bad I hardly noticed when Dad climbed up onto the planks next to me. When I looked over at him, I saw that he was crying too, out of sympathy.

I searched for another half hour but found no spent cartridges, no more spikes, nothing. By now the trees had swallowed up the sun, and dusk was closing fast. A light snow had begun to fall. I took a final look at the spot next to the fallen birch where I'd found him, then started for the car, setting a hard pace for myself, nearly running for the edge of the woods, dodging branches, stumbling over deadfalls and smashing through snarls of bramble.

The engine turned over grudgingly, then fired and roared to life. For a minute or two I sat there behind the wheel, eyes closed, and tried to catch my breath. Nothing anymore could be simple or easy, could it? Nothing anymore could be fair. My life was over — I was screwed, and I'd better get used to it. I shoved the gearshift into drive, did a U-turn on the gravel road and headed for town, furious with myself for imagining I could waltz out here and in half an hour put my finger on the piece of evidence that would nail my uncle.

As if he'd leave an empty cartridge behind him in the woods.

As if he were that stupid.

In a deeper place, though, my anger had no focus — if, in fact, it was anger at all. Because in large part it must have been fear.

What if my best instincts, my truest impulses, were dead wrong? What if I couldn't trust my own eyes and ears? I didn't know which scenario was more threatening to me: my uncle, a murderer, walking free, or my own mind, for reasons of love and grief, hatching a conspiracy that had no connection to anything real.

II

BELOW ZERO

7

There was nothing very elaborate about the trap I was preparing to set, and nothing designed to play on Clay's conscience either, because I doubted that he had one. As I think back on it now, I have to admit it was clever in its way, especially considering it was hatched out of psychological duress by a kid with everything to lose. A letter is what it was — photographs too — and that night in my bedroom I spent an hour on it. I used a ruler for a straightedge and wrote in generic capitals half an inch high with a number-two pencil on standard typing paper. Finished, it looked like the product of a grade-school student striving for an A in penmanship — or of some deranged soul with a limited education. Here's what it said:

I KNOW WHAT YOU DID AND CAN'T HELP WONDER-
ING, HOW WOULD YOU LIKE A TASTE OF WHAT
YOU GAVE YOUR BROTHER? HERE IS WHAT YOU DO.
COME ALONE TO THE BEACH ON BATTLEPOINT, THE
CHANGING HOUSE, AT ELEVEN FRIDAY NIGHT, AND

I'LL TELL YOU WHAT YOUR LIFE IS WORTH TO ME.
BRING A DOWN PAYMENT, FIVE HUNDRED DOLLARS.
IF YOU'RE NOT THERE BY ELEVEN FIFTEEN, I'M HEAD-
ING HOME TO CLEAN MY RIFLE.

A few hours earlier, at dusk, I'd driven out past Clay's place with an old Polaroid camera Charlie Blue had lent me in ninth grade for a science project I was doing on cloud formations. I parked in a dense stand of poplars half a mile beyond his driveway, walked back along the willow-crowded lakeshore, came up on Clay's house from behind the barn and from thirty feet away snapped a shot of him through his kitchen window, sitting at the table, his face tinted blue from the reflected light of the TV. Then as luck would have it, he stepped outside to toss his coffee grounds, and having retreated to the corner of the barn I snapped another shot.

I wasn't sure there was enough light for decent exposures, but in fact the pictures turned out all right — or well enough, at least. At my desk at home, with compass and pencil, I scribed on both photos a two-inch circle around Clay's fuzzy image. Then I added crosshairs that intersected on his body, one at the shoulder, the other at the hip, producing reasonable facsimiles of how Clay would look through a rifle's scope.

For a couple of days I'd been calculating the risks involved in the trap I was setting, considering the possibilities, trying to look at the thing from all sides. I knew there was a chance — probably a good one — that Clay's first impulse would be to suspect me. If I *had* seen him, though, what in God's name would have prevented me from going immediately to Sheriff Stone? In fact that's exactly what I would have done, and Clay, no fool, would realize it and rule me out.

Or so I reasoned.

It also occurred to me that Clay might call my bluff. But in my all-or-nothing, zero-sum, seventeen-year-old, grief-damaged brain, the notion that he might be innocent was not a real possibility — and no way, I told myself, would a man capable of planning and carrying out the murder of his brother have reason to question the ability of another man — whoever he might be — to commit violence for the sake of gain. What if he lost his nerve, though? Wasn't there a chance of that? I thought about it long and hard and decided the possibility was slim. At the memorial Mass, in the church basement and afterward at our house, Clay had struck me as self-possessed, almost gratefully so, like a man embarking on a new life — a life I was certain he would fight to keep. I might hate him with every twitch of every muscle, but I also knew him well enough to believe he was a desperate coward, not a shrinking one. If he was guilty, he *would* show up at the changing house on Battlepoint Beach, I felt certain of it.

And that was the beauty of the plan: if Clay arrived, as I fully expected him to, it would mean one thing to me: he had done it. I had to be careful, though, in case he showed up with the intention of doing me harm — which is why *I* had no intention of meeting him that night. Adjacent to the beach was a heavy stand of lakeside woods, part of the Gary Sinclair farm, twenty or so acres that developers had been trying to get their hands on for decades. It was high land — uncleared, brushy — and from the edge of it, I would have an unobstructed view of the changing house, fifty or so yards away. It would simply be a matter of finding a lookout perch on Friday night and waiting.

The trap wasn't foolproof — I see it now and probably saw it then. And yet at the time, thinking things through and setting them into motion made me feel empowered, confident, nearly euphoric. I was *doing* something. In the universe of my imagination my uncle was becoming my pawn. Soon I would know for sure. Soon I'd be in a position to make *real* plans.

Before going to bed I addressed an envelope, using the ruler once again, and the same block letters. I fixed a stamp to it, drove downtown to the post office and mailed it. It was Sunday night, late. Most likely the letter and photographs would be delivered the next day. That would give Clay the rest of the week to deliberate, ponder and second-guess himself. Stew in his own juices.

And me? I had five days to kill. Five days.

8

Monday morning — I woke up thinking, *Clay's letter day* — the temperature was ten below according to the big round thermometer Dad had nailed to the tree outside the kitchen window. There was also snow in the air, a lot of it, not to mention a gusty wind blowing it around, and the houses across the street faded in and out of view. Today Mom was sending us back to school.

Magnus and I sat at the kitchen table listening to the radio, hoping the storm was bad enough to keep the buses parked. The trouble was, we knew that Superintendent Fitzer counted on the weather judgment of Tryg Pearson, a retired army colonel who drove a military-issue jeep and believed that if he could make the six-mile drive into town from his place, then the school buses should be able to get through, no problem. When the announcer on KQAR finally read off the cancellation list, Battlepoint wasn't on it. Magnus said nothing. He was hunched over his oatmeal, his face and hands red from walking his paper route through the storm.

We haven't had a snow day in three years, I said.

He laid down his spoon on the tabletop and said, You know what I hope? I hope one of the buses goes in the ditch or runs into a marsh and gets stuck, and the kids all freeze to death. I hope they don't find them till the snow melts. And I hope those dead kids haunt Fitz for the rest of his life. That'd teach him.

Before I could get to my locker that morning, the school counselor, Maggie Toms, tracked me down and insisted I come to her office for a chat, which turned out to be a long string of questions to which I responded with single-word answers. Maggie was two or three years out of college, more than pleasant to look at and well meaning too, but I didn't have the patience right now to play along. The Friday before, I'd met with Pastor Lundberg, and so I'd already been probed and prodded, scrutinized for evidence of emotional trauma that might lead to problems I couldn't handle. Pastor Lundberg's main goal had been to let me know I wasn't at fault.

Please understand, Jesse, he'd said. Nothing you did or didn't do had any bearing on what happened. You can't allow yourself to take this on.

You don't have to worry about that, I told him. Believe me.

By the time Maggie let me go, my English class was more than half over. I stole into the room and took a seat at the back. My classmates didn't seem to notice — they were all under the spell of Mr. Bascom, whose eyes were lost in the storm outside. He pulled at his little goatee, carrying on about the piece he'd assigned as if the people in it were his own friends or family. It was a Hemingway story — a boy and his father sitting close together in a rowboat, at night. I hadn't read it, but Bascom's low voice brought me there. I could smell the rain-washed air and hear the hollow bumping of water against the wooden hull, the dip and splash of the oars. I could see stars shimmering on the face of the lake.

Nick lay back with his father's arm around him, Bascom read, and I imagined that *I* was in the boat and that Nick's father was my own, his thick blunt fingers resting loosely on my forearm, his three-day beard scraping against my ear as he bent to squeeze me, his breath like potatoes. I felt the pain of tears at the back of my eyes.

They beached the boat and moved through the dark to a small Indian shanty, where the boy's father, a doctor, delivered a baby by Cesarean section. The husband lay on the bunk above her, absorbing his wife's screams.

I was appalled by the woman's situation, by the dinginess of her home, the crudeness of the surgery being performed on her, the pain she must be feeling.

Bascom stopped reading. Except for the storm whining at the windows, our classroom was silent. From my hiding place behind Joey Trundle — the fattest kid in my grade — I glanced around at my classmates. They looked prematurely old, their faces pale, maybe from the gray sky, maybe from the ranks of fluorescent bulbs mounted on the ceiling.

So, what happens next? Bascom asked. After the baby's delivered, I mean.

I caught a movement over by the windows and turned to see Christine Montez. She was staring right at me, her face drawn, dark eyes alarmed. Her tongue made a nervous trip from one corner of her lips to the other. I wanted to ask her, *What? What's wrong?*

What happens next? Bascom asked. Come on.

At the front of the room a hand shot up. Overachiever Becky Ulmer. Bascom blinked at her, waiting.

We learn the husband killed himself, Becky said. He slit his own throat.

My stomach shriveled, turned in on itself.

Why? Bascom asked.

He couldn't stand things. That's what it said.

It said? Who's it?

The doctor, I mean.

What couldn't he stand?

I don't know. His wife's pain?

I squeezed myself lower in the desk and tried to think of how I was going to escape.

He's been listening to her screams all night, Becky said. He can't stand it anymore. A person can take only so much.

Hey, it's *his* fault she's pregnant, right? This from Mary Apple, in front of me and to the right. Maybe the guy finally figured that out, she added.

Mary lived in a cabin north of the lake with her two older brothers. A couple years ago their mom had gone on vacation to Las Vegas and ended up staying there.

So, Mary, you're saying he did it out of guilt? Bascom asked.

Yeah, the guy's a wimp. Look, they've got a doctor there, and he still freaks out. Leaves his wife behind, and the kid too, not to mention a mess to clean up, all that blood. That's sick. It's a sick story.

From far off on the lake came a tremendous boom, massive ice plates shifting in the cold. Then, as Mr. Bascom moved to the front of his desk, he caught my eye — until now he hadn't realized I was there. I could feel the room registering my presence too, everybody turning my way, but somehow I wasn't able to take my eyes off Mr. Bascom, who stared straight at me. The muscles of his face squeezed into a complex of hard figuring. I wanted to scream, *Dad didn't kill himself!* — but was paralyzed. And Bascom seemed helpless as well, until a voice came from the window side of the room, Christine Montez, in that singsong but oddly melodious tone of hers.

Go get him, Vince, she said.

I felt the weight of the room — thank God! — tipping away from me, and I saw the pressure leave Bascom's face. His eyes broke from mine, and I followed them to the window. Outside, Officer Kaeler's black patrol car, red lights flashing, had pulled over a white delivery van on Lake Street. From the front of the room, Jarod Bloom barked out a laugh.

Vince Kaeler, a couple of years out of the academy, was ambitious, and Jarod already had a few citations under his belt. Some of my classmates scrambled out of their desks and hustled over to watch. Mr. Bascom clapped his hands.

Pop quiz, he said in his most commanding voice. Take out some lined paper. He glanced in my direction, his face drained.

The students issued a general moan. In front of me, Joey Trundle whimpered and clasped his pudgy hands on top of his head.

Twenty points, Bascom said. He went to the blackboard and started scraping out an essay question with his yellow chalk.

I left my textbook on the desk, slid from my seat and fled, quitting the building by the nearest door, a fire exit that opened onto a platform at the top of a zigzag stairway bolted to the brick wall. The cold was crushing — it felt like steel, except that I could breathe it and move through it. My coat and cap and gloves were still in my locker, but I left anyway, my feet ringing against the iron stairs. To the east, faintly, a pink and yellow sun dog shone through the snow. I cut through the playground and then across Third Street into the lumberyard. At the back of it, I scaled a six-foot chain-link fence and dropped down next to the train tracks. The cold was brutal. I passed the abandoned depot, the body shop with its rusty acre of cars, the grain elevator. My eyes ached and watered, then froze up, blurring my vision. It was like driving through a wet snowfall, wiper blades clogging and crusting over. I stuffed my hands into the front of my pants for warmth, turned around and tried walking backward to protect myself from the wind, but then tripped on a railroad tie and went down hard, cutting my palm on a piece of crushed rock. The blood was dark, almost purple. There wasn't any pain, though. I couldn't feel a thing.

I just sat there, my right hip wedged against the steel rail, and stared at the gash in the pad of my hand. I brought it to my mouth and probed the broken skin with my tongue. My blood tasted salty, hot.

It's true what you read about the cold, how it can lull you to sleep, and that was my temptation now, to lie down and let everything go — to let winter come and settle over me. The tightness in my shoulders began to loosen. As I adjusted my hip against the rail and made myself comfortable, an image came, a dream or the memory of one — I wasn't sure which. Dad carried Magnus on his shoulders, the two of them moving through a landscape of rocks and boulders, some the size of small cars, Dad negotiating them easily in a series of vaulting leaps. And then by some turn of dream logic, he became a horse, an angry, stamping roan that threw Magnus off and galloped away.

The dream was disturbing enough that I pushed to my feet and started moving again. I thought of Dad, broken and lost at the edge of Crow Lake, and couldn't help but remember a sermon of

Pastor Lundberg's, something about Satan appearing as an angel of light. What if it hadn't been Dad I'd seen, but some apparition out of hell, tempting me? The wind coursed into my brain. Through my crusted-over eyes I couldn't see much of anything — a blurry, white-gray world. But then, along the back of the bowling alley where the tracks intersected First Street, something yellow winked in front of me. I heard the idle of an old engine, the halting syncopation of its rhythm. I lifted my arms and waved it off. *Keep going, I'm fine. Please.*

It stayed put.

I pawed at my eyes, clearing them enough to see a dented yellow truck parked squarely on the tracks in front of me. In the driver's seat was Christine Montez, her glorious face centered in the cranked-down window. *How did you get here?* I wanted to ask. She waved me forward.

Heater works, she called to me. A little, anyway.

I stumped around to the passenger door, which she had shoved open for me, and climbed in. When I tried to say thanks, my lips, numb from the cold, managed only an *aa* sound.

You're welcome, she said, and shoved the gearshift into first.

The truck lurched, and off we went, bouncing and sliding down the snow-rutted street. Christine reached over as she drove and took hold of my cut hand. Her own felt warm, smooth, and at the touch of it something hard inside my chest broke open and surged through me. I thought of all the times I'd watched her in the cafeteria — off in the corner where she sat with her cousin — and the way she always blessed herself before eating that terrible food the school cooks served us. With shame, I thought of the picture I conjured, nights, in bed: Christine's bare feet padding on my wooden floor, and the cool air as she lifted the blankets to slide

in beside me, the heat of her skin. Her small generous hands. The
heady press of her soft lips. Her warm breasts, their nipples as hard
and tight as licorice nubs.

Here, she said now.

She'd removed a clean white handkerchief from her pocket — it
had lacy edges and a flowered design stitched into one corner —
and she applied it to the cut on my hand, held it there.

Thanks, I managed to say, my throat thick, clogged with
feeling.

Are you all right?

I nodded. She squeezed my hand harder.

You followed me? I asked.

I saw you cross into the lumberyard, from Bascom's window.
Just as the bell rang. He shouldn't have done that story today. That
was so stupid.

He didn't think about it, I said.

It's his job to think, isn't it? Isn't that what he tells us all the
time? *You're here in school to learn how to think, people.* Isn't that
Bascom's big thing?

I guess so.

She pulled over next to the curb in front of my house, brakes
shrieking. I glanced down at my watch, and it occurred to me that
now I'd have to go inside and explain to Mom what I was doing
home at ten in the morning.

Could I ask you for another favor? I said.

Christine nodded, her eyes glancing my way, and I remembered the cool moistness of her lips.

Maybe you could drop me off at the Valhalla instead. I've got
a key to get in.

Your mom?

Yeah.

She put the truck in gear again and gunned the engine. At Main we turned left, then rolled through downtown. The pain had started in my hand, and I kept Christine's handkerchief pressed against it. She pulled up diagonally in front of the Valhalla and stepped on the emergency brake.

I just wanted to tell you how sorry I am about your dad, she said, finally turning and looking at me. Her dark eyes burned in my belly. Neither of us looked away. I allowed her eyes to come into mine, and mine to go searching in hers for what I sensed she'd been holding for me. I couldn't have described it then, but now I think I understand what I experienced in that moment — the future jarring itself loose somehow, turning, and trying to lay its hand upon me. If I'd had the courage, I would have reached over and pulled her close, held her. Instead I grabbed the door handle and yanked on it. Nothing happened.

Sometimes it doesn't work, she whispered. You've got to do it just right.

She leaned across me, her warmth against my lap for two gorgeous seconds as she snapped open the door, then straightened up again, averting her face. I saw the line of her cheekbone, the heavy black sheen of her hair. In the lobe of her ear a bright red ruby. All around us the air swirling and gusting with snow. I thought of the stories I'd heard about the damage her father had inflicted on Rudy Foss — a fractured skull and broken ribs, lacerated kidneys, four smashed fingers. And here was his daughter, so composed, serene. I thought of the kiss we'd shared in the darkroom and felt a buoyancy in my lungs. I desperately wanted her not to leave.

I pushed open the heavy door and climbed out.

Hey, she said to me.

I looked up at her.

You're going to be okay, she said. Your life, I mean. It's going to turn out all right.

She smiled at me, then leaned across the seat, pulled the door shut and backed away from the curb, wheels spinning in the new snow. Before driving off, she rolled down her window and called back to me through the wind, Get a bandage on that cut!

I stood there nodding in reply until her truck rolled completely out of sight. Then I let myself into the Valhalla with my key.

Beowulf was gone. Mom had called Demetrius Moon, asking if he was interested in buying him back, and Demetrius told her yes — out of pity, I figured. The head could be refixed to the shoulders with wood epoxy, Demetrius said. I turned on one of the big ovens in the kitchen and stood in front of its open door. When I was warm — or warmer, at least — I shut off the stove and walked into the lobby. The sun had slipped in through the bluster of snow and wind. The sky was brushed aluminum: brilliant, hazy.

I didn't know what to do with the crush of thoughts in my brain — there was too much to sort through, too many people, all with their own demands. My dad and mom. Clay. And of course Christine. I could still smell her, still see the orangey pink of her lipstick. How did *love* survive, I wondered, in the face of terrible acts and betrayals? There must be something defective in my character for being able to accommodate, as I could now, such a surge of love and vengeance, both at the same time.

Instead of going back to school, I went down into the basement to be close to the furnace. It was a dark, low-ceilinged place, cracks snaking across the concrete floor, gray walls lined with commercial-size cans of ketchup, gravy, beans, corn, peas, coffee. In one corner a toilet and sink. At the center of the room was the large, green, humming furnace, and next to it the canvas military cot that Dad had napped on sometimes after the dinner rush. I lay down on it and pulled the red camp blanket up to my chin, catching in it just a hint of Dad's smell. For the first time since he'd died, I allowed myself to cry, to let go completely — and the tears, so long in coming, burned my eyes. I cried so hard my stomach hurt, and when I was finished it struck me that he might well be close by, that if I wanted to see him, here was a likely place. I wondered what he'd say to me this time. I wondered if by now he'd shed his bloody coat, if the wound in his head had begun to heal. I wondered if he was watching me, waiting for the right moment.

As it turned out, he showed himself to me only after I'd fallen asleep, when I had a dream about the first time I'd carried a gun into the woods with him. We'd stayed in our stands that morning until ten or ten thirty. Then he came wandering over and asked if I'd like to share a thermos of coffee. I climbed down and together we lay back against the tree trunk, the sun on our faces, our legs stretched out in the dead grass. It was unseasonably warm that day. We laid our guns beside us.

Dad had been bragging me up to his friends and predicting that I was going to change his luck.

I've been skunked four years running, he'd tell them. But you just watch. Opening morning, everything's different.

As it happened, though, there was nothing astir in the woods, probably on account of the pleasant weather, and I felt personally responsible, afraid I'd let him down somehow.

I must have fallen into a trance brought on by the sun and

too many warm clothes, because it wasn't until Dad nudged my foot with his that I saw the young spike buck standing above us, not four paces from our upturned feet. He was the color of maple syrup and amply muscled, his nose probing the air for a scent, probably ours. Moving only my eyeballs, I peeked over at Dad, whose expression was saying, *Go on — take him, Jesse.* In my head I recalled the advice he'd given me: *Don't think to yourself, I'm gonna kill it,* he'd say, *but think of your rifle as an extension of your arm and the tip of the barrel as your finger. When your deer comes along, just reach out and touch him.*

Which is what I did. Using only my right hand, I tilted the rifle up from the floor of the woods, set the hammer with my thumb, and imagining the barrel as the tip of my finger, I reached out and touched that spike buck. He leaped away at the sound of the shot, took half a dozen bounds and fell dead. I let the gun drop back to the ground and looked over at Dad, still lying there next to me.

Guess you were right, I said.

His smile was so big, I could see the glare of the sun in the gold fillings of his back molars.

Of course I was right. You're my lucky boy.

I woke up with that vivid image in my mind — Dad lying next to me in the woods, up on one elbow, smiling.

My watch said three ten, which meant school would be letting out in twenty minutes. I lay there on his cot, dreading the cold walk home without cap or mittens, and gazing at the orange flicker that showed through the joints and rusted cowling of the furnace. Finally I got up and climbed the stairs into the cloakroom, where I found a long wool overcoat that someone had never retrieved, and a cap too, one of those squarish fur things with earflaps that you might see on a Russian spy in a cold-war movie.

As I walked the alleys and side streets home, hoping nobody would recognize me, I reminded myself that even though his death had left me in a terrible way, life with Dad had been mostly a joy.

9

At home I learned from Mom that Dr. Milius had called saying we needed to meet with him. He'd gotten word from the state coroner's office.

Mom's jaw and her shoulders were fixed in a straight line. She was standing in the entryway, wrapped up in her winter coat. She said, He wants to see us right away. I dropped Magnus off at Brian's house after school. Come on.

On the way to the hospital, I allowed myself to hope that some fresh bit of evidence had come to light, that we'd be happily surprised, that something had been found that would point to homicide. Maybe the weight of Dad's death was about to be lifted from my shoulders. Maybe I'd be able to share at last the knowledge I had, describe my talk with Dad, explain about the trap I'd set for Clay.

I knew it was too much to hope for.

At the hospital entrance we were met by Pastor Lundberg, there on Mom's request, and he led us to a conference room. He'd made an effort to comb his unruly hair, which was still damp and plastered down. Instead of his usual jeans or khakis he wore a pair of neatly pressed dark slacks, also his black tunic and white collar. He nodded for Mom and me to sit down at the large oblong table, then seated himself across from us.

Have you talked to him yet? Mom asked him.

He shook his head, but I could tell he wasn't coming clean.

Then Dr. Milius glided in, phlegmatic as ever, and laid a large manila envelope on the table. He sat down next to Pastor Lundberg and brought his fingertips to rest on the envelope. I'll start, he said, by noting that every difficult decision, like this one, is provisional in a sense. If new evidence were ever to come to light, the case could be reopened.

My lungs clenched, and I forced myself to breathe. *Okay, let's get this over with,* I thought, and looked at Mom, who nodded at me, her bottom lip tucked inside her mouth.

As you know, a death certificate has to be completed, Dr. Milius continued. A cause of death must be assigned. Given the evidence at his disposal, the medical examiner has decided the most likely explanation in this case is a self-inflicted wound from a high-velocity rifle.

Mom didn't blink. I could see that she'd prepared herself for this. Not that we'd talked about it. In fact, she and I were learning how to avoid each other, how to live in the same house without communicating about anything that mattered.

What does it say on the form? she asked. Suicide?

He put on the pair of half-glasses attached to a leather cord around his neck and opened the manila folder. From it he drew a one-page document that he slid across the table to us. He touched a fingertip to the line labeled *Cause of Death*, and there someone had typed the words DECEASED SHOT SELF.

Do you have any idea what this ruling is going to mean for me? Mom asked.

I'm afraid I do, Dr. Milius said.

There must be an appeal process. A federal body of some kind. His death *could* have been an accident.

I'm sorry, Genevieve. No.

Dr. Milius reached to the floor next to his chair then and brought up another envelope, which he placed on the table. He drummed it with his fingers. There are some personal effects that you'll be getting back today. If you're ready. I have the list here.

He glanced over at Pastor Lundberg, who stood up and left the room. He was back in a minute, carrying a tall narrow box the size of a golf bag, plain brown cardboard. He set it on the floor between Mom and me, then opened it for us and removed the items one by one: Dad's rifle, his wool hunting trousers, the shooting gloves and his boots, which still looked supple and waxed. I remembered how he took pleasure in heating up his blue tin of beeswax in a shallow pan of water on the stovetop and then rubbing the hot yellow liquid into the leather uppers with a piece of checkered flannel. There was also a plastic bag containing his wallet and car keys. His hunting coat wasn't there, and neither was the shirt he'd had on, or the blaze-orange vest or the orange stocking cap I'd seen hanging on the branch of the caragana.

I cataloged these things in my head. Mom had started to cry, silently.

What about his change? I asked. He always had change in his pocket. I heard it jingling that day, walking out to our stands.

Dr. Milius turned and scrutinized me over the top of his glasses. He tapped the list with his finger and scanned down through it.

I don't see anything about coins here. Damaged or soiled clothing, of course — that kind of thing they retain as evidence, or else destroy. But no, I can't say why the coins aren't here. Unless they came out of his pocket when he fell and simply weren't found. I could certainly put a call in to the medical examiner.

I'd like that, I said. Let him know we want everything back.

All right, then. He pushed back his chair and straightened up. If there's anything else I can help with, please call.

And just like that, it was over.

Pastor Lundberg carried the box out to our Toyota and stowed it in the backseat, anxious, it seemed to me, to be rid of it. When he asked if we'd like to pray with him, Mom said no, we had to be going. There were things she needed to do.

At home she went upstairs to her room and shut the door. I hauled the box full of Dad's things into the attic, behind the sauna, so Magnus wouldn't find it. I was still wondering about the coins. It bothered me to think of them lying on the floor of the woods, along with bone fragments from his skull — though if they'd still been there I would have found them with the metal detector. It bothered me even more to imagine somebody in St. Paul shoving them into a pop machine. I wanted them back. I wanted to carry them in my own pocket and listen to their music. I wanted to be able to reach down and touch them as I walked.

Two days later, on Wednesday, we buried Dad. Sawmill Cemetery is where we put him, in the far northwestern corner where the pines were trying to come back, seedlings sprouting thick as weeds around the winter-cracked gravestones. It was a private ceremony, only a few people there, with Father Dittmer officiating. He read from John's Gospel, the story of Lazarus, ending with the words of Christ: *I am the resurrection and the life; whoever believes in me, even if he dies, will live* . . . I half expected Dad to come walking out of the woods to join us.

When the brief service was over, Dwayne Primrose stepped from Jack Runion's hearse and lifted his gold cornet, pink wrists glaring from his sleeves, elbows jutting like a pair of sharp feather-less wings. He blew taps with an unforced vibrato, each note pitch-perfect, taking his time. It was a cold day but there was no wind, and a metal-gray sky bore in upon us. Primrose lowered his horn and let it dangle from one hand, the last smooth note — a middle C — lingering beyond this movement.

Clay, who'd been standing behind us, stepped forward and took Mom's arm, edging me aside. She gave him a thorny look, and he bit his top lip, sucking a few stray mustache wires into his mouth. He glanced around at me with a flat smile. He'd received the letter, of course, and the pictures — I could see it in his eyes, which had an opaque, distracted quality. He was making calcula-tions, weighing his options.

I looked right through him. Let's go, I said to Mom.

She stepped away from Clay and pulled Magnus close. As I led them toward our car, I could feel my uncle staring after us.

We were just turning in to our driveway at home when Mom put both hands on her head and groaned. I think I forgot my purse, she said. At the cemetery. Damn it. You know that big gravestone that says Vorland, the one with the praying hands and the flat top? I think I put it down on that one when I retied my boot. I'll have to go back.

She sat there diminished and pale. She hadn't spoken all day.

I'll do it, I said. You and Magnus go inside.

She didn't argue or thank me but simply popped open her door and shoved it with her shoulder. Magnus got out too, and I watched them walk single file up the sidewalk, heads down, Magnus in the lead. He opened the door and stepped aside for Mom to go in first, then glanced at me and shook his head. I didn't blame him if he was angry with me. Or jealous. I wouldn't have wanted to be sitting at home with Mom right now either.

I took my time driving out and halfway there met the grave digger in his rusty one-ton truck, pulling a flatbed with a Bobcat digger on it. He waved his cigarette at me and nodded, as if we were old friends. At the cemetery I parked just inside the gate next to Clay's Austin and sat for a while before getting out, wondering why he was still here. Instead of following the path, I picked my way stone to stone, moving toward high ground until I could see him. I leaned against the shadow side of a monument to the man who had founded Battlepoint, a sawmill owner named Halverson. Clay stood on the dirtied snow before the black rectangle of earth, arms straight down at his sides, head hanging forward as if his neck were broken. He sobbed, his shoulders moving in a rhythm of jerks. Several feet away Dwayne Primrose sat waiting on the Vorland stone.

I don't know how long Clay cried, but it was long enough to make me promise myself to be careful — go back over everything I'd seen and measure it, consider anything I might have missed. I didn't know if he was crying out of guilt or loss or both. But finally he straightened up and turned around, tugged his collar tighter around his throat. Primrose stood from the gravestone. They both started toward me. When they were twenty yards off, I stepped away from the monument into their path. They stopped, then came on again.

Bet you're looking for this, Clay said. He was holding Mom's purse, which he lifted now to show me.

I nodded.

Well I'm going home, he said, handing me the purse. And you know what? I'm gonna get drunk. What do you say to that? Your dad wouldn't approve, would he? He was like our old man that way. But tough shit, he was the only brother I had — he might just understand.

Clay walked past me toward his car, his stride purposeful yet plodding, like a tired soldier's. Dwayne followed after him, pink wrists and pink knit mittens poking out from the sleeves of his ragged coat. Abruptly, Clay turned and looked right at me. I waited for him to speak, but he only watched me for a few moments, then lifted his hands as if to say, *Okay, we're done here.*

At the Austin he ducked into the driver's seat and closed himself in. Dwayne went around to the passenger's side. I followed them into town and all the way pleaded with Dad to come back and set things straight, tell me what was true and what wasn't. Why did it have to be so hard? I asked him. Why was everything left up to me? Dad had always known what to say when the world seemed crooked or wrong. He'd always been able to see straight to the heart of things. That was the talent *I* needed now, and Dad could give it to me if he chose to. I knew he could. He could tell me what to expect at the changing house on Friday night and how to prepare myself for it. He could tell me if my plan was going to backfire. He could tell me if I was in danger.

But even though I smelled in momentary gusts the soap he used, his cheap aftershave, the gunpowder and beeswax — and even though I thought I heard his voice at one point and slowed the car and cranked down the window to listen — he stayed away.

10

It was a terrible week. Mom's very presence infuriated me, and Magnus seemed to require a support and love that was beyond my capacity to give. There was no one to talk to about my fears, no one I could trust. For that matter, there was nothing I could find to occupy myself or take my mind off my upcoming engagement with Clay.

I don't remember how it happened, but after supper on Thursday evening I found myself behind the wheel of the Mercury, heading north and reliving in my mind the way Christine had rescued me three days earlier — coatless, my eyes frozen closed. I drove up to Little Mexico and turned onto the perimeter road that skirted the back of her trailer house. I still had the embroidered handkerchief she'd used to stanch the bleeding on my cut hand, and I'd taken to carrying it around in my back pocket. I went in slowly and parked well back of their place, which was light gray in color, plywood around the bottom. Sitting next to it, like an old dog yawning, sat a station wagon, hood sprung open. In the yard, a crooked metal swing set and a wooden storage shed. The yellow truck was parked beneath the corrugated roof of their carport.

The hollow sound of my knuckles on the wooden door reminded me that I had no idea what I was going to say. I would have turned and sneaked back to the car, except a light snapped on inside and Christine appeared, indistinct through the frosty window. At her shoulder was another, smaller face — her baby sister, with a yellow ribbon in her hair. They both watched me, their eyes identical and solemn.

It's just me, I said.

She swung open the door and stepped aside. I shuffled my feet on the welcome mat and bent to remove my shoes, but she touched my shoulder with three fingers — I felt the press of each one — and said, Leave them on. In the narrow kitchen she gave me a chair at the table and sat down across from me. She leaned down and spoke to the baby on her lap.

This is the silent boy, she said, and looked up at me, a little smile playing on her lips. Christine had a way of overwhelming me with her eyes, and that's what she did now. It was like she could turn on the power with a lever. I didn't know if I was ready for this.

You're alone? I asked. The two of you?

Mom's got nights at the plant this week. Next week it's me. We switch off. That's why I'm late to school sometimes.

I nodded.

We were just going to have some toast, she said, and motioned toward the counter where a loaf of dark bread and a jar of jelly sat next to a gleaming four-slot toaster. Want some?

No thanks, I said.

The baby reached up and grabbed hold of Christine's lip and tugged on it.

What's her name? I asked.

Renata.

Christine stood and went to the sink and turned on the tap. She tested the water with her finger, filled a plastic peanut-butter jar halfway and spooned in cream-colored powder from a blue canister. She shook this mixture together, poured it frothing into a plastic bottle, then plucked a brown rubber nipple from the counter-top and attached it to the bottle with a screw-top ring. Finally she took four pieces of bread and dropped them into the toaster. Renata observed all this from the crook of her sister's elbow, fingers holding tight to a hank of Christine's shining hair, and when they sat down again, she went full-force after the bottle. Her eyes glazed over, satisfied.

So, what are you doing here? Christine asked. Her voice was serious, but her eyes seemed to be making fun of me, and I wasn't sure what to feel about that.

I reached into my pocket for her embroidered handkerchief and pushed it to the center of the table. I'd tried to wash it out, but there were still bloodstains.

She laughed. Did it make you nervous, having that? You didn't want to keep it?

Maybe I just needed an excuse, I said.

She thought for a while, her eyes fastened so tightly on mine that sweat broke out on my forehead and the back of my neck. Then the toast popped up, and she handed Renata to me, dangling her by her armpits. I didn't have any choice.

You sure you don't want any? she asked from the counter. She was buttering the toast.

Sure, why not. It looks great.

Renata tipped her head back, trying to get a peek at the stranger she'd been handed over to. She blew a spit bubble. The smell coming from her diaper had a sweetness I couldn't identify.

I think she might need a change, I said.

Christine retrieved her sister from my lap, set the plate of toast on the table, picked up a piece and took a bite. She'd applied a thick coating of jelly, and the flavor was almost too strong. Bitter and fruity. I pointed at my mouth and nodded.

Wow, I said, between swallows.

Renata buzzed and squirmed, tipped her bottle higher.

I wanted to thank you, I said. For picking me up the other day, giving me a ride.

Christine lifted a finger to say *Hold on*, and went to the counter, where she laid Renata down on her back and opened her yellow flannel pajamas, unsnapping them at the crotch. She peeled them up to expose the diaper, the cloth kind with plastic pants over the top. A few expert movements of her fingers freed Renata from her diaper, which Christine balled up and dropped into a white plastic bucket on the floor next to the sink. Renata's legs pedaled in the air.

Ooh! Christine fanned the air with both hands. *Hermana del hedor*, she said, then wiped her little sister with a cloth she'd dampened under the kitchen faucet, and replaced the diaper with a dry one she took from a stack on the counter, deftly fastening the pins despite Renata's pumping legs and arching back.

You're good, I told her.

Bedtime, she said, and disappeared with Renata down the narrow hallway.

While she was gone, I got up and looked around. Children's artwork hung in homemade pine-board frames, and there were photographs of Christine when she was small, posing for the camera in a sun-baked country I could barely imagine. Between the kitchen and living room was floor-to-ceiling shelving cluttered with knickknacks: a collection of carved animals, a line of plaster lighthouses, and on the top shelf a row of yellowing baseballs, each on its own cork pedestal. A framed black-and-white photograph showed a man with a bat on his shoulder.

Your dad? I asked.

Christine had come in from the hallway and was rubbing her eyes against the light. He played in the winter league down there, she said, taking down one of the balls. I grew up watching him. We'd spend summers in the fields west of here in the valley, or else in Washington or Iowa, wherever the best work was, and then go back down there, where he'd play all winter.

She handed me the ball. The old leather was dry to the touch, and the red stitching had faded to a dull pink. In pencil somebody had written, *Daniel Montez home run. 448 feet. June 21st 1979. Saltillo.*

He almost had a chance to play for the Cardinals once. This scout wanted to sign him up, but then somebody came along and checked his records, somebody high up in the organization. At least that's how Dad tells it. And he was over thirty already, so they dropped him. That's when he decided the world's against him.

I handed Christine the ball and she put it back, then sat down across from me and started on the piece of toast still left on her plate. Her eyes went off to a corner of the room.

When are they letting him out? I asked.

February, March. Maybe earlier. Depends on this hearing that's coming up just after Christmas.

She stood and went to the window that faced the back of the lot and gazed off into the dark, her face softened by the dim light of the kitchen's single bulb. From outside, in the distance, came the sound of an engine whirring, refusing to start. I'm going to tell you something, she said quietly. Something I've never told anyone.

A chill passed through me. Christine looked over, solemn, her face the loveliest thing I'd seen. I remembered the touch of our lips that day in the darkroom and wondered if she remembered too.

There's this old guy who lives just up there, she said, pointing to the north. A couple blocks. Johnny something or other. I mean, he's old. Close to a hundred.

Johnny Johnson, I said.

Everybody in town knew him. He spent mornings in the post office with his cronies, speaking Norwegian. Bone thin, nearly deaf. It was said that he'd come over as an infant the same year the *Titanic* went down.

Dad used to do stuff for him, Christine said. Shovel his driveway, mow his grass. That's where he went the night of the fight, after it was over. He hid in Johnny's basement, not that *we* knew it or that Johnny did either. Dad called the next morning, early, and told us where he was. Told us he was getting out of town as soon as he could. But here's the thing. I was walking to the store later that morning, and Vince Kaeler pulled up next to me in his cruiser and told me to climb in. He goes into this speech about how bad it's going to be for my dad if he doesn't give himself up. He asks if it matters to me if I never see him again outside a prison cell. He asks if I want to see him shot by some bounty hunter. *Gunned down* is how he put it. There's this guy, he told me, who's killed four men with a shotgun, all of them on the run like my dad. He scared the hell out of me, Jesse. And when he asked me where Dad was hiding, I told him. Johnny's house, I said. In the basement.

Christine turned from the window. She'd always had a thought-

ful look about her, and I'd imagined her as a girl given to contem-
plation, but now it seemed as if the habits of her face — the vertical
lines in her forehead, the arch of her brows — had more to do
with fear.

Do you know what it feels like? she asked. Giving up your
dad? Vince Kaeler dropped me off here, and it wasn't five minutes before the sirens came. I ran over there, and so did Mom and
some of the neighbors, and we watched them haul Dad out of
Johnny's basement. They've got him cuffed behind his back, and
he's all bloody, and he's looking around for us. Then you know
what happens? Vince gives me this little thumbs-up, and Dad *sees*
it. I can't tell you the look on his face. It was the end, and I knew it.
He looked at me like he'd been shot dead, and I was the one who
shot him.

I reached across the table and put my hand on Christine's small
wrist. In the distance somebody shouted — a man's voice, guttural
and questioning, a desperate sound — and then an engine fired
up and tires whined for traction in the snow.

That was the last time I saw him, she said. I haven't gone with
Mom to the prison, and she can't understand why. He asks about
me, I guess. Where's Christine? he says. But he knows, and he
knows I know he knows. He'll never forgive me.

He's your dad, I said. Give him a little time, he'll understand.

No, he won't. But here's the thing. He's still my dad, and I love
him. No matter what he thinks, no matter how much he hates me.

He doesn't hate you, I said.

Christine tried to pull her hand away, but I held on. Then the
late coal train rumbled into town, and we turned our heads toward
the whistle blast. As in my own house, the passing of the train set
up a vibration in the walls and rattled the dishes in the cupboards.

We sat and watched each other, letting the weight of her story lift and dissipate, and when it was quiet again, she moved her hand beneath mine, turned it so that our fingers laced together. In them I felt the pulse of her heart like a small rhythmic shudder — or maybe it was my heart.

There's something I'm going to tell you too, I said. About *my* dad.

She leaned toward me and gave my hand a squeeze, making me know I had all the attention she could give.

He didn't kill himself, I said.

Christine's expression remained unchanged, but her eyes darkened. I told her everything — about seeing Dad on the night after he had died and the message he'd had for me, about the trap I'd set for Clay. It was so easy, talking to her. The words came as if she were prompting them out of me, and when I was finished, she stood up, led me into the living room and sat us down on the big wicker couch there. She said nothing at first, and I took that to mean she pitied me, that she thought I'd lost my mind. I didn't hold it against her because the moment was perfect anyway — her baby sister asleep in the next room, the scent of garlic and peppers still lingering from whatever they'd had for supper, the sound of the fridge buzzing like a dragonfly. And Christine, of course, smelling as she did of sour baby's milk and sweet perfume and some girl-smelling soap. She produced a book of matches and lit the holy candle sitting on the coffee table. It was enclosed by a frosted glass painted with an image of Jesus, arms reaching toward us, red nail holes visible in his palms. The robe he wore was the color of a dyed-blue Easter egg, his skin a dull pink.

What do you make of it? I asked her. Do you think I'm nuts?

She fixed her gaze on me — dark, warm, without judgment —

and when I leaned forward and kissed her, she kissed me back, took my head in her hands and moved it just so, her lips the comfort I'd needed, the assurance that life wasn't all cruelty and unknowable calculation.

After a few minutes, she pulled away.

What? I asked.

I believe you, she said.

Everything? All of it?

Yes, she said.

She may as well have wrenched open my chest and climbed inside. I pushed my face into her hair, into her neck. I tried to disappear into the smell and the softness of her. It seemed to me that she lived and breathed in a place cleaner than my own, and I wanted to go there and stay with her, leave my own world behind. She was sun and water.

But then she pulled away again, and the look in her eyes frightened me. Jesse, she whispered. What about your mom? I mean, what does she know? What did she *do*? How is *she* involved in all this?

My stomach turned. It was the question I'd been avoiding, the question with no reasonable answer — or none that could both convince and satisfy me. I didn't even want to think about it. The whole state of affairs was crazy, beyond belief, and sitting here now with Christine, having unburdened myself, I could see that. Yes, beyond belief. In fact her presence had the effect of making harmless phantoms of all my fears. Everything looked suddenly different.

Look, it's all bullshit, I said. All right? I just had to get things off my chest. I mean, *ghosts*? I'm such an idiot. I don't know what I'm talking about.

Christine shook her head.

What? I asked, and laughed.

She slid away from me and crossed her arms in front of herself. I felt the distance between us like a ball of compressed air in my lungs. She said, Where I come from, people don't always stay gone after they die. I mean, it's not that unusual, Jesse.

What do you mean? I asked.

My grandma, for one. Whenever Dad started drinking, I'd go hide in my closet, and Grandma would come and sit with me. This is a year or two after she died. She'd cover my ears so I couldn't hear my parents yelling, the sound of Dad slamming Mom around, and Mom begging. Grandma would braid my hair, tell me stories, sing lullabies. I don't know what I would have done without her.

Whoa, I said.

Christine sat there at the other end of the couch, not moving, her eyes boring into mine. I didn't know which thing to take up first.

So, he hit your mom? I asked.

She nodded. And I'm telling you the truth about my grandma too. She always smelled like peanuts — that's what she loved to eat more than anything. And when I cried she'd wipe my face with her fingertips. They felt cool and slippery, like polished leather.

Your dead grandma, I said.

That's right, and I shouldn't have to convince *you*, for heaven's sake. You know what *you* saw.

I'm sorry.

And you know what else? This thing you've got going — this trap for your uncle? I'm not sure it's such a good idea. I mean, if he shows up, he's pretty much admitting he did it. Why would he want to do that?

Because he doesn't have a choice. That's how blackmail works, Christine. He doesn't want to get shot.

What's to stop him from bringing a gun? Why wouldn't he just kill you and be done with it?

He's not going to see me, remember?

And what if he doesn't show at all? What'll *that* mean?

He'll be there, I said.

But what if he isn't?

Then I have to rethink everything. But that's not how it's going to be. You should've seen the look on his face at the cemetery yesterday. He was crapping his pants.

Christine slid close to me again and laid her head on my chest. She put her fingers against my mouth and then slipped one through my lips. The taste of it reminded me of black olives. I thought of the Madonna's fingers in the painting above Dad's office desk, slender and somehow terribly naked despite the rings she wore. I lifted Christine's face up to mine and kissed her. She kissed me back, deeply, her teeth clean and smooth, like glass. Then she took my head in her hands and moved her lips to my nose, which she kissed, and then to my eyes, kissing each in turn, and then to my ear.

I have to tell you something, she whispered. I'm not letting you go out there alone tomorrow night. Into the woods. I'm going along. Mom'll be home to watch Renata. She's got the night off.

Is that right? I asked.

Yeah.

Fine. And I've got something to say too. If your dad ever hits you, I'll kill him.

You will? she asked.

Damn right.

Ooh, big man, she said.

Later, as I left the trailer house, dizzy with the smell of her, she touched my face — just the side of her index finger against the front of my chin, but I felt as if every nerve in my body had received a gentle stroke. Then the trailer's heat was rushing out with me into the cold. In the Mercury I refused to let myself look back at her. All the same, I knew she was there watching, and that later she'd be thinking of me as she lay in her bed that night, just as I'd be thinking of her as I always did, and at least in that way we'd be together.

On my way home the air was thick and frosty, every surface coated with rime: the sides of the houses, the parked cars and their antennas, the trees and lampposts and electric lines. As I drove, I had the sensation of my body wanting to come apart, dissolve in the cold fog.

I know it wasn't very big of me, but when I went into Sinclair's woods the next night, I was more than happy to have company. By ten thirty, Christine and I were in position. I was sitting on the wide branch of a huge, dying white pine similar to the one in which Dad had built his stand. My back rested against the bark-less trunk. Christine was perched on a branch a foot or two below mine and thirty degrees to my right, where she could keep watch on the lake, to our north, and the woods behind us. We were ten feet off the ground and maybe fifty yards from the changing house on the beach. I'd left home in my running clothes at ten, after Mom and Magnus had gone to bed. I headed east on the lake road, ran out past the town line and the beach too and met Christine at the old Skaggs place, where she parked her truck behind the barn. We doubled back through Sinclair's woods, tromping our way through deep snow and threading willow clumps and tangly brambles until we found an easy tree to climb, one with the right view.

We watched.

The sky was clear, the moon gleaming, the air crisp. What wind there was came from behind us, carrying forest sounds: the ticking of dead leaves and the occasional distant call of an owl. I wore a stocking cap pushed up on my head to leave my ears free — if there was anyone behind us in the woods, I wanted to know it. Whenever I glanced over at Christine, her lips were moving soundlessly.

Every few minutes a pair of headlights approached from town, and each time my stomach clenched. But none pulled into the beach lot.

He's not coming, Christine said at last.

No? I asked.

No, she said.

Just wait, I told her.

At ten forty-five Officer Kaeler drove by in his patrol car. He didn't slow down, didn't even glance in our direction. From our perch I could see his profile through the driver's side window — his chin lifted high, as if he were pondering some deep thought — and the burning orange speck of his cigarette. Soon he passed by again on his way back into town.

It's cold, Christine said.

A few more minutes, I told her, thinking as I said it, *Maybe he's watching us right now.* I reached into my pocket for my watch and glanced down at the glowing hands.

Eleven o'clock. Zero hour.

Then somewhere behind us, a branch snapped. At the sound, my neck jerked and I slammed the back of my head against the tree trunk. I held myself still, didn't release the breath I'd taken. Christine froze too. Out the corner of my eye I watched as she turned to scan the woods behind us — or the part of it, anyway, that she could see. I strained to hear movement, a step in the snow, the click of a safety button. What came to mind was a picture of Dad on his tree stand, turning his head in to the cold muzzle of Clay's rifle. Icy hot needles pricked the inside of my gut. I tried to reason with my fear: *There's no one there, get a grip*, I told myself.

Still, I could feel him — or something — behind me. And so I resolved to jump, take him by surprise. Silently I counted back from ten, then swung my leg over the tree limb and pitched myself toward the ground, twisting a full hundred and eighty degrees as I fell. I lost my balance on landing but caught myself in time to see a large doe — eyes luminous — wheel and bound away, the white rag of its tail zagging through the night woods, branches snapping beneath its hooves.

My God! Christine said from above me.

Relieved, I dropped to my haunches and knelt there until my heart slowed down and my breathing calmed. But when I stood up again, a movement drew my eye. Turning, I saw — or thought I did — a figure slip into the changing house.

You see that? I asked.

Christine shook her head no. She was still facing into the woods, the wrong direction.

Wait, I told her. Hold still.

Clay's Austin wasn't in the lot, but I imagined him hiding down there, just inside the entrance, watching the woods for movement. Or maybe waiting on one of the changing benches. And so we stayed in place, Christine and I, just inside the tree line. I was afraid to bend over and scratch the itch on the side of my foot, afraid to check the watch in my pocket, afraid even to blink, for fear I might miss him as he ducked away. I don't know how long this went on, five minutes, ten, fifteen, but finally I'd had enough.

We better have a look, I whispered.

In answer, Christine flung herself off the branch and landed gracefully beside me in the snow. We started down the hill, at first on foot, then going to our hands and knees, and finally to our bellies. By the time we reached the corner of the building, the tightness had leaked out of my chest. My sense of anticipation was gone. No way would he just sit here, waiting all this time. Would he?

The changing house was a simple shell of cement blocks, open to the elements — no roof, no doors at the entrance or exit — and as we crept along the outside of it, I heard a soft sound, like a kitten crying. Then I heard nothing. I moved to the end of the wall and peeked around inside.

It was hard to make out, but the moon was bright and the image clarified. A sleeping bag, filled to bursting, was balanced on a pair of benches that had been pushed together to form a bed. Inside the bag their bodies moved. Their heads, no more than four feet away, were visible to me. I knew them, two kids from school: Jeremy Black, who lived a few houses west of me, and Mary Apple, from my English class. I could have sneezed — I could have sat down right there and cried out of frustration — and they wouldn't have noticed a thing.

Still on my hands and knees, I backed away. I turned to Christine and pressed a finger to my lips. Her eyes in the moonlight said, *Well?* I shook my head, pointed toward the trees, mouthed the words *Come on*, and then we ran for the woods. No sooner had we entered the tree line, though, than a pair of headlights rounded the curve from the east, coming on slowly. Christine and I dropped down and pressed ourselves against the ground. The Austin turned in at the beach drive and pulled up to the changing house.

Clay shut off the engine and cut his running lights but at first made no move to leave the car.

What's he doing? Christine whispered.

As if in response, Clay pushed open his door and rose from the bucket seat. The night was quiet, and across the fifty yards between us came the squeak of his boots on the snow. Stealthily — bent double, shoulders hunched — he approached the changing house, paused at the entrance, glanced all around, patted the front chest-pocket of his coat and then ducked inside. For several seconds there was nothing at all. Then we heard the husky voice of Mary Apple, who didn't shout or even sound particularly angry when she said, Do you *mind?*

Clay's flight from the building to his car was quick and stiff — he looked like a boy who'd been spanked. Somehow his pinched movements and uncertain gait made it impossible for me to summon the feeling of triumph I'd been dreaming of all week. My trap had been snapped, certainly — but instead of catching Clay in his guilt, all I could say for sure, I saw now, was that I'd given him a good scare.

III

THE SOUND
OF THE TRUMPET

11

That month I shoveled the walk and the driveway almost every morning. Twice I hauled the aluminum extension ladder out of the garage, leaned it against the house, climbed up on the roof and shoveled that off too. The snow was coming as if it meant to stay, as if it meant to displace the air, as if one day in some infernal boardroom they'd decided to make winter a permanent season.

Despite the way things had turned out at Battlepoint Beach, a part of me felt perversely pleased. My plan had worked. The problem was it had worked too well — I'd designed it too efficiently. The trap wasn't discriminating enough. For all my scheming and despite what I knew in my gut, logic told me that Clay's appearance at the changing house proved nothing more than a desire not to be shot.

If he's guilty, though, he's going to screw up, Christine said. He'll make some mistake. Isn't that how things work?

Needing to be reassured, I decided yes, I agreed with her. I would wait him out, exercise a little patience, if that was possible.

In the meantime Christine moved to the dead center of my life. If love is one part escape, my experience tells me it's the largest part. Each day on waking it was the image of her face in my mind that chased away my troubled dreams. Nights — at least those when she wasn't working the late shift at the turkey plant — we'd go to movies at the Bijou and make out in the worn leather seats that smelled of bodies and popcorn grease. When it wasn't too cold, we'd drive out into the woods in the Mercury, zigzagging the back roads and pulling off at gravel pits and logging trails. Mostly, though, we studied together at her place or mine — hers was better because her mom worked the shifts Christine didn't. I'd help take care of Renata: feed her, walk her, change her diaper, read her stories, put her down for bed. After, we'd do our assignments at the kitchen table until the gravitational pull made us shove our books aside.

We retreated into the refuge we made of each other, and if in our case there was more to retreat from, that might account for why our bond came to feel so permanent so fast.

Meanwhile, Mom performed a retreat of her own. Mornings she slept in, and each night after supper she escaped to her bedroom, where she listened to the classic rock station, sometimes singing along. Magnus grew adept at fending for himself. He made his own school lunches — peanut butter sandwiches, mostly — and figured out how to use the washer and dryer. He stopped inviting friends over to play. When he needed something from Mom, he'd leave a note — always formal in tone — on the kitchen table:

Our class is taking a field trip to the county zoo next week. Please sign this permission slip and make out a check for $3 to Battlepoint Public School.

Mom showed no interest in Christine. She asked me nothing about my first experience with love. We spoke only about the
commonplace events and demands of the life we were pretending
to share: what we needed from the store, where to take the Toyota
for a new clutch. As far as I could tell, she wasn't looking for
work or doing anything to address the uncertainty of our future.
She stayed clear of the Valhalla and ignored a proposal from
Rich Castle, who'd been Dad's cook, to reopen as a chef's training center with help from a small-business grant. To her credit,
though — at least by all appearances — she was avoiding Clay. He
hadn't come by the house in more than a month. For years Mom
had made a point of going to listen whenever he had a gig nearby,
but when his band, Liquid Dogs, played the Deep Freeze, a local
club, she stayed home. I couldn't decide if my letter trap had
managed to scare him off, or if I'd simply been dead wrong from
the start.

At one o'clock or so on Christmas afternoon, Pastor Lundberg
came to our door with a gift. He looked, as usual, earnest and
thrown together, his black stocking cap inside out, its red tag jutting from the top, toothpaste dried at the corners of his mouth.

Merry Christmas, he said, peering past me into the house.

I invited him in, apologizing for the tree. I'd gone out and
picked it up the night before, and it wasn't decorated yet.

Hey there, he said to Magnus.

My brother was lying on the living room floor playing the
game he'd invented using baseball cards, a Popsicle-stick bat and
a ball made out of tightly crumpled masking tape. I went upstairs
to Mom's room to fetch her, but she refused to come out. She was
in bed with the lights off and shades pulled, lying like a corpse

beneath the bedspread, her arms outside the covers and straight at her sides. The radio was going softly, a standard by the Eagles, Hotel California.

Tell him I'm not feeling well, she said.

He'll want to come up. You know he will.

Tell him I'm not home.

That's great, Mom. I'll say you're out looking for work. I'll tell him you're meeting with a real estate broker. How's that? I'll tell him you're up here figuring out the future for us.

Tell him anything you want, she said, and turned to the wall.

Downstairs, Pastor Lundberg was spread out on the living room floor next to Magnus. He was trying to snap the tape ball with the Popsicle-stick bat, and he had one ear flat against the Persian rug.

That's not how you do it, Magnus said, reclaiming his game pieces. You've got to put your finger here, see? And then flick it like this. The tape ball rose in an arc toward the unlit fireplace and struck the edge of the mantel. See? That's a double, he said.

Mom's out buying a turkey, I told Pastor Lundberg. I forgot she left.

Magnus looked at me quickly, and I shook my head at him. Pastor Lundberg pushed himself up from the floor. He took the small gift he'd set on the coffee table and added it to our sad little pile beneath the Norway pine.

She must be feeling better then. Tell her I stopped in, okay?

Magnus and I spent the afternoon in the boathouse, scraping away on the wooden-hulled Chris-Craft that Dad had bought at auction a few summers back. Although he'd paid a guy at Battle-point Marine to overhaul its engine and replace a section of the rotting hull, he had never launched it. I held my scraper in both hands, pulling and pushing in even strokes, just like Dad had taught me, and it wasn't long before I was numb to the elbows. The varnish came off in yellow scales, crisp and curved.

That night Magnus and I heated up a frozen dinner one of the churchwomen had brought over: hamburger, potato and green-bean hotdish. Mom had promised that we'd have our traditional supper — boiled shrimp and sourdough bread — the next night, and that we'd open our gifts then, though if she'd gone out and bought any, I didn't know where she'd hidden them.

I'll feel better tomorrow, she had said, fingers grasping the neck of her gown. Her eyes looked vague, loose in her head, as if their only purpose were to let light pass into her skull. As she turned and left, her white gown floated about her narrow body in such a way that she might have been hovering over the floor.

My brother and I sat on opposite sides of the table, silent, picking at our food, and when the doorbell rang, we both jumped in our chairs before racing each other to the front door. Clay was standing casually on the front step, a large computer box propped against one hip. It was wrapped in the Sunday comics. Despite the cold, he wore his short leather bomber jacket, its collar turned up, and a pair of thin doeskin gloves.

Where's your mom? he asked, glancing past us into the living room.

Asleep. She's not feeling well.

I stayed put in the doorway, but Clay slid past me like oil. He set the box on the floor of the entry, leaned against the wall and pried off his boots, balancing on one leg, then the other, yanking with both hands. The boots clumped to the floor.

Smells great in here, he said, striding into the kitchen.

Magnus and I had no choice but to follow after him. He went first to the archway and took a quick look up the stairs, then came back and sat down at the table.

What's in the box? Magnus asked.

Christmas present, Clay said. But you can't open it until your mom's here. He lifted his face toward the ceiling and projected his voice, as if trying to reach Mom's room upstairs.

I told you, she's sleeping, I said.

Oops. He brought a finger to his lips, hiked his eyebrows and made a face, then went over to the stove and lifted the cover off the pot in which I'd heated the hotdish. He leaned down close for a smell.

I haven't eaten yet, he whispered. Sometimes you forget, living alone.

I gave up and sat down at the table. Help yourself, I said.

Clay flipped open the cupboard door and took down a white dinner plate and a glass, then clattered a fork and spoon from the silverware drawer. When he'd filled his plate and taken a seat at the table, he said, Anything to drink?

I pointed at the fridge.

For all I could tell, he'd gone without food for days. He bent close to his plate and shoveled in huge forkfuls. It was a wonder he didn't skewer his lip. Between bites he complained about having to spend the day fixing a broken sewer main at the trailer park. He also described the new fish house he was building, a four-holer, three for angling and a large square one for spearing. The Sons of Norway Lodge was sponsoring a spearing contest, with a thousand-dollar first prize going to the fisherman whose take of pike for the season added up to the most weight, and Clay planned on winning it.

And you better believe I could use the cash, he said. I'm out of work on May first — that's when everybody's got to be out of their trailers. They want to break ground by the start of June.

Clay looked from Magnus to me, his eyes widening as if he expected sympathy. He didn't get any.

So, I said. Where are you going to put it?

Put what?

Your fish house.

Oh — Oscar's Bay. But don't tell anyone. I had it all to myself last winter, and you should've seen the lunkers. Nobody thinks of that spot for northerns. Most of the guys try the shallows north of Battlepoint, you know, just off Sinclair's woods? Say. He pointed his fork across the table at us, and for a moment I thought I saw an iron gleam in his eye, dull and savage. Then it was gone. Sometime the two of you'll have to come out there with me. How about it? I know your dad took you fishing once in a while, but I bet he never took you spearing.

That's right, he didn't, I said, and held my uncle's gaze until he looked away. *Sinclair's woods?* I thought. He was messing with my head, the bastard. But he wasn't going to beat me — I wasn't going to let him see a thing.

I don't like fish, said Magnus. I don't like how they smell.

There are things a guy's gotta overlook, Clay said, chewing. His face was pleasant now, even vacant.

That's right, I agreed, and forced myself to smile at him. Then I offered him more hotdish.

When he'd finished his second helping, Clay pushed himself

away from the table and leaned back in his chair. With both hands he swept his gray hair back behind his ears and propped his hands behind his head. Any coffee in the house? he asked.

I got up and filled the pot at the tap, then took down the can of grounds and scooped some into the filter. Magnus watched me unhappily from the table.

Ah, will you smell that, Clay said. If that doesn't get your mom down here, nothing will.

She needs to sleep, I said. And at that moment I heard the soft sound of her step on the stairs. We all turned as she entered beneath the archway, her hands tucked in the pockets of her fuzzy red winter robe, her head tilted to one side as if she were pondering something or simply too exhausted to hold her neck straight.

I thought it sounded like you down here, she said.

Clay stroked his black mustache and told Mom she looked rested. In fact, her lips were white. Fleshy lavender pouches hung beneath her eyes. Clay shot a dazzling smile at her.

What's going on? she asked.

I brought something over, a little present. Nothing big. And the kids persuaded me to stay and eat. So...He lifted his hands at the inevitability of it all, then got up and went to the counter where the coffeepot had filled.

Oh, no, Mom told him. You can't have that. I'll put some milk on.

Clay offered a pleasant scowl, then sat back down and let her heat up milk for his bad stomach. He'd suffered from ulcers for years, and it was a point of pride for him that he didn't listen to his doctor. At our house, though, Mom didn't let him get away with anything, no citrus or strong spices — and she always made sure that he drank some kind of milk with his meals.

After he'd finished a big mug of cocoa, he stood up and put his palms together. Time for a little surprise, he said.

We followed him to the front door, where he picked up the box, and then into the living room, where he set it down gingerly on the Persian rug. Instead of inviting us to open it, he knelt beside it himself and carefully removed the newspaper wrapping. Then he lifted the cardboard flaps at the top and reached inside.

He paused dramatically. Ready? he asked.

None of us spoke. I resented the anticipation I felt.

He lifted his hand from the box and held up a small gray kitten, its head and tail squirming where they stuck out from his fist. Its whiskers were electric white. Its marbled-yellow eyes blinked. A scratchy grunt came from its mouth. Clay, stroking its tiny skull, fastened his eyes on Mom, who somehow managed to look both tranquil and surprised, as if the kitten were something of great value that she had lost and now recovered. She reached out for it, and Clay placed the wiggly thing in her hands. She brought it close to her breast and began to rock it back and forth.

Is it one of yours? she asked.

Are you kidding? he said with a sour look. Those barn cats are filthy, full of lice. I'd never bring one in here.

He took the kitten back from her, tipped it upside down and peered at its pink underside. I think it's a her, but it's hard to tell when they're little, he said.

Mom lifted the kitten away from him and sat down on the couch, where she nestled it close against her. The kitten yawned, reached up with a single paw and set its claws neatly into her robe.

Clay said, I was at the Laundromat yesterday and saw this notice on the bulletin board. Free kittens, you know, to a good home. And something clicked. It just seemed like the thing to do.

Leaning against the fireplace mantel, Clay looked comfortable and pleased with himself.

Mom pushed her face into the gray fuzz. She kissed the sharp white tips of the kitten's ears. This is perfect, Clay, she said.

I don't like cats, Magnus said, glaring over the top of his glasses. I'm allergic. They make me sick. I get stuffed up.

You don't either. That didn't get passed on to you.

I like *dogs*, Magnus said. And Dad told me we were getting another one. He promised.

Mom sighed, exhaustion showing in her face and shoulders. She said, I guess I'll be the one who takes care of her then. I'll get to have all the fun.

Dad promised me. I want another dog.

Hey, we better see if she's hungry, said Clay. I haven't fed her yet.

In the kitchen he poured milk into a bowl, warmed it for half a minute in the microwave and set it on the floor. The kitten's head ducked in and came out quick, milk frosting its whiskers and nose. Its tongue darted out and flicked back and forth. Then it walked a slow circle around the bowl in that jerky, uncertain way kittens have, as if they're moving through a strobe light. Clay stood watching, hands on his hips. Baby animals, he seemed to think, were an invention all his own. He picked it up and gave it a peck on the top of the head.

He was about to hand it off to Mom when he sneezed. The kitten sprang out of his grip and attached itself to the yellow curtains on the kitchen window. But instead of dropping to the floor, it ran straight up the curtain and leaped to the top of the cupboard. For a long moment we all stood staring, the kitten staring back down at us, its head only inches from the ceiling.

It doesn't like us, Magnus said.

Clay reached up, clucking his tongue. Good kitty, he said, stay there now.

But it edged away and then teetered toward the other end of the cupboard.

Good kitty, don't jump. Clay's voice was anxious and tight, out of all proportion to the situation. The kitten peeked over the lip of the cupboard again.

Clay grabbed one of the spindle-backs from the table and climbed up on it. Then he lunged, catching the kitten by one leg but losing his balance in the process and falling sideways onto the mint-green Formica counter, a two-point landing, elbow and hip, the kitten dangling from his hand.

It should have been funny, but no one laughed — certainly not Clay, who rubbed his arm and insisted he hadn't hurt himself. Mom took the kitten back from him. I felt sick all of a sudden and went upstairs, where I knelt before the toilet, my stomach clenching. I gripped the sides of the ceramic bowl, not caring about the piss stains there, and held on as the bathroom wheeled about me, the floor up around my ears. A prickly sweat broke out on my neck and shoulders. Magnus had followed me upstairs, and now he stood a couple of feet back, his fists at his sides.

Are you all right? he asked.

Shut the door, I told him.

Are you sick?

It's about time you learned to pee straight, I said. Then I threw up, my stomach convulsing again and again. I felt as if abiding parts of me were being dislodged and expelled. I saw the look in Clay's eyes when he mentioned the spearing houses off Sinclair's woods. When I could breathe freely again, I let myself fall back on my butt and leaned up against the shower stall.

Should I get Mom? Magnus asked.

Are you kidding?

My throat was on fire and my mouth tasted like rancid cheese, the kind Dad liked — he'd leave it in the fridge for months, until Mom finally threw it away. I felt light-headed but also euphoric, lucid. I allowed myself to enjoy the postpurging calm in my stomach and the air in my lungs. Magnus filled a glass for me at the sink, and we sat together on the bathroom floor waiting for Clay to leave.

For ten or fifteen minutes neither of us spoke. I was remembering the story of Mom and Dad's first wedding anniversary, at a rustic bed-and-breakfast on Rainy Lake. At three in the morning Dad had woken up, choking on phlegm. When Mom turned on the bedside lamp, she saw that his eyes were shot with red, two bloody globes shining in their sockets. She went to the bathroom down the hall for water, and when she came back, Dad was sitting on the plank floor in his boxers, laughing to himself and petting a large yellow cat he'd discovered beneath the bed. Apparently the old tabby was used to sharing its room with strangers.

That was how Mom had learned about Dad's cat allergies.

And he never once, she liked to say, mentioned this before we got married. Not a word about it.

It was an omission that rankled her.

I wish he'd leave, Magnus said. It's Christmas, he shouldn't be here.

He'll be going soon, I said, though downstairs we could hear the drone of his voice, and it sounded like he'd settled in for a while. I told Magnus I needed to lie down. I was tired and still didn't feel well.

I think Mom likes that cat, he said, following me out of the bathroom.

She had them growing up, I said. What do you expect?

Well, I'm getting a dog. I'm getting a Newfie, like Sonny was, and that's what I'll name him. He'll be mine.

Do you know how much they cost? I asked.

I have money. You wait and see.

Hey, that'd be great, I'm all for it, I said. Then I went into my room and shut the door behind me.

Sonny — the first Sonny — had been Dad's dog, a colossal full-breed that welcomed guests by clapping his paws on their shoulders and slobbering over their clothes. Children he simply knocked down and held in place until he'd licked all the salt from their faces. Whenever he felt like it, he scrambled over the wire fencing meant to keep him in our yard and roamed happily through town. A couple years back he'd died of old age.

I felt cold suddenly and went to my closet for the fleece pullover that Mom had gotten me for chilly nights playing trumpet at football games. I was searching through a week-old pile of dirty clothes when I heard the sound of Clay's Austin starting up. Through my window I watched him back out of our driveway and move off down Lake Street to the east. He hadn't gone a block, though, before the Austin rolled to a stop beneath a streetlight. For a minute, maybe two, Clay stayed behind the wheel, probably asking himself whether the notice he got for driving an exotic car was worth the effort it took to keep it running. Finally he climbed out, walked around to the front and popped the hood. My eyes were drawn to the closet, where my .30-30 stood propped against the side of my shoe rack. I went over and got it, pulled my desk chair up close to the window and sat down.

Clay was bent under the hood, tinkering. When he straightened again, I shouldered my rifle and laid its sights on him. At that distance, a hundred yards or so, his body was half the height of my little finger. I put a fine bead on the side of his head. A white puff of breath issued from his mouth. While sighting in my rifle before hunting season, I'd placed six shots within an eight-inch circle at this range.

I levered back the hammer with a forward snap of my right wrist, took a breath and held it. The small iron bead on Clay's head didn't move. I squeezed the trigger and the firing pin slammed with a dull click into nothing. Had there been a live round in the chamber — one of the hollow-points Dad and I used for deer — Clay would have been flat on the street now, half his head missing.

He slammed shut the hood of his car, got back in and drove off.

My first thought was to call Christine, who would understand, but she was out of town. Her mom had convinced her that she ought to be present at her dad's parole hearing at the penitentiary in Wisconsin the next day, and they weren't due home until the twenty-seventh. I waited until my heart slowed to its regular beat before putting my rifle away. Then I went to my dresser and took from its bottom drawer the Baby Ruth candy bar that I'd found in Dad's pocket. I removed its wrapper and tucked it inside my confirmation Bible. Then I sat down on my bed and ate the candy, taking my time and savoring each bite.

I miss you, I said. And though I listened hard for some response, none came.

Downstairs I found Mom in the kitchen, putting the kitten to bed in a cardboard box she'd lined with one of her old flannel robes. She'd wrapped a wind-up alarm clock in a bath towel, and this, she explained, would serve as a stand-in for the kitten's mother.

You think that'll actually help? I asked.

We have to do the best we can, don't we?

The next morning, for the first time in weeks, she got up early and cooked a full breakfast for us — bacon and eggs, toast, hash browns, pancakes — what Dad would have called a hunter's breakfast. Before we sat down at the table, though, she warmed a bowl of milk in the microwave and lifted the kitten out of the box. As it drank, its tail trembled with pleasure.

12

Mom washed the dishes in a whirl of splashing and clanking, then cleaned out both the pantry and the fridge, filling a garbage bag with boxes of stale cereal and big chunks of frozen hotdish the churchwomen had brought over. Finally she got down on her hands and knees and scrubbed the kitchen floor. It was as if Clay's visit had given her a shot of some wonder drug, and she couldn't contain herself. She was more vital than I'd seen her in years. She wore a tight-fitting denim work shirt with pearl buttons, sleeves rolled to her elbows, and she'd tied back her platinum hair in a red bandanna that matched the lipstick she'd put on that morning. For some reason I was reminded of a hot summer day long ago when she'd taken me to a beach, I think on the lake's west side. I couldn't have been more than three years old. She gave me a spoon and a little pail, ordered me to stay out of the water, and lay down on a towel to tan herself. I didn't intend to disobey her, but I must have, because the next thing I remember is the lake bottom disappearing beneath my feet and the suffocating flood of fishy water in my lungs — and then Mom's strong hands, pulling me up. It's painful, thinking back, to realize that in my earliest years she was the one I counted on most, the one who made me feel safe, the one I ran to when I got hurt. As a child I never questioned her strength, never wondered if she'd be there when I needed her.

So, she said now. Who's going along with me? She was lifting her olive-green parka from the hallway closet. It was twelve noon.

Where? I asked.

Opportunity. The mall. It's not too late for a little Christmas shopping, is it? She smiled fiercely, as if daring me to challenge her. Because of how she'd applied her makeup, one eye looked deeper and larger than the other, and it gave me the creeps.

I'll go, Magnus said, jumping up from the table. He'd been watching Mom all morning, sifting and weighing, and apparently he'd come to some positive conclusion. Head down, he ran to the hall closet and started digging through the mess on the floor for his snow boots.

How about you? Mom asked me.

Guess I'll stay here.

Don't you need any clothes?

Not really.

Your jeans are looking pretty raggy. We could get you a couple new pairs.

That's all right.

Have it your way, then, she said, zipping her parka.

Where are you getting the money from? I asked. We don't have it, that's for sure.

Mom gave me a look that was dark and punishing — as if I had no right to question her, as if I had no comprehension of the mess we were caught up in.

Clay? I asked.

Be so good as to let *me* worry about our finances, she said, and took hold of Magnus by the shoulder and steered him toward the door. I glared at her back, hoping she could feel it. The door slammed behind her, and I lifted my hands and gave her both my middle fingers, which I held there straight up and trembling until the Toyota started up and whined down the street. When it was quiet again, I went upstairs to put on my running clothes.

It wasn't really warm enough for it, but today I needed to think, to make a plan, and it always seemed as if my head was clearest when I was pushing myself hard, my body running on fumes. I put on two pairs of thermal long johns and over them my nylon pants to break the wind, then a pair of cotton socks and over these a pair of wool ones. On top, a thermal undershirt, a sweatshirt, a fleece pullover and a nylon jacket. Finally, a stocking cap and a pair of lined buckskin mittens. I ran for at least an hour and a half, maybe even two — up through Little Mexico, back downtown, east on Lake Street to Battlepoint Beach, past it and nearly all the way to Clay's place on the lake, four miles out of town, before turning back. Though I hadn't been running in weeks, there was nothing to it, I was hardly aware of my legs and feet beneath me. I felt like a naked brain, surging through the cold air above my body.

Clay's visit, and more to the point, mom's reaction to it, had shaken me. Christine was right, and I could feel the damned truth of it all around me — it was in the bitter flavor of the air I breathed. I had come full circle, all the way back to that night with Dad by the icy lake, and the intervening weeks were lost. I'd wasted them. From now on I needed to consider any doubts I had as signs of my own weakness. I was drowning in self-hate, keenly aware of my limited options. I could try to persuade Sheriff Stone to continue his investigation, in spite of the state coroner's ruling. I could break my oath to Dad and go tell Mom everything, in the hope she might believe me. Or I could take things into my own hands.

I couldn't help but think of Hamlet again. In English class Bascom had spoken of him as a man caught between two worlds, pagan and Christian, obligated to avenge his father's murder but unwilling to violate Christ's law of forgiveness. Nothing had changed, had it? The choice was still impossible: cowardice on the one side, grave sin on the other. What would Dad himself have done? I wondered. Which hell would *he* have chosen? I thought of his quickness to forgive me when I disobeyed, broke things or talked back to him. I thought of how he'd never spoken poorly of his own father, though he had good reason to. Two times, though, he had hit me — once when I was ten and he learned that I'd cheated on a history test, and a few years later when I told him, for no reason I can recall, that I hated him. And I remembered a conversation we'd had about capital punishment. There had been a murder in Battlepoint, the only one in more than a century. A man had molested and killed his next-door neighbor, an eight-year-old girl.

No, I don't believe in it, Dad said. But if I were that girl's father, it'd be a different matter. Real different.

At home I stood beneath the shower until my bones thawed, and when I got out to dry myself, the phone was ringing. I considered not answering but knew I had to — something told me it was important. I sat down, took a breath and picked up the receiver.

Hi Jesse, it's Mom.

Her voice sounded strained, as if something had caught in her throat, and I saw a picture in my head of the Toyota in the ditch, smashed, and Magnus trapped inside.

What's wrong? I asked. I tightened my gut against the rush of acid there.

Nothing, nothing. I just remembered something.

I considered hanging up on her, but didn't. Always the dutiful son.

I was supposed to meet with Phil Bolt this afternoon. The monument guy. Remember?

No, Mom, I don't remember.

He was going to show me these two stones at the cemetery — so I'd be able to order the right color and style. I was going to meet him out there.

You never told me, I said.

I think I did. Anyway, that was the plan.

He's got a showroom, doesn't he? There are samples you could look at there.

Yes, but he's put up a couple stones lately that he thinks I'd like, and he wanted me to see how they look on site. We were going to meet out there at four, but Magnus and I won't be home by then.

I'll call and cancel, I offered.

Mom was silent for a few moments, then said, I was hoping you could go out there for me.

I thought. *What's wrong with you?*

I think it's better that *you* do this, Jesse.

Better for you? I asked.

She didn't say anything. I felt confused, angry too, but even more than that, disgusted with myself for the sudden panicked sense I had that every moment from now on was going to require more than I was capable of — more courage and cunning and self-possession.

I wouldn't know which one to pick, I said.

You'll do fine. Whatever you choose will be perfect. And Phil is a decent guy. He used to be in real estate. He was the one who sold us our house, remember? He's easy to work with.

I don't want to go out there, Mom.

She exhaled into my ear. You and your dad were always so close, she said. He'd want *you* to pick it out, I know he would.

I doubt that.

Please, she said.

At three forty-five I went outside and climbed into the Mercury, but when I turned the key to start the car, nothing happened. The motor didn't even turn over. All I heard was a little clicking sound, like a penciltip on a desktop. I tried again. Same thing.

This had happened to Dad once, and I remembered how he'd taken a hammer and crawled underneath the front end and tapped on the starter a few times. But not too hard, he'd said. You don't want to break anything — just loosen things up in there. It worked for him, of course, but not for me today, and so I went inside and gave Charlie Blue a call. We hadn't seen or talked to each other since school let out for Christmas. He answered on the first ring, and I thought he sounded irritated, his voice flat, the spaces of silence measured. I explained about needing a ride out to the cemetery, and he told me sure, he'd be right over.

Five minutes later he pulled up next to the curb, right behind the Mercury. He sat there behind the wheel of his mom's four-by-four, peering at me from underneath the brim of his blue Twins cap. His hair stuck out from beneath it like feathers. He was wearing a pair of the furry yellow work gloves you can still buy at most hardware stores for a couple of bucks. I opened the passenger door and climbed in.

Christine must be out of town, he said.

I told him she was.

Have you checked your battery wires?

Nope.

He hopped out and walked up to the Mercury, reaching into his pocket for a pliers as he went. I followed after him. I haven't mentioned this, but Charlie was a motor head — sort of. Maybe not the kind with grease under his nails, but he knew how things worked, how to take them apart and put them back together. His dad had taught him a lot before he died. They'd torn apart snowmobiles and chainsaws and trucks and boat motors, all the machines that composed the family business. As a kid, whenever I had trouble with my bike, it was Charlie I'd bring it to, not my dad, who was impatient when it came to any kind of mechanical tinkering.

He lifted the hood, then stood cracking his knuckles, one finger after another.

We don't have time, I said. I was supposed to be out there at four. Maybe you could just give me a ride.

Charlie's hands roamed across the engine, his fingers tapping, tugging, pausing, moving on. He made several flourishes with the pliers and told me to climb in and give it a crank. It started right up, of course, the big eight-cylinder howling to life. I felt like an idiot.

He slammed the hood and played an air-guitar riff on his red-

handled pliers and then executed a low bow. His baseball cap fell
to the street. I rolled down the window and stuck my head out.

Loose battery cable, he said. Always the first thing to check.

I shrugged.

You're supposed to say, Thanks Charlie, you're a genius.

Thanks, Charlie, I said.

Want me to ride out there with you? he asked.

That's all right.

Hey, I've got nothing else to do. You might need the company.

It's up to you, I said.

He performed a little syncopated beat on the car's roof and then
went around front and got in the passenger's side, moving so fast, so
light on his feet, it made me nervous, made me wonder if there was
some pleasure to be had for him, watching me pick out a gravestone
for my dad. I threw the car into drive and accelerated down the
street. The sky was heavy with snow clouds. Charlie made small
talk at first — the novels he was reading, spots on the lake where
the crappies were hot — and he fidgeted. He opened the glove box
and whacked it closed, lit a cigarette and sucked on it, cranking
down the window a few inches each time he exhaled. Then he
turned silent and leaned back against the seat. He was upset with
me, I could tell — and he probably had a right to be. I'd been avoiding him. I couldn't bear the comparisons he seemed determined to
make between himself and me, the satisfaction my grief apparently
brought him. He made me think of a buzzard, a turkey vulture like
the ones we'd see on the side of the road sometimes, picking at the
carcass of a car-struck deer or dog — his complexion red, his nose
long and curved, his shoulders hunched. Lately I'd pictured him
watching me, predatorially, his small eyes patient.

It's not the sort of thing you want to do by yourself, he said as I pulled onto the gravel turnoff into the cemetery.

Dusk had fallen, and Phil Bolt was waiting. His silver blue Mercedes sat just inside the iron gate, and I could see the man's tall silhouette against the trees on the far side, where we'd buried Dad. At a hundred and fifty yards he looked like a scarecrow in his full-length coat.

You can wait here, I said to Charlie.

Whatever.

I glanced over at him to gauge his tone, but he looked away. When he blinked, the lids of his eyes moved down and up, by degrees, like mechanical shutters.

The meeting with Phil went better than expected. I explained that I was here in place of my mom, and he simply shrugged, then led me on a tour of his recent sales. I followed, watching him tiptoe through snowdrifts in his loafers and listening to his spiel, the gist of which suggested that Dad was lying beneath our feet fully sentient and afraid we might slight him by choosing a stone too small and too similar to those of his permanent neighbors. Phil wasn't interested in color or texture or shape. He was all about size — and though I'm not sure why, I found the man's transparency refreshing.

Now this one, see, this one's invisible. Who's going to notice it? It's like a beige split-level in an aging suburb. Know what I mean? He was pointing to a knee-high brown marker with a flat top.

And this one. My Lord, here's what you want to avoid. A fifties rambler. I swear, the sod'll be creeping over the top of it in five years. As you're my witness, Jesse, if my kids do that to me when I'm gone, I'll scratch my way out of the ground and give them an earful.

He showed me a few more stones, and when I made my choice — a standard black-granite model that came to mid-thigh — he nodded in approval and made no attempt to keep me further.

Perfect. Bold but not boastful, he said. Excellent curb appeal. A nice, solid two-story. And I'm certain your father approves. He glanced quickly toward the corner where Dad lay.

Thanks, I said.

Phil Bolt lifted his arm to check his watch, then held out his hand. We shook. With the deal behind us, he finally showed me his smile.

By now the sun was gone behind the trees, and I couldn't help but notice that the quality of light was much like it had been on the night Dad died, the same press of darkness filtering up out of the forest floor, a light shower of snow falling. I found the similarity unsettling. Behind the wheel of the Mercury, I started to cough and couldn't stop. I felt as if a hot set of fingers were probing my lungs. Charlie sat hunched in his seat, arms crossed over his chest, his hooded eyes aslant in my direction. When I could breathe again, I tried to start the car, but the engine didn't fire. Charlie groaned. I pounded the wheel with both hands, cursing, and tried again. It sputtered and caught hold. I nursed it along with just enough gas to keep it running but not enough to flood it, and after a few minutes the rhythm evened out. Then I turned us around and headed for town, anxious to be out of the woods.

13

This time he didn't smell like gunpowder and beeswax, but instead like he'd smelled on those nights when he got home late from closing and came into my room to check on me. I'd be lying in bed awake, having heard the whine of the side-door hinges, his heavy steps on the stairs and the sound of the faucet flipping on and off about twenty times as he brushed his teeth in the bathroom on the other side of my wall. I never let on that I knew he was there, but I looked forward to those moments, Dad standing above me, making certain I was all right. He always reeked of cigarettes from his night at the Valhalla, but there was also a hint of his spearmint toothpaste and the soap he was partial to, a tangy brown bar soap peppered with mysterious black granules. It was this combination of smells that made me glance up now into the rearview mirror as Charlie and I neared the edge of town.

Dad was in the backseat watching me.

He looked the same as before, the dome of his head sheared off, his skin ashen, like modeling clay. I turned around in my seat to make sure it was him. He had on the gray-checked flannel shirt he'd worn beneath his hunting coat the day he died and a pair of red wool long johns. That's all. His blood-spattered pants were gone. His khaki hunting coat was gone. His blaze-orange vest was gone. He didn't seem confused or lost this time but knew where he was and who I was. There was recognition in his one remaining eye. His face looked troubled, though, as if something he'd seen had cracked his soul.

I swung around to face the road, but then Dad spoke. In a gravelly voice I could barely make out, he said, Don't you know I'm waiting, Jesse?

Beside me, Charlie flinched.

I turned again on the Mercury's bench seat and looked right at Dad. The red stubble on his face sparkled, and his single blue eye glimmered, a thing apart from the rest of him. I remembered how he used to watch me sometimes, gravely, as if my presence were a noteworthy event.

What do you want? I asked him.

Who are you talking to? Charlie asked.

I aimed my thumb toward the backseat.

Hey! Charlie shouted, snapping my attention back to the road. I corrected my drift across the centerline just in time to avoid an oncoming car, which had run off onto the opposite shoulder. The lake was on our left and the turkey plant just coming up, tents of glowing snow suspended from the high outdoor lights of its parking lot.

You're wacked, Charlie said. You know that? You're certified.

In the rearview mirror I saw Dad reach into the front chest pocket of his flannel shirt and take out a candy bar, not a Baby Ruth but some brand I'd never seen before, with a green and gold wrapper. It was huge, king-size and then some. He tore off the paper at one end with his teeth — which looked yellow, untended — then stripped off the wrapper and took half the bar in a single ripping bite.

Please tell me, I said to him.

He chewed for a few moments, and then his neck pumped hard, as if it hurt him to swallow. He said, You have to do it *for* me, Jesse.

Do what? I asked, knowing but not wanting to know.

Charlie's hand flashed in front of me, grabbing the wheel and easing us back to our side of the road. Then he swiveled around and looked into the backseat. He sucked in his breath.

Mother of God, he said.

I was aware of the road ahead and the prudence of staying on it, but Dad's presence pushed everything away. Nothing else mattered.

Look at what's happened to us, I said, crying now, glaring at him through the rearview mirror. How could you let him *do* that?

Keep your eyes on the road, Charlie said. There's nothing back there.

And now you want *me* to make things right? It's not fair.

Dad leaned closer, and I felt his cool breath on my neck, his fingers pressing against my shoulder, then grasping hold of the shell of my jacket.

You can't just let him take it all, he whispered to me.

Jesse, for God's sake! Charlie yelled.

I felt a lightness in my chest as we hit a frostheave in the road and went airborne. Charlie grabbed the steering wheel, I touched the brakes and we slid off the road on the junkyard curve, flattening a mailbox on the way. We bounced a few times and spun to our left, coming to rest half in and half out of the ditch, the

Mercury's rear end plunged into the snow. I gunned the engine, but we were tipped too far backward and stuck fast, the high beams spotlighting a billboard the city council had spent parts of three meetings on: BATTLEPOINT, it said. BIG FISH — FRIENDLY PEOPLE. And beneath the words, a bikini-clad girl riding a walleye the size of a horse.

The first thing I did was check the backseat. He was gone. He'd left without the thing he had come for — the promise he wanted from me. I shut off the engine and unsnapped my seatbelt. The tailpipe was buried in the snow, and I could already smell exhaust in the car. Charlie sat with his fingers pressed against the dashboard, his head jammed against the back of the seat, as if he weren't convinced yet that we'd stopped moving.

You saw him, didn't you, I said.

This is crazy. You almost killed us.

And you heard him too, I said.

Shut up! said Charlie. Stop that shit.

He cut the air with his hand, then he cracked his window open and stuck his head out to breathe. When he turned to look at me, his eyes glowed with venom. He was sucking lungfuls of air and expelling them in quick bursts of white vapor.

You think you're so special, don't you? You think it all has to fit together somehow. The fact that he might've just been miserable, that's not good enough, is it? Not for you.

I don't know, I said. I tensed up, ready for attack. Something was buzzing inside my chest, rumbling, like a large insect.

You're just like your mom. What do you think, that you're too good for something like this to happen? It's like those monkeys sitting in a row and covering up their faces and ears. But you're worse, you won't even believe he's gone. If you had any sense you'd leave things alone.

You're jealous because *your* dad didn't ever come back.

Charlie laughed and twisted around, peered into the backseat.

Yeah? If he loves you so much, then where is he? Listen, Jesse, this whole thing's a lot simpler than you think it is. There's stuff you don't know. The truth is, your dad *did* have a reason to leave, and a good one — but if I told you what it was, you couldn't handle it. You'd call me a liar.

If you told me what?

Charlie was quiet for a time. When he spoke again, he sounded less sure of himself. I promised Mom I wouldn't say anything, he said.

My heart stopped for a beat, then came back with an extra-hard kick. My mouth went dry. Now you're obligated, I said.

Across the road a dog had started barking, and now it moved closer — a long, big-bellied, yellow dog, stopping every step or two in order to check the air for our scent.

Charlie sighed, then cleared his throat. You remember the night of the election, in November? he asked.

Of course I do.

Remember your mom wasn't home?

I know that, I said. Clay called us from Cat Creek about supper-time. His car had broken down up there. He needed a ride, and so Mom drove up to get him. Dad was waiting out the returns.

Okay, Charlie said. But my mom happened to be up there too that night. She buys minnows, wholesale, from this guy on Big Island Lake. She was in the gas station there, getting some coffee for the drive home, and she saw Clay and your mom coming out of that little motel beneath the water tower. This is about ten thirty at night. They came out of the motel together, and then they both got into their own cars and drove off separately.

The buzzing in my chest stopped. I tried to understand what Charlie was saying. I put his story into pictures to see if it was something I could accept — to see if it fit with what I knew about my mom. I tried to imagine them coming out of the little green motel in Cat Creek and discovered that yes, I could do it. I could even see what she was wearing — an open jean jacket and a lacy white blouse. And I could see how Clay sort of leaned to the side as he walked, one shoulder angled down toward Mom, a single finger touching her waist.

You don't have to believe me, Charlie said.

I don't. There's any number of ways to explain it.

Of course. Forget I said anything. Charlie laughed, mocking me. We better go find someone to pull us out of here, he said.

Clay could've had the car towed into town, I said, and then gone over to the motel and called us from there. He probably didn't think anyone would be able to come get him until the next morning.

Sure, Jesse. Forget it. Just forget it.

Or his car might've broken down right there in town, next to the motel.

I said forget it.

Charlie unlatched his door but couldn't push it open far enough to squeeze out. The snow was too deep on his side of the car. I tried mine, leaning against it with all my weight, and managed to get my head and shoulders outside, then the rest of me by pushing against the car's frame with my hands. All the while, the dog complained from the edge of the road. As I stepped up onto the gravel shoulder, shooing it away, I heard the stutter and growl of a tractor. Forty yards off, in the direction of town, Councilman Bull Foss came swinging out of his driveway, heading for us. I lifted a hand. He waved back and throttled up.

Quite the job you did on my neighbor's mailbox, he said after he'd shut down his tractor. Had a great view from my kitchen.

Bull was smiling, as if we'd done it all for his amusement. He had on a wool shirt, rolled to the elbows, and no jacket or coat of any kind, though the temperature was close to zero. His gray head was bare, and his hands were red.

So let's get you out of there, he said, jumping down. He took a chain from beneath his seat and walked past me to the Mercury, knelt down and stuck his head under the front end. I heard him muttering under there, then some clanking. When he withdrew, he was still smiling.

This could be tricky with the slick road, he said. Don't know how much traction I'm gonna find.

He found enough, and five minutes later Charlie and I were on our way again. As I drove back to my place, Charlie looked diligently out the passenger window, avoiding my glances. I parked in the street behind his four-by-four and turned off the engine. Before popping open his door to get out, he hesitated — and I think it was that moment of delay that allowed me to speak.

You saw him too, I said.

Charlie turned and glared at me, outraged — but frightened, I was positive. In a brittle voice he said, You'll get over it.

It was ten when I got home. Magnus was in bed, and Mom sat in the living room, watching TV. She motioned me in to join her, but I needed to work myself up for the talk we had to have, and so I went upstairs to shower. I stood in the stream of water until it wasn't hot anymore and imagined Mom glancing all around as they left the motel, flinching at the touch of Clay's finger. I didn't have any illusions about my uncle's scruples, but up until now — despite what Christine had said, and despite the pull of sheer logic — I hadn't applied myself with any diligence to the question of Mom's fidelity. For all her weaknesses, transparency being one, she was true, wasn't she? But now Charlie's story had me looking for something I'd missed, a moment in which she might have given herself away. What came instead was a memory of Dad, an incident I'd forgotten — or buried, more likely.

It was the end of the summer, three months before his death, and I woke up one night, thirsty, two or three in the morning, and went downstairs for a glass of cold water from the pitcher we kept in the fridge. Lifting it, I heard a sound on the porch — the neighbor's cat, I thought. It was getting old and several times lately had wandered, yowling, into our garage, and once into our house. I crossed the kitchen in my bare feet and peeked through the window of the porch door. Sitting there on the plank flooring, head between his knees and hands folded over the back of his neck, was Dad, crying — not loud, but with unqualified sorrow, his shoulders shaking, his groans coming in soft bursts. It didn't occur to me to go out and ask him what was wrong. In fact what troubled me most was the chance that he might look up and catch me there, a witness to this unfatherly display. And so I retreated. I escaped to my bedroom, and by morning the moment had already begun to seem unreal, a fabrication or a dream — probably because I couldn't find any context for it.

As I stepped from the shower I heard the hiss of steam above me and realized that Mom was in the attic sauna for the first time since Dad died. I felt indignant, betrayed. The sauna had been their rendezvous spot, the place they'd steal away to when Magnus and I went to bed.

I dried myself off, put my clothes back on, and climbed the narrow attic steps. At the wooden door that Dad had salvaged from an old church before it was torn down, I lifted my fist to knock, then dropped it. I didn't want this conversation. It wasn't fair that I had to confront my mom like this. It wasn't fair that everything rested on me. All I wanted was to go back to how things used to be. I remembered helping Dad build the sauna during our first winter in the house — how we used two-by-sixes for framing and lined the inside with sweet-smelling redwood that Manfred Miller had special-ordered from California, how we stood there on the day we finished, a white winter sun squeezing in through the skylight we'd cut in the roof and the scent of wood in our nostrils, and how I'd closed my eyes and imagined trees so tall their branches made a green sky, so wide you could tunnel highways through their trunks.

Mom, I said through the door, I'm coming in. I knocked.

I gave her a few moments to cover up before I released the latch and shoved the door open — harder than I meant to. It slammed against the wall and rebounded. I shoved it open again and stepped inside. Below the single cloudy bulb, through a veil of steam, Mom sat on the top tier of the redwood benching, legs crossed and canted to one side, graceful as always. Her skin glowed. She'd wrapped herself in a pale blue towel.

For heaven's sake, she said. Look what you've got on, Jesse. It's a hundred and thirty in here. You'll burn up.

I peeled off my shirt and threw it behind me, down the attic steps. The air felt like syrup boiling in my lungs.

And shut the door, she told me.

I ignored her.

Where'd you go tonight? Christine's?

The cemetery, remember?

I mean after that. It couldn't have taken you that long.

Charlie went out there with me. We talked a while.

Thanks for doing that for me, she said. She pursed her lips and cocked her head to one side. Watched me.

Do you want to know what I picked out?

Not now, she said. With a modest tug she adjusted her towel, and in doing so revealed a flash of breast, its nipple like a flattened plum. Her eyes shone with a light I couldn't translate. They looked feverish and large.

What's this about? she asked.

Clay.

Haven't you already made yourself clear on the subject of your uncle?

I didn't answer.

What you don't seem to appreciate, Jesse, is that Clay has been a help to me.

What sort of help? I asked.

He's given me advice. And emotional support.

Is that what you call it?

What do you mean?

Was it emotional support you were getting at the motel in Cat Creek? The night of the election?

What are you talking about?

Just tell me what happened, I said.

Mom's lips had gone white. The gleam disappeared from her eyes. They looked flat and hard, like painted marbles without any depth.

There's nothing to tell, she said. Her voice was hushed, and the pitch of it fell an octave. His car broke down, and of course your dad couldn't go pick him up, so I drove over and got him.

You were at the motel with him.

Oh, my Lord, she said, and laughed. Whoever got this thing started has a little too much imagination. Was it Charlie's mom? Diane? The motel in Cat Creek — I can't believe it.

I waited. Sweat trickled into my eyes, stinging them, making tears flow, and I hoped Mom wouldn't think I was crying. I used my fingers to wipe them dry.

Listen, she said. Clay's engine overheated on the other side of town, and he called from a farmhouse. By the time I got there, he'd figured out that all he needed was a radiator hose. He was able to drive the Austin into Cat Creek, stopping every couple of miles to let the engine cool. Then he had to find a replacement hose and put it in. I ended up in the lobby of the motel, waiting for him. It was the only place open that time of night, except for the gas station across the street.

The gas station would've had a hose.

We stopped there, but they didn't have one that fit, so Clay went off to this garage, some guy he's gotten parts from before. It must have taken him an hour, and then we drove home. I was here by midnight, remember? In plenty of time for the celebration.

Mom crossed her arms in front of herself and glared at me, resting her case. Sweat stood out in large beads on her lip. Her nostrils quivered. She said, I can't believe I'm having to defend myself like this.

I just want you to level with me, Mom.

And tell you what, exactly?

I stood my ground, waited for my head to blow up, for my lungs to pop. What was I supposed to say? How was a son supposed to speak of such things to a mother? What perversity in her would let it come to this — to the point of sitting before me and forcing me to assemble my questions like a prosecutor?

You want me to tell you there was something going on between your uncle and me? she asked. No, I won't tell you that.

Mom, I'm not a fool. I want you to tell me there was *nothing* going on. I want you to tell me that Diane was wrong, that Charlie's wrong, that you never messed around. That you're not messing around *now*. And that you don't plan to. Ever.

She brought her full, pointed lips together in prim, yet oddly coy, denial. She gave her head a small shake, as if that dismissed every accusation and doubt. She was calm, even confident. She uncrossed and then recrossed her legs. She smoothed back her wet hair, sat up, pushed out her chest and faced me straight on. The heat was crushing me. I stepped back toward the door and took hold of it to keep from losing my balance.

All right? she asked.

I searched my brain. *All right?* I didn't understand what she meant. Then suddenly my attention was drawn to the left, to the corner of the room, where Dad was sitting on the top tier of the red-wood benching. He wore only his longjohns, no shirt at all, and though he still had some of his bulk, he was beginning to waste away, his formerly ample torso slackening, sagging. He lifted both hands in a universal signal that meant stop. Fat dangled from his arms. He shook his damaged head.

Let her be, Jesse, he said. Give her a break, here. Please.

So she's innocent? I asked.

He shrugged, and then got up from the bench and lurched bearlike to the door and disappeared. I turned back to Mom. She was laughing, head thrown back to show me her pink, unlined neck.

Innocent? she asked. Is anyone *innocent?* God, Jesse. A pained smile crossed her face, and she put out her arms and beckoned me, her narrow fingers quivering.

I looked away, up, escaping into the skylight above us where a bright jet streaked through the small square of dark sky. I heard its far-off roar and could almost feel the lift and power of its great body.

Come here, she said to me.

I let go of the door and moved through the heat toward my mother. I waded right up to her, the air an icy-hot brine threatening to seize up my limbs and stall my feeble line of thought, the resolution I'd just made to myself. Mom's eyes were glowing again, an unhealthy luster. She looked ill. She reached up and touched me. Her fingers burned my shoulder.

I wish I had your strength, she said to me. I really do. Things might be different.

You don't need him, Mom.

I loved your dad, Jesse. You have to believe me.

I'm moving out, I said. I'm leaving.

She ran her fingers down the length of my arms and took my hands in hers. She tried to laugh again, but the sound came out wrong and caught in her throat. I can't believe that, she said.

I gave her hands a brief, merciless squeeze, grinding the bones against each other, telling her in this way what I thought of her. Then I tossed them back and stepped away. She rose from the redwood platform and came toward me. For a moment I thought she would slap my face, but instead she spun past me and through the door in a careless pirouette meant to show me just how much she knew about the world and how little I did.

I waited that night until I was certain she was sleeping and then longer, until I felt settled inside, or settled enough. It was nearly one a.m. In my closet I found my canvas duffel and stuffed it with fresh underwear and socks, a couple pairs of blue jeans, a sweatshirt and a wool sweater, some T-shirts, my alarm clock, my textbooks for school and the toiletries case that I'd packed earlier in the bathroom when I was pretending to get ready for bed. I stole down the steps, careful to avoid the ones that squeaked, and through the darkened kitchen and living room to the entryway, where I put on my parka, my cap and my insulated boots. As my hand touched the doorknob I remembered my trumpet, which I'd nestled into its case and set in the middle of my bed, so as not to forget it. For some reason my old silver horn seemed like the center of the life I was leaving. I took my boots off and crept back upstairs to get it.

Outside, the cold pricked at the hairs inside my nose. The sky had cleared, but there was still a faint sparkle of snow in the air. I guided the Mercury into the alley behind the Valhalla and parked where Dad always parked, beneath the sign that read RESERVED FOR OWNER. Inside I turned up the thermostat and went into the kitchen to scrounge.

My head was feeling light and my stomach irritable, as if I'd been fasting all day. I found a package of bacon in the freezer and fried up the whole thing and ate it. I spooned peaches and syrup from a gallon-size tin and spread a pile of soda crackers with peanut butter. For dessert I had vanilla ice cream topped with frozen strawberries. When I was full I sat down at the booth in which Dad had parked himself on slow nights to work the books or interview new help. I smoothed my palms across the tabletop and closed my eyes, letting my fingertips follow the grain of the wood. I pictured him sitting across from me, imagined the rustling of his breath leaving his nostrils and the scent of the cheap cologne he favored, as he watched me, patient, scratching at his red, bristly cheeks and smiling, reading my thoughts.

If there was something between Mom and Clay, I said, and you *knew* it, why didn't you do something? Why did you let it go so far? And how could you let him come up from behind you like that, get the jump on you?

He didn't answer me, of course, and when I opened my eyes he wasn't there. He wouldn't appear on demand, and I thought, *Good for him.* Maybe, at least in some ways, the dead did things on their own terms.

Out of the silence came the whistle of a Burlington Northern coal train and, closer by, the howl of a dog. I sat for a while longer, wishing somehow for a glimpse into the next stretch of time, wishing I hadn't had to leave, and wondering what I was going to do — though I have to say, I was aware too of an unexplainable, tingling excitement in my lungs.

In the basement I lay down on Dad's cot and tried to sleep. It was a cold night, and the green furnace labored. For two or three hours I listened to the aluminum ductwork sigh and knock and the oil burner kick in every so often with a *whump* that made my breath catch in my throat. Finally I got up and took my trumpet from its case and moved to the middle of the basement floor and started to play. I blew a low C and climbed slowly to G above the staff, holding each note four counts. Then I played a chromatic scale, working my fingers fast and ending on a high C that I held as long as I could, pushing from my diaphragm, like Skogen had taught me, and taking care not to press too hard. When I stopped for air and lowered my horn, the sound continued on, an uninsistent high C coming from someplace above me — in the ceiling or the ductwork. Unconditionally on pitch, sweet, unforced.

I lifted my horn and blew a few measures of the solo I'd been practicing for Mr. Skogen. A difficult piece that required range and control, plenty of quick trips between the top and bottom of my register. After twenty measures or so I stopped to listen, and sure enough it all came back in a flawless echo. I pictured Dwayne Primrose in his second-floor rooms, settled on a kitchen chair, directing the bell of his horn down between his knees toward a furnace vent or cold-air return. I could see the blur of his fingers on the valves and the furrow in his brow as he solved the problem of the notes, his lips curving up in a grin as they always did when he played, as if he were discovering a part of himself he'd thought was missing. I put the horn back to my lips and this time played the whole piece straight through. When I was done, I sat down on Dad's cot and listened as it all came back again, note for note.

Dwayne's apartment had its own entrance, accessible by means of a door adjacent to the Valhalla's, and I climbed the enclosed, unlit stairs to his small cold landing and knocked quietly on the pebbled-glass window of the door. Immediately his tall backlit silhouette appeared. A sour smell like boiled cabbage grew more pungent as the door swung in. He greeted me with cornet in hand, his face expectant yet grim. In the weak light his long thin nose with its bulging tip struck me as odd. Thinking back I'd say it was somehow medieval in its shape, a peasant's nose out of Brueghel. His eyes looked cloudy in their sockets, disoriented, as if blowing his horn had knocked him silly.

Sounded good, I said.

I've got that one here someplace. He nodded toward a small

wooden table stacked high with CDs. I think it's got a purple case. Chuck Mangione. He plays a flügelhorn.

I'm doing it for the solo and ensemble contest this spring, I told him.

He shrugged and nodded. I did Hayden's Trumpet Concerto at my last contest. You know that one?

Yes, I said, but chose not to tell him I'd found it too difficult.

That was twenty years ago. My judge was the band director at St. Olaf College, and he said he liked my tone. He gave me a star. He asked me if I wanted to come play in his band.

Primrose looked off to the corner of the room, his out-thrust bottom lip pulsing. There were squiggles of blue veins on the inside of it. He suddenly lifted a fist and thumped the side of his head with his knuckles, as if testing a melon for ripeness.

You're an amazing player, Dwayne, that's for sure.

I heard my mom talking to this doctor one time. Know what he told her? He said I was just smart enough to know how dumb I am. You want to sit down, Jesse?

He gave me his sofa, a high-backed relic upholstered in faded burgundy, and took for himself the edge of his little iron bed, which was pushed up against the opposite wall. The room was narrow — only a few inches separated his knees from mine — and it opened at one end into a kitchen with yellowing knotty-pine cabinets. He hadn't bothered to clean up after supper. A pot still sat on the stove, and dishes were piled on the counter next to the sink.

That's a lovely horn you've got, I said. May I?

He was sitting straight on his bed, his back like a post — an orchestra player anticipating the rise of the baton, his polished gold cornet in the vertical position, bell resting on one knee. He made no move to hand it over.

Clay gave it to me, Dwayne said. For a Christmas present. It's a Getzen. He said I should have a good one. The old one I had, the finish was coming off. Clay said it looked like a rusty car you don't dare wash anymore. You're afraid it'll come apart. He went to Minneapolis and bought it for me. There's a music store down there as big as the high school. They've got an acre of grand pianos.

You and Clay are good friends.

He's my brother-in-law, Primrose said, gravely.

I know that, Dwayne.

He got me that too. See? He angled his thumb toward a small stereo system that rested on a shelf fixed to the wall at the head of his bed.

Who do you listen to? I asked.

The trumpet players. He leaned over and stood his horn bell-down on the maple floor, then looked at me cautiously, his bottom lip still wobbling. Why are you staying down there? he asked, pointing to the floor.

Had a fight with my mom.

He frowned and bit his lip. My mom used to kick me out too, he said. I stayed overnight in the school one time. Down in the band room. In that closet with all the uniforms. It was quiet in there. Hot too. It smelled bad, I couldn't sleep. And once I busted her candlestick holder on Thanksgiving. It was made out of special glass, and I broke it when I poured the apple juice. I cut my hand and got blood on the tablecloth, and she had to throw it away because the blood wouldn't come out. She yelled at me and hit me. Right here. See? Bending over, he parted his hair to show a small pink scar.

But Clay never hits me. He didn't even hit me when I left his car door open and it rained on the leather seats. They got cracked, and you could see the white stuffing. He never yells at me either.

Abruptly he stopped speaking, and he cocked his head at me. I'm sure she'll let you come back, he said.

Oh, she didn't kick me out. I just needed to get away for a while, that's all. It's okay.

He peered at me for a while, moving his head on his shoulders as if to get a better angle on something I was hiding. Then he clamped his mouth and breathed in hard through his nostrils. I was jarred by the thought that I was someone Dwayne Primrose felt sorry for.

There's something I have to ask you, I said.

He put up his hands, palms out, and shook his head. Then he stood up and led me into the kitchen, to a Formica table pushed into the corner. His big hands were nervous, not sure what to do with themselves as we sat down in the only two chairs. Arranged across the tabletop and flush against one wall was a neat row of books and folders standing propped between a pair of bookends. Primrose lifted a flesh-colored spiral tablet from the middle of the row and opened it between us. It was a scrapbook, browning pages filled with clippings: articles from *Trumpet Player* magazine, photographs of jazz greats like Miles Davis and Maynard Ferguson, glossy color advertisements for Olds, Bach and Getzen horns.

Look here, he said. I cut this out of the paper the day after he died. See? Primrose touched a finger to the date, which had been printed by hand at the top of the page: July 7, 1971. The headline of the clipping read, *Jazz Legend Armstrong Dies*.

And here. Primrose flipped some more pages, stopping at a small, curling news story taped to the middle of a lined page. Ever hear of Lee Morgan?

No, I told him.

Cornbread. That's the album I've got. He died in 1972. His girlfriend shot him. He was thirty-three. They said he would've been the greatest ever. His teacher was Clifford Brown, and he *was* the greatest ever. Clifford Brown died in a car accident. June 26, 1956. He was twenty-five.

Why are you showing me these? I asked.

He made a face, as if trying to push a large chunk of thought through some narrow passageway in his brain. I don't know. I was thinking about your dad. I don't know. I'm sorry. He lifted his hands to his face and covered his eyes. His lips were still trembling.

Maybe you better go, he said to me.

I reached out and touched his elbow, and that seemed to calm him. He sighed and lowered his hands to his lap.

I have to ask you something, about Clay, and then I'll leave, I said.

He nodded.

Do you remember last November, one night in the middle of the month when Clay's Austin broke down on him? It happened over near Big Island Lake.

Primrose blinked at me, frowned, then made an odd popping sound with his lips before shaking his head no.

He never told you about it? I asked.

No.

It looked like you were remembering something.

No, I wasn't.

I sat watching his long pale face, which needed a shave. The stubble on his cheeks and chin was multicolored, brown, gray and red. His eyes were calm but alert. Wary, I thought.

Are you sure you don't remember that night? Anything about it?

No. Dwayne's eyes tightened on mine. Why? he asked.

It's really important, I said.

You don't like Clay very much, do you? he asked.

I don't like him spending time with my mom.

Why not? Clay's a good person.

Was he good to your sister?

He's good to me.

I have to go, I said.

He nodded, rose from the table and disappeared into the bathroom off the kitchen, closing the door behind himself. I walked through his narrow living room and out into the stairwell, which was black and dank-smelling, like the inside of a rotting tree. I took hold of the wooden handrail and descended through the dark. As I reached the bottom, the door squealed open above me, and I heard Dwayne Primrose's off-pitch voice: There's one thing, he said.

I turned. He was at the top of the stairs, his stamped-tin silhouette black against the weak yellow light from his little living room.

Yes? I started back up, careful not to move too quickly and startle him. Halfway, I stopped and sat down.

I'm listening, I said.

He grabbed on to the handrail and lowered himself to the landing, then swung his legs around and thumped his stocking feet on a wooden step. Outside, a car engine whined and cranked before starting with a clamorous roar.

When I was little, my dad had this gun, Primrose said. A rifle he used for deer hunting, and he kept it in under his bed. When he and Mom died, I was the one that got it. But I left it there. Marnie kept it for me. She kept it in the closet of the spare bedroom. I stayed in that room when I went to visit.

And it's where you stay now, right? When you go out and visit Clay? I've seen you walking the tracks.

I grew up in that house. I like it out there on the lake.

Do you still stay in the same room?

Yes, he said, and the word sounded faint and hollow, as if he were speaking from inside a barrel.

A weight pushed down on the top of my brain, and it was suddenly hard to think against that pressure. A voice whispered inside my head: *You're cursed.*

Tell me, I said to Primrose. Go ahead.

I don't know what time it was. I was in my room, watching TV.

You're talking about the night my dad died, right? I asked.

He nodded. It was in the afternoon, he said. Almost dark. Clay came in and got the rifle out of my closet. I said to him, What are you doing? I think he told me he had to give the gun to a friend who wanted to go hunting. I'm not sure what he said, though. Clay doesn't like to hunt. He doesn't like guns.

He left then?

Dwayne nodded. My eyes had adjusted to the black of the stairwell, and I could see his face now, chin elevated, lips cracked and trembling, unhealthily purple. He stared at the wall beside him as if trying to make out a message written there.

When he came back it was dark, Dwayne went on. It was snowing. I watched out the window, and I saw him drive in and get out of the car, carrying something. He went down to the lake and tipped the boat over, right side up. He pushed it out on the ice. He pushed it till he reached the part that was open. He got in and rowed till I could barely see him anymore. Then he tossed something into the lake, and that's it, that's everything I saw.

Primrose gave out a heavy sigh, and his head dropped between his shoulders.

The rifle? Was it a rifle you saw him toss into the lake? I asked.

I think so. Yes. He didn't have it when he came back in.

He didn't have it.

No. I didn't see it. He tossed it.

But you *saw* him when he came back in the house, right?

I saw him in the kitchen.

What did he say?

He said he was tired. He went up to bed.

That's it? He didn't mention the rifle he took from your closet?

Primrose shook his head.

And you didn't ask him?

Primrose shook his head again. He took a deep breath and blew it out in a long sigh.

I climbed up the stairs to him and put a hand on his shoulder, which felt warm to me, hot almost, despite the fact that he wore only a thin cotton shirt in that cool stairwell. He was slumped forward, elbows on his knees. I took hold of him beneath his arms and helped him stand, and then I led him into his living room and put him on the burgundy couch. I knelt down on the floor in front of him and asked him if he'd be willing to tell Sheriff Stone everything he'd just told me.

His eyes flicked up and snagged at the edge of mine before glancing away. He said, It won't make any difference, will it? What I say to Sheriff Stone?

It will, Dwayne, I said.

That's what I thought. He ran his tongue around the perimeter of his lips. I don't want it to, he said.

I stood and looked down at him.

Eight thirty in the morning, I said. I'll come up and get you, and we'll drive over to Sheriff Stone's. All you have to do is tell him what you told me. And I'll be there the whole time. Okay?

Primrose nodded. His eyes were closed, his purple lips trembling, starved, it seemed, for blood. His flesh clinging to the sharp bones of his face.

Eight thirty, I said.

Instead of going back into the basement, I walked around to the rear of the building and got into the Mercury and drove out of town, past the public beach where I'd seen Dad's ghost, to the double bridge that spanned Boy River. I pulled over just short of it and walked out to the middle and stood there, staring down at the ice and rocks thirty feet below. Over on the east shore lay a pile of boulders that covered an area the size of a city lot and extended out toward the center of the river. The night was still — and the sky light enough that I could see what looked like a book lying spread-eagled on the ice. Probably because people had died here, the place had become a receptacle for sacrifices, treasures thrown over the edge for good luck. Like a wishing well. I'd seen teddy bears, hats, shoes, dolls, photographs, money. Once I'd climbed down and found a pocket watch faceup on the snow and still ticking. I wished now that I had something to toss down but couldn't think of anything I owned that was valuable enough to serve as a sacrifice for what it was I needed.

I felt spent, used up, exhausted. In English class Bascom had read us a Frost poem about a man out walking in the woods — a weary man, a man who's tired of life. He comes upon a stand of birch trees, high narrow ones of the sort he used to climb as a boy, shimmying all the way up to the top and then throwing his weight to one side and letting the springy trunk carry him back to the floor of the woods. If only he were young again, he thinks, and able to get away from earth a while, even a little while, just leave it behind! Anyway, for some reason — I guess I was on my way to becoming the book nerd I am today — I had memorized the poem, and now as another Burlington Northern coal train rumbled out of town, heading my way, some of Frost's lines ran through my head. I understood them now.

> *I'd like to go by climbing a birch tree,*
>
> *And climb black branches up a snow-white trunk*
>
> *Toward heaven, till the tree could bear no more,*
>
> *But dipped its top and set me down again.*

Of course, I had no way to leave the earth, much as I would have liked to. In fact, I felt as if my body weighed a thousand pounds. And heaven? Heaven seemed far off.

14

At seven thirty I was already dressed, my stomach full of crackers and canned peaches. I had washed up in the basement sink and brushed my teeth, and now from the lobby of the Valhalla I watched the sun's first light delineate the spire of Pastor Lundberg's church. Across the street old Mr. Blue, Charlie's grandpa, stepped out of the door that led up to his apartment above the Sons of Norway lodge. He bent to pick up his newspaper from the sidewalk and then he stood there looking around at the morning. He wore an orange bathrobe and a pair of slippers. His bare ankles, thin and bony, looked too frail to bear the weight of him. He smacked the rolled-up paper into an open palm, a couple sharp pops, and then turned and went inside.

When I couldn't wait any longer, I left the lobby and climbed the stairs to Dwayne's second-floor landing and knocked on his door. I had a miserable feeling. I knocked again and waited, then tried the knob, which turned freely in my hand.

His bed was made, and the half-empty cup of coffee on his

kitchen table felt cool to my fingers. I ran back down the stairs and out to my car and drove Lake Street east along the railroad tracks — Dwayne's walking route to Clay's place. I drove all the way out there, three miles, past the town beach and the double bridge, and pulled into the end of Clay's driveway, which cut through a stand of birch trees, their naked white branches pink in the new sun. I didn't drive in. I felt certain Dwayne wouldn't be there — and if he was, Clay would be there too, and I couldn't imagine what I would say to him. And so I turned around and headed back to town, swearing at myself.

How could I have been so stupid? How could I imagine that he would have the nerve to tell Sheriff Stone what he'd told me? We should have gone and talked to him in the night. God only knew where Dwayne was now.

I found Sheriff Stone at his office, of course, but it took him a while to come and unlock the door. Yeah, yeah, he called from inside. Just hang on.

Something thudded on the floor, and then he cursed, and finally the deadbolt clicked and the door swung in. In bare feet and longjohns he stood rubbing his elbow and blinking, his eyes so veined and puffy it was a wonder he could see. Or maybe he couldn't. He waved a hand in front of himself as if to clear smoke from the air or shoo off a fly.

Jesse?

Yes, I said.

He wore a gray T-shirt, badly stained, and his breath was foul. It smelled like alcohol and bad cheese. He turned to survey his office, turned back to me and invited me in, pointing to the couch — it was covered in a mess of blankets. I pushed them to one side and sat. He retreated to his desk, where his brown sheriff's pants lay in a heap next to his belt and holstered revolver. He put on the pants, hopping on one foot, then the other, and striking his knee against the sharp edge of the desk. He swore.

There's something I have to tell you, I said.

He lifted a hand to shut me up, then took his shirt from the back of his desk chair and put it on. He sat down and put on his socks and boots too. When he was dressed, he moved unsteadily to the back of the room and poured two mugs of coffee from the electric pot he probably never unplugged and came back and handed one to me and finally sat down.

Okay, he said.

I started to speak, but he cut me off once more and pointed to the wall clock, which showed five minutes past eight. For the record, he said, my workday starts at eight thirty. He nodded for me to begin.

As clearly as I could, I told him what Dwayne Primrose had told me last night, explained what he had agreed to do and how this morning he was gone. I tried to stay unemotional. I listened for any wavering or uncertainty in my voice. Sheriff Stone watched me out of one eye while working over the other with an index finger. When I was done, he waited long enough to make me wonder if he'd listened. He closed his eyes and frowned. With his fingertips he massaged his bald head.

Pretty serious stuff, he said finally, and took a pack of cigarettes from the desk drawer. He shook one free, plucked it out with his lips and lit it with a kitchen match that he struck on the iron turtle-shaped ashtray that sat on the corner of his desk. His hand trembled.

How much did Dwayne volunteer, and how much did you drag out of him? he asked.

I didn't drag anything out of him. He volunteered it.

And he saw Clay toss a rifle into the lake from his boat. He *saw* that.

He said it looked like a rifle, yes. He said Clay never brought the rifle back into the house.

Looked like a rifle, said Sheriff Stone. And *where* was he watching from?

A window.

A hundred yards away, minimum. And Dwayne told you he was willing to talk to me himself?

Yes.

How willing?

I had to convince him.

Ah. Sheriff Stone drew on the cigarette and held in the smoke as he watched me, his eyebrows poking up into his forehead. With his knuckles he rubbed at the skin of his temples, just above his ears.

There's something you might want to consider, he said to me.

All right.

If you go down this road you're on, you'll end up someplace different than you are now, and it might be uncomfortable there. It might be an untenable place to be, if you get my drift. He ground his cigarette into the ashtray and stood up. So what do you think? he asked.

What do I *think?*

Yeah. I mean, does it make you feel better, telling me what you did? Is that good enough? Or do you want me to go ahead and be the sheriff now?

Be the sheriff, I said. I wouldn't be here otherwise, would I?

Fine. He stood up. We better go see if Clay knows where his brother-in-law's at, he said. Oh, and your mom called an hour ago, worried half out of her skull, no idea where you were. I think we better stop by on the way and pick her up. She needs to hear this story too, don't you think?

He looked down at me, hands at his sides, waiting. I stayed put on the couch. If I'd wanted Mom to know everything — and Clay too — I'd have gone and talked to them myself. This wasn't at all what I'd had in mind.

You need to understand, Jesse, everything you told me is secondhand. That's called hearsay. I'm not saying it's untrue, but it doesn't amount to much. Legally, nothing. Not only that, the guy you heard it from is retarded, all right? What the hell do you expect me to do?

You're saying we just go out there and tell Clay what Dwayne said? Do you think that's the best way?

Sheriff Stone lifted his gun belt from the desktop and strapped it on. He squeezed his red-fox-fur cap onto his bald head and winked at me.

This is Battlepoint, he said. Not TV. Come on, let's go.

At my house he went up to the door and knocked while I waited in his Jeep. Mom answered, and I saw her peer over his shoulder at me, her face all knotted up, before she disappeared back into the house. Sheriff Stone followed her inside. For ten minutes I sat there wondering how much he was telling her and how he might be framing things for her. I wished I hadn't gone to see him in the first place. But where else could I have turned? I was sick to death of waiting, tired of holding out, alone, fed up with living in the dark hole of what I knew. Maybe it was best this way — bring it all out in the open.

When they appeared again, I could see Mom was angry. Her usual grace and fluidness were gone. Her feet pounded the sidewalk. She had her fists jammed into the pockets of her coat, and she looked right at me as she came, squinting hard, trying to get a better view of me through the tinted window of the Jeep. I got out and let her climb in front next to Sheriff Stone. I slid into the backseat. He started the engine and turned around in our driveway and headed east on Lake.

After a block or so Mom swung an arm over the front seat. She turned to look at me as if I'd just uttered an obscenity. Do you have any idea what you're doing? she asked.

Sheriff Stone lifted a hand from the wheel and reached over and laid it on my mother's shoulder. I have to ask you for your patience, Genevieve. Hang tight here. Indulge me. Jesse did the right thing, coming to see me. What Dwayne Primrose had to say is plenty disturbing.

You can't take somebody like him seriously, Billy. For God's sake, he's not normal. Everyone knows that.

Maybe so. But we can't just let this thing twist in the wind. That wouldn't be fair — not to Jesse, and certainly not to Clay. Besides, we have to find out where Dwayne's at, right?

He let his hand remain on Mom's shoulder, and it seemed to have the effect he intended. She didn't say another word as he drove. At the birch grove we turned in and followed the curving, quarter-mile driveway that led to the old farmhouse that Marnie and Dwayne's grandparents had built a hundred years before. A narrow two-story, white with green trim. Clay stood on his front step waiting, head tipped forward on his long neck. His eyes looked skittish as he glanced around at the three of us. It was like he was trying to take us all in at once, read the expressions on our faces to learn where he stood. Sheriff Stone had called to tell him we were coming, I knew, but I wasn't sure how much he'd said.

No sign of Dwayne yet? Sheriff Stone asked.

Clay came down off the steps to shake hands with Stone. Nope. And he usually walks out here Saturday mornings. I think he must have gone to Minneapolis.

Oh?

He's done it a couple of times before. Like after Marnie's funeral. He was upset because I had her cremated, which had been her wish. Dwayne wanted her buried next to their parents.

Who's in Minneapolis? Sheriff Stone asked.

Relatives, I guess. No one that Marnie ever talked about. He was gone for a couple weeks that time. No, it was more like a month. Didn't leave a note or anything. He can be like that.

How would he get down there?

Stick out his thumb, I suppose. But we can check with Lyle to see if he took the bus.

I'll do that. Sheriff Stone brought his hands to his mouth and blew into them. Can we go inside? It's a little cold out here.

Clay didn't move. Tell you one thing, though, he said. Dwayne'll be back sooner this time. He's my partner in the spearing contest, and he's all hyped about it, thinks we're going to win. We've been doing pretty good too, by the way.

Let's go inside, said Sheriff Stone.

Clay shrugged and led us toward the house. Hope you don't mind a mess, he said.

He sat us down in his kitchen and poured coffee all around. When he filled my cup, his hand jerked and he spilled some on the table, then wiped it up with a dishcloth. He kept clearing his throat, and once he walked over to the sink and spit.

Damn it, this cough, he said.

The place was cluttered but wasn't the mess he'd called it. He and Marnie had married shortly after the death of her parents, and they'd moved into a furnished house, hardly changing a thing. It looked like a crowded, undusted museum, none of the furniture or fixtures less than sixty years old. The kitchen floor was red linoleum, well-worn, with a yellow geometric pattern. The fridge and stove had rounded edges and lots of chrome, the faded wallpaper covered in tiny pink roses. During the couple of years that Clay and Marnie were married and living here, they'd had us over maybe half a dozen times. It was more typical for them to come to our house, maybe because Marnie was unhealthy, maybe because Clay as a long-standing bachelor was used to being hosted.

Okay, then, he said. What's this about? He was standing at the sink and his eyes came to rest on me.

Sheriff Stone spoke in a genial voice, offhand. Like I told you on the phone, Clay, Dwayne said a few strange things to Jesse last night. Please, sit down.

My uncle took hold of the chair opposite Sheriff Stone, spun it around on the linoleum, swung his leg over and straddled it. He sat lightly.

Across the table Mom watched me, her eyes smoldering. I couldn't help but think that in that moment she wanted me dead.

Sheriff Stone was brief and plainspoken, and he left nothing out. Clay, as he listened, tipped his face lower and lower until he was looking out the tops of his eyes, peering through his dark brows. Once in a while his hand came up to stroke his mustache or smooth back his long gray hair. When Sheriff Stone got to the part about the boat and tossing the rifle into the lake, Clay laughed.

What?

No. Go ahead, finish up.

According to Dwayne, you never brought the rifle back into the house, Sheriff Stone said. Is that true?

Mom remained stiff in her chair, arms wrapped around herself as if she were cold, her eyes shooting thin beams of dark light.

True, did you say? Question is, is any of it true. Where do you want me to start? Clay asked.

You're not obligated to say a thing.

Ask me a question.

Did you come and get a rifle from Dwayne's room that night?

I did. I had to shoot a dog. Clay turned and looked right at me.

Not a cat? I said to him. You sure it wasn't a barn cat you had to shoot? That's what I was thinking you'd say.

Sheriff Stone sat with his hands steady on the tabletop, palms down. He'd sobered up nicely.

My uncle glared at me. I've had to take some of those too, he said, screwing his neck to one side and then the other — it cracked like a nut. I was on my way home that afternoon, he went on. Must have been around dusk, and I saw this pack of dogs going after a deer on that Bywater field across from the township hall. They were all over it, dragging it down, four or five of them. I don't like to see that sort of thing. I figured, what the hell, I'll go home and get the rifle.

You say this happened around sundown?

That's right. It wasn't dark yet. By the time I got back with the gun, the dogs were busy on the carcass, sort of hopping around and snarling. They ran off when I got close, all but one of them. Which I shot.

Then you drove home?

Clay breathed in, coughed, went to the sink, spit and sat down again, straddling the chair. He said, I went up to the dog I shot — it was a hound of some kind, thin, not big — and I saw it had a collar on. And that's when it dawned on me I might be in trouble. I mean, this was somebody's pet. So I dragged it back to the car and threw it on top of this burlap bag I had in the trunk. At home I put it in the bag and weighted it down with a couple of rocks from the shore, and I pushed out the boat and dumped it in the lake. That's what Dwayne saw. He saw me dump that goddamn dog in the lake.

Clay lifted both hands as if to say *There you go.*

What about the rifle? Sheriff Stone asked.

For what seemed a long time Clay sat watching us, slumped in his chair, elbows close to his sides, his eyes dense with thought. With a finger he spun his coffee cup on the table. At the corner of his mouth, beneath his mustache, a smile twitched. Did he think this was funny?

In the basement, he said, nodding toward the floor. I took it down there after Dwayne had gone to bed.

Can't say I remember anyone reporting a missing dog, Sheriff Stone said.

Clay shrugged. Mom groaned but didn't speak.

Can I see the rifle? Sheriff Stone asked.

God, Billy. I'm a criminal now?

You're not obligated. I just want to put all this behind us.

Clay shrugged again and got up and went to the basement door and disappeared down the steps.

The three of us sat without speaking. Across from me Mom's face looked as hard and cold as aluminum. She hated me now, I could see that. She hated me because she wasn't sure if Clay was telling the truth. I'd upset the balance of her life, made her see just how precarious it was.

Sheriff Stone shifted in his chair. He lit a cigarette. I was starting to think Clay had gone out a basement window when his boots sounded on the wooden steps, and then he emerged with a rifle in his hands and laid it on the table, the barrel's mouth pointed toward me. It was an old bolt-action model, most of the blueing worn off the barrel. The stock was dented and battered. There was rust at the breech and along the trigger guard. A .30-30, I figured, by the size of the bore.

Marnie's dad's, Clay said.

Sheriff Stone picked it up and rubbed the stock with his fingers and drew a hand down the length of the barrel. Mom sighed and offered Clay a smile, as if the gun proved anything. It looked like it hadn't been used in decades.

I think Dwayne told me it was a lever-action, I said, though I knew he had not. In fact, I couldn't recall what sort of gun Clay had used that long-ago day on the cat in his front yard.

Dwayne can't tell a shotgun from a rifle, Jesse. This is the only gun Marnie's dad owned, far as I know. The only gun in the house.

I had an urge to tear it from Sheriff Stone's hands and use it to bludgeon Clay, smash his mouth, shut him up, ruin the smirk he wore beneath his mustache.

All right, Sheriff Stone said, handing back the gun. He stood up from his chair and stretched, took a deep pull on his cigarette, which had burned down to the filter.

That's it? Mom said. You ask all these questions, make allegations, and then just get up and leave?

I wouldn't call them allegations, Genevieve.

What should I call them?

Let's not overreact here. It's all on the table, and Clay's had his say. And I'm sure if Dwayne had been here to listen, he'd be feeling a lot better, this whole mess behind us.

Mom shook her head. It's cruel, Billy, just throwing this in our face — in *Clay's* face — like that. It's not right.

What gets under my skin, Clay said, shaking his head, facing me, is that you'd think I'm *capable* of something like that. What am I supposed to do? Tell me, what do you think I am? Judas Priest, Jesse, you think I'd shoot your dad?

Whoa, Sheriff Stone said. He stepped forward and dropped the butt of his cigarette into his empty coffee cup. Slow down now. This wasn't *Jesse's* story, Clay. You think it's been fun for *him*?

Clay stood up now too, set his hands on his hips. He said, What I'd like to know is how much of it came from Dwayne and how much Jesse put into his head.

I'm right here, I said.

So you are. Fine. Clay looked right at me. You haven't been yourself for a while, Jesse, and you know it. We all know it, he said, glancing at Mom. The truth is, you need help.

I think we better go, Mom said, standing. Come on. She came around the end of the table toward me, touching Clay's arm on the way — a mediating touch, gentle and firm at the same time, a touch I read to mean she had chosen to believe him.

If you don't mind, I'd like to drive Jesse home, said Sheriff Stone. Maybe Clay could give you a lift back to town, Genevieve. That work okay? He glanced at my uncle.

Sure, Clay said.

Sheriff Stone had moved to the door, and now he rapped his knuckles on the door frame. Let me know when you hear from Dwayne, he said to Clay.

My uncle nodded.

I let myself be guided across the snowy yard to the Jeep and before climbing in looked back and saw Mom and Clay standing side by side in his kitchen, watching me, their faces as solemn as death.

Sheriff Stone started the engine and stepped on the gas, and beneath us the tires spun on the icy, rutted driveway. Just like I said it would be, isn't it? he said.

I agreed that it was, then listened as he explained how the only way to reopen the investigation would be to convince the county attorney that new evidence had come forward.

Trouble is, we don't have much to go on here. Nothing, really. You can see that, right, Jesse?

What if Dwayne came back and talked?

And held to his story, you mean?

Yeah.

Then we'd have *next* to nothing.

Even if we found the rifle in the lake?

Sheriff Stone didn't take his eyes off the road. Above us the sky was dark with snow clouds. He said, It's a hundred and fifty feet deep off that point, and it's rocky structure down there on the bottom. Big rocks, little ones. I fish it a lot. I've got a sonar system. We're talking a patch of lake bottom the size of a city block. The divers would need lights and time. That requires money. The fact is, the chances of finding that gun, if it's there — and frankly I don't think it is — are slim. Are you with me?

But what if we found it?

Like I said, I'd have to persuade the county attorney that it's worth the time and money to perform the search.

But what if we found it?

Circumstantial evidence, Jesse. That's all it is, unless we put Clay in the woods at the time your dad was shot. Which is what we'd need to do in order to get the county attorney's attention in the first place. Do you see?

We pulled up in front of the law-enforcement annex, and Sheriff Stone shifted the Jeep into park and left the motor running. He said, Listen, here's what I can do for your peace of mind. I'll interview everybody that lives within a mile of the spot where your dad died. See if anyone noticed anything out of the ordinary that night.

That's what you said before, the same thing. Back in November.

He shrugged. Never got around to it, he said, and he reached out and laid a big paw on my shoulder, fatherly. I shook it off. He turned to wave at mailman Darrel Pickett, driving past in his red and blue postal truck.

I'm not sure why, but I wasn't angry with Sheriff Stone. In fact I felt oddly calm. I glanced over and waited for him to turn and look at me. When he did, I could see that he wasn't embarrassed — not for himself, anyway. There was pity in his eyes. He was embarrassed for me.

He cleared his throat. Do you really think Clay would do something like that? Can you believe that about your uncle?

I wanted to say, *Yes.* I wanted to say, *It's not a matter of think — I know he did it, and I can tell you exactly how it happened and why. He's been jealous of my dad his whole life, and he's in love with my mom, and he wanted her all to himself. And now he's got her.*

That's what I wanted to say. Instead, I shook my head, thanked him for the ride, stepped from the Jeep and drove the Mercury home. I felt like a stranger as I went up the sidewalk toward my house, Dad's house — the old familiar elm trees that overhung it so vivid I could barely stand to look at them, the rock-and-timber walls immovable and grand, the air so fresh it almost hurt to breathe. And though I wasn't certain why at the time, I was absurdly happy.

15

I remember a night when I was five or six years old and riding in the car with Dad. We were coming back from Duluth, where his own dad was in the hospital after suffering a stroke. It turned out to be the last time we saw him alive. This was in the winter, Christmastime, but the air was mild and loaded with moisture. The low clouds had trapped the evaporating snow, and the result was a fog so thick we couldn't see beyond the long hood of the Mercury. Pea soup, Dad called it. To stay on the road he had to open his door and lean out and use the centerline for a guide. It was dangerous, and I remember how nervous I was. I felt cut off from the world, with no idea how far we'd gone or how many more miles we had left to go. It was the middle of the night, and though it seemed as if the road was ours alone, I kept listening for the sound of a car or, worse, a semitruck bearing down from behind. I imagined the accident that would kill us, pictured in my mind what they'd find in the morning when the fog lifted: our car all crumpled up and lying on its roof, the two of us thrown free of it, lacerated and broken beyond recognition.

I don't know how far from home we were when it happened. We were creeping up a hill, Dad of course leaning out the door, when suddenly in front of us, white and round and glowing like the face of a lucky child, was the moon, hanging there in a sky riddled white with stars. Just like that, the fog was behind us. Dad laughed, yanked his door closed and stepped on the gas. I cried, I was so happy.

That's how I felt now. It was as if nothing was hidden from me any longer. I could see my way forward. My uncle was guilty, even if Mom, out of self-preservation, might have to pretend for a time that he wasn't. More important, it was now plain to see that *Clay had gotten away with it.* There would be no exercise of justice. He was free and clear.

This may be the hardest part, explaining how it's possible that I decided to kill a man, to murder my father's brother. How can I put it? I guess in the end it was like the decision you make to eat when you're hungry, not a decision at all, because it happens at the level of the cell. Getting even, I think, is the most natural thing in the world, a physical law, like gravity. Somebody hits you, what do you do? Hates you? What do you do? There was this little toy that my dad had when I was small. I think it was called Newton's cradle. He kept it on his desk in the basement. A line of five steel balls hung suspended, each by two strings, within a wooden frame. When you lifted a ball at one end and dropped it against its neighbor, the force of the strike transferred itself through the line of balls, causing the one at the other end to rise. When that one dropped, the original ball on the opposite end rose again. And so it went. If there were no such thing as friction, the back-and-forth motion would have gone on forever.

Most people, of course, don't *act* on their thoughts of revenge. I realize that. But I'd argue that one way or another, they do manage to purge them. They snap at their wives or husbands, kick the dog, eat the last slice of pizza, curse the driver in front of them, disparage their co-workers. In my case it was simply a matter of directing all my energies into one pure stream.

It was still morning when I left Sheriff Stone's black Jeep and drove back home. Mom hadn't returned yet. Magnus was in the living room playing Popsicle-stick baseball again. I lied, telling him I was going over to Charlie's, that he and I needed to help his mother move some fish houses.

You never hang out with Charlie anymore, Magnus said.

It's a big job, and I promised. Tell Mom, okay?

I wish you'd stay home sometimes, he whined.

But I needed to get away and think. I needed a few hours to myself in a place where I would be unbothered, where I could plan my next move, study the details of the country before me. I drove to Bob's Grocery and bought at the deli counter a summer-sausage-and-cheese sandwich, a banana, a carton of chocolate milk and a Baby Ruth candy bar. With no idea where I was going, I got back into the Mercury and started driving. The clouds had begun to give up their snow, and the air was full of it, huge flakes coming straight down. I didn't have to go far. I didn't even make it out of town. When I came to the block on which the water tower stood, I knew where I'd be left alone.

I parked as close beneath it as possible, right behind the old brick creamery, closed for years. From the trunk I took a sleeping bag — Dad always insisted that we keep them in the car during the winter — and I threaded one of its straps through my belt so the bag hung behind me. I pushed my paper sack full of lunch into my coat pocket, and then I started to climb the narrow ladder.

Its steel rungs couldn't have been more than a foot wide, and there was no safety cage. I took my time. Every few steps I stopped and peered down to check my progress, but the snow was coming so thick and heavy I couldn't tell how high I'd climbed. It was hard not to think of that night with Dad in the fog.

Halfway up or so I took a direct hit in the eyeball from a crystal flake of snow and instinctively jabbed at my eye, throwing myself off balance. I swung out, flailing with my right arm. My right foot slipped from the rung, my heart slammed against my ribs and my lungs emptied. I managed, though, to hook my left knee around the ladder and hang on. Minutes later I reached the catwalk at the base of the tower's bowl and flopped down onto it. I lay there on my back and let the snowflakes crash against my face. With my fist I knocked on the steel tank wall and listened to the hollow bell sound of the echo inside.

After I'd caught my breath, I got up and circled the tower, one hand on the hip-high railing of the catwalk, the other brushing against the tank. At the tower's access door — it looked like the escape hatch of an airplane — I stopped. Two of my classmates, Josh Ruby and Ricky Bragg, had gone inside for a night swim last summer and gotten themselves caught by Vince Kaeler. Now the door had a new hasp and a shiny padlock. I took out my lunch and sat down facing what I thought was the lake, though in this whiteout it was hard to be sure. The summer sausage was sharp and the bread chewy, underbaked. I bolted it down, then ate the banana and drank the carton of chocolate milk. Finally I took out the Baby Ruth bar and ate that too, taking my time in honor of Dad. I could feel him with me and wondered if ghosts could fly or if they were bound by land and water as we are in life.

The snow had let up, and soon I was able to make out the ground below, the faint green blur of the Mercury and, off to the north, the buildings of downtown, which from this height and distance looked like oversize children's blocks neatly arranged in a snowy yard. I thought of Christine, the fullness of her lips, and felt almost panicked relief at the idea of seeing her again, talking to her — someone I could trust! And yet I was afraid too. She'd been gone just three days, but it may as well have been years for how my life had been tipped and shaken. I didn't feel like the same person anymore, and it struck me that I might *look* different too. What if Christine noticed? What if I scared her, if she wanted nothing more to do with me?

I burrowed into my sleeping bag, leaned back against the cold steel wall and watched the snow clouds move off to the east. A bit of blue brightened above me, and before long it filled half the sky. The lake itself, flat and white, stretched away from the edge of Battlepoint, north. I started to count the shacks that made up the shantytown of fish houses on the two-mile bar and lost track at seventy-five. They came in all colors — red, blue, silver, black — some no bigger than a piano crate, others the size of a garage. A few had two stories, a sleeping room above.

It probably happens to everybody. You're moving through your day, and something you see or do or something you smell brings back a dream from the night before — a dream you may not have remembered at all when you first woke up. That's what happened to me now as I looked across the frozen lake toward the point that sheltered the narrow bay where Clay's fish house sat. The dream came back in full color as if I'd just wakened out of it: Clay adrift in crystal-green water, his arms and legs waving like the fronds of a lake plant, his face ice blue, dead eyes staring. I could smell him, cold and ripe, like a freezer full of lake-caught fish, and the plan tumbled into my lap wholly formed.

It was going to be easy. Nothing to it. His fish house sat alone in that bay, no one out there to see me arrive or leave. I'd make a friendly nighttime visit, bring him a thermos of hot cocoa for his bad stomach — cocoa spiked with Halcion — ask him to show me his catch, sit down and stare with him into that square green hole. Sure, he might be nervous, my showing up like that — but, in fact, by then I would have admitted my error, professed my shame, begged forgiveness. Mom, Clay, everyone, would understand that grief had knocked me out and filled me up with lies, thrown me, for a time, completely out of orbit. I'd be on a steady diet of humble pie, and Clay for his part would be rolling around in my guilt like a dog in its own shit.

And so I'd watch him drink the Halcion-spiked cocoa and watch his eyelids thicken, and when he couldn't stay upright any longer, when his head fell and his body dropped, I'd shove him into his spearing hole and push him under the ice.

16

I stayed up on the tower all afternoon, and when I got home that evening I found a note on the kitchen table.

> *Jesse,*
> *Pastor L. and his wife invited us all for supper. Magnus and*
> *I left at 5:30. Please drive over as soon as you get home. Don't*
> *make everyone wait.*
>
> *— Mom*

I crumpled it up and threw it across the room, retrieved it and tossed it in the wastebasket beneath the sink. I sat down at the table and blew into my cupped hands to warm them. Up there on the tower the cold had worked its way through my clothes and gotten inside of me. I closed my eyes and tried to picture summer — leaves, green grass, clouds like dandelion puffs, a breeze that didn't cut — but the images wouldn't come. All I was able to conjure was a white landscape filled with black trees. What would it be like, I wondered, to sit in my pastor's living room on the same day I'd decided to murder someone, and pretend to be a man like he was, dedicated to doing the right and godly thing? It seemed outrageous, more outrageous even than the act I was going to commit, and it made me want to laugh. I didn't, though. The laugh muscles in my stomach felt dead.

Motivated by a sudden grip of hunger, I went to the fridge to see what I could find. A fist-size brick of Swiss cheese, a tube of hard salami, a jar of pickles, a carton of milk, an orange. I took a knife from the block of knives on the counter and carried the food to the kitchen table and sat down before it. I began to eat. My appetite was monstrous.

I'd polished off half the cheese, a dozen pickles, a good five or six inches of the salami and the orange when the phone rang. It was Christine.

We're home, she whispered, and the sound of her voice, warm and earthy — it always made me think of coffee grounds and sun-warmed soil — had an immediate effect on me. The muscles in my shoulders loosened. The tension left my eyes.

Can I come over? I have to talk to you, I said.

Now? She still whispered, as though it was late at night and her family was sleeping.

It's not a good time?

I guess it's okay. She coughed, cleared her throat. You can meet my dad, she said. They let him out. We brought him home.

I couldn't tell how I was supposed to respond to her news, and in any case I was so caught up in my own head that I found it was hard to care.

Is this a good thing? I asked.

In the background Renata shouted in her baby voice, and

below that I heard a droning male sound. I don't know yet, Christine whispered. I just don't know.

I knocked several times before her mom came and peeked out the window at me. She opened the door, but only a crack. Her face had a hard red glow about it, as if she'd just been scrubbing at it with rough soap.

Jesse? she said. Normally she would have grabbed my arm with her little fingers and yanked me inside, beaming. Now she couldn't even look me in the eye.

How was your trip? I asked as she brought me in. Christine told me to come over. Hope that's okay.

Maria glanced behind herself into the kitchen. Her face seemed cloudy, confused. Then from behind her came her husband's voice, and she jumped.

Bring the boy in, he said.

Maria managed a smile. Then pushed me forward. From the kitchen table her husband watched me sideways as if I were some dim-witted salesman or a missionary bent on saving him. He wore a crisp blue workshirt rolled halfway up his arms and sat with his elbows propped on the tabletop, dark fingers meshed in front of his chin. Green veins like strands of twine jutted from his forearms. I couldn't tell if he was smiling or recalling something funny — a joke, maybe, from one of his fellow inmates, I thought ungenerously.

Daniel Montez, he said. Even as he offered his hand, he kept his face averted.

Jesse Matson. Glad to meet you, I said, and we shook. I was prepared for an iron grip but got a limp fish instead.

Jesse Matson, huh? Are you looking for my daughter, or was

it me you wanted to see? Daniel Montez laughed, face angled to one side, not quite looking at me. His teeth looked strong and yellow, his lips taut. His fingers moved against the table rhythmically. His black hair gleamed like a showroom car. Harold Matson's son, right? he asked.

That's right, I said.

I'm sorry about your father. There was a good man.

Thanks.

Life's a bitch, isn't it, Jesse Matson — when you look at what happens to good men?

I guess it is.

Daniel Montez nodded, took a breath. When he exhaled, he said, We're always having to pay the price for somebody else's sins, aren't we? Christine! He lifted his voice to reach the far end of the trailer. There's somebody to see you. Get the hell out here.

Maria pulled out a chair for me, and when I sat, Daniel turned himself away so that I could see only the left side of his face. Still, I could tell that the other side had been crushed, the cheekbone flattened. Thick red scar tissue had formed where bone was supposed to be.

People don't know what matters anymore, he said. Things like loyalty, who it is you owe your *life* to. You know what I mean, Jesse Matson?

I wasn't sure but nodded anyway.

And then you've got a few left like your old man, willing to give somebody a hand up once in a while. Hey, thanks to him we might be able to move out of this rat hole, buy a house. And my wife probably told you. He made sure she got that job at the plant. I asked him to do it, and he did it. Called him up one night before my sentencing — before that goddamned jury had me every which way, and those goddamned lawyers. And I said to him, Look, I voted for you and now I need a favor. I'm leaving a family, a pregnant wife, for God's sake. And he listened to me. He wouldn't of had to do it, he didn't owe me a thing. Hell, he wasn't even family. Not that family counts for shit these days.

Christine entered from the hall and gestured awkwardly, lifting an arm as if she had spotted me off in the distance and needed to flag me down. Her dad glanced over at her, popped up from his chair and left the kitchen without speaking. In the living room he turned on the TV, cranked the volume, dropped himself on the couch. Christine came up and touched my cheek with her lips, which felt cold and dry, then gave me a brutal hug. She smelled like heaven.

Let's go for a drive, she whispered. Get out of here.

It seemed like a fine idea, but then Maria flew in, Renata balanced on one hip, and asked if I would stay for supper.

Please, I insist, she said, and took hold of my arm above the elbow and squeezed so hard it hurt.

Christine shook her head. *We're leaving*, she mouthed. But her mother looked toward the living room and raised her voice: Isn't that right, Daniel?

Isn't what right? he asked.

That Jesse should stay for supper.

Jesse should stay for supper, he answered.

Maria lowered her eyes at us.

Christine, though, didn't give up. Do you need anything at the store? Jesse and I'll go pick it up for you, she said.

In fact I do. Maria nodded. I could use a package of chicken breasts.

From the living room Daniel piped up again: *I'll* go to the store. Need the fresh air. And I've gotta pick up some cigarettes, anyway. He got up from the couch and swept past us through the kitchen fast, head down, grabbed his coat from a hook and left without a word, chin tucked into his collar.

While he was gone, we watched TV — at least Christine and I did, with Renata propped between us sucking on her bottle and rocking herself back and forth. Maria worked in the kitchen. By the sound of it she was trying to tear it down, whacking shut cabinet doors, clanging silverware, slamming dishes on the table and stomping her feet uncharacteristically. Yet the smells that came floating out were sharp and spicy and full of summer sun, almost intoxicating.

Christine's dad was gone a long time, at least an hour, and when he came back, he looked exhausted, shoulders sagging. Maria sat us down to eat. There was no chicken in the fajitas, though — Daniel had apparently forgotten to buy it. She'd used spiced beef instead, and gave us rice and refried beans and canned corn on the side. We drank Mexican Coke from glass bottles. At the head of the table Daniel sat brooding, eyes never lifting from his plate. After each bite he wiped his mouth with his napkin and sighed. He spoke little, and when he did, it was to contradict his wife as she tried to keep silence at bay.

I hear we're getting some weather, she said. Freezing rain, maybe some wind. It might get bad, they say.

Goddamn weathermen, always whining, Daniel said. They've just gotta have something to talk about, makes them feel important. Don't know their ass from a hole in the ground.

Maria said, We have a guest, Daniel.

Her husband tipped his head in my direction, just barely. And I'm pleased that we do, he said.

Thanks, I told him.

Maria, sitting straight in her chair and putting on a bright face, tried again, explaining that Father Dittmer was doing a special Mass tonight to commemorate the workman who had died when they were building the church.

Remember when that happened? she asked.

Poor bastard, said Daniel. Fell off the steeple, didn't he? What sort of fool goes up there without a safety rope? Seems to me if you're going to commemorate somebody in a Mass, you ought to pick a person you can look up to. One of the saints, maybe. A president. Not some damn idiot.

Well, I was thinking it might be nice to go to Mass, all of us together. The whole family. You'd be welcome to come along, Jesse.

Daniel shook his head and pointed with his fork at his mouth, chewed for a few moments, then swallowed. He said, I'll be dead before anyone drags me into that church again, at least as long as that priest is there. What did he do for me when I needed help? Hmm?

What could he have done, Daniel? Maria asked.

He could've come in front of the court and spoke on my behalf. People *listen* to priests.

But he wasn't a witness, Maria said.

With deliberation, Christine's father set his silverware beside his plate, leveled his shoulders, and squared his damaged face to us, let us have a good look. He said, That man, my priest, let me down, and I won't forgive him for it. If he were here right now, I'd spit on him. You hear? I'd spit on him, break his nose and throw him out on his ass. You live long enough — Daniel's gaze moved straight to Christine, and his eyes blazed — you live long enough, you learn who you trust and who you don't.

Christine got up from the table and left the room. Daniel stood too. We'll stay home tonight, he said to his wife. Watch TV or something. I'm tired. You kids, though, he added, glancing my way, if you want to do something, go someplace, that's just fine.

What we did was go for a drive in the Mercury. We cruised town, up and down Main, then drove north into the woods and followed the backroads I knew from Sunday-afternoon car rides with Mom and Dad. Despite Maria's warning, the skies had cleared for the night. The trees were so close on either side that to see the stars and moon we had to peer straight up through the windshield. The inside of my head was crammed full, humming with everything I needed to say. It was the same for Christine, I'm sure. Her anxiety was palpable, I could almost smell it. The fact is, both of us that night required exactly what the other could not give — someone with an unencumbered soul, someone able to listen — and it strikes me now that the problems we have with those we love can often be explained in this way. Attracted as we are to kindred spirits, to those with similar strengths or facing similar crises, often what we need from them simply is not available.

And so we kept everything to ourselves, the distance between us growing wider and colder as we drove. Christine pressed up against the passenger door on the far side of the big bench seat. A couple of times I tried to break through, tried to push away my own concerns, give her an opportunity to talk, get things off her chest. But my heart wasn't in it, and I'm sure she sensed that. What I really wanted was for her to question *me*, listen to *me*. I didn't have enough room inside to absorb her pain, take on her troubles. Not tonight. But like I said, I tried.

What's he going to do? I asked. For a job, I mean.

Who knows? Christine snapped.

What happened to his face? I said, a mile or so later.

She shook her head.

Has he spoken *at all*? I asked. To you, I mean.

She lifted her feet to the dashboard and curled herself away, toward the window. I gave up and turned around at the entrance to a logging trail and started back for town. We were a mile or so north of Little Mexico when she finally spoke.

I'm sorry. It's just too much right now, and you're not ready for it.

I'm sorry too, I said.

Take me to the double bridge, she told me.

I looked over at her. She was still hunched up but peeking at me past her shoulder.

There's something I want to toss in, she said.

Superstitious all of a sudden?

No. Desperate.

She slid over and nestled up against me, wedged herself beneath my arm and wrapped hers around my chest. In the bright darkness of that night her eyes burned up at mine.

I wish I could do something, I said.

You are.

No, I'm not. I'm thinking only about myself.

Hey, she said. You came over, you were there with me tonight. You're here now. That's something. You can't live my life for me, Jesse. I'm the one who needs to figure it out, and I will.

I don't know if you should even stay there, I said. I don't think it's safe.

She waved me off with an odd little gesture, wrist loose, fingers outflung. I'll be fine, you'll see, she said.

We drove past Little Mexico, past my place and Charlie Blue's and past the public beach with its cement-block changing house. At the double bridge I stopped where I had before, and we got out and walked to the middle of it, where she reached into the pocket of her coat and pulled something out. She held it up before the sky for me to see. It was a baseball, an old one by the look of it, scuffed and stained.

One of your dad's? I asked.

She nodded. He won't miss it, she said. There must be a dozen of them. Without hesitating, she brought her arm back and sent the ball in a long arc toward the river. Her throw went wide, though, and struck one of the boulders at the edge, caromed back toward the middle of the channel and came to rest on the snow. We could see it down there, a speck in the white. I wasn't sure what she believed she had just done, but it seemed to have helped.

There, she said. She stood with one hand on the railing, her breathing heavy and cathartic — white ghosts in the chilly air. I stood with her until she was ready to go. A winter owl called from a shoreline tree. Far below us a night animal, a raccoon or mink, scurried among the rocks.

Back in the car I started the engine, but she put her hand on mine and said, Let's just sit here a while. You need to tell me what happened while I was gone.

That was all it took — she didn't have to drag it out of me. I told her everything: Dad showing up in the backseat, Charlie's story of Mom and Clay at the motel in Cat Creek, my night in the Valhalla and the talk I had with Dwayne Primrose, my conversation with Sheriff Stone, the tense meeting at Clay's afterward.

Hearing myself talk, I found it hard to believe that so much could have happened so fast, and I watched Christine's face for signs that what I was telling her was beyond the scope of reason. She only nodded and made little listening sounds. When I was done, she pressed herself against me, her face on my neck.

So Sheriff Stone is looking for the gun, then, right? she asked. In the lake? And he's trying to find Dwayne?

He won't find Dwayne, I said.

How do you know that?

I just do. Dwayne's gone. He won't be coming back.

You think he's dead?

That, or as good as.

You think he went out and told Clay what he told you? You're saying Clay killed *him* too?

I have no idea. I just know he won't be back.

For a while Christine was silent. Then she said, Sheriff Stone can't just ignore what you told him, though, can he?

Sure he can. It's all too hypothetical, too slippery. It doesn't line up with the way he's got it figured out. And if you think about it, why *should* it make sense to him?

Because now he's got somebody's testimony.

Dwayne's? Dwayne's not here. And nobody would believe him if he was. Sheriff Stone's right about that.

Christine worked her hands under my coat and then under my shirt and wrapped her arms around my back, her skin warm against my own. Clay got away with it, didn't he? she said. We know that now, right?

We do, I said. And you want to hear something crazy? I feel pretty good about it — knowing for sure, I mean. It's like I've been swimming under water all this time, holding my breath and seeing everything through a haze. And now I can breathe again, I can *see*. Things look sharp to me, it's all clear. And I know what to do.

A tremor passed through Christine, and I looked down into her eyes. It was like peering into a mirror. In a way that was horrifying and normal at the same time, I could feel her mind inside my own and knew that she understood, that she knew what I was planning.

She shook her head. You can't do that, Jesse — you have to promise me. Do you hear? You have to promise me you won't.

I looked out the window and saw in the distance, out on frozen Crow Lake, the moon reflected on a patch of bare ice. I felt an urge to unwrap myself from Christine's arms, slip out of the car and run.

She squeezed me harder. Her breath was coming fast. You have no idea, she said. Look at my dad. Whatever he touches, he kills. You saw him tonight. You saw my mom.

I'm not your dad, Christine.

No, but you're not God either. Can't you see? *He's* the only one who can take life, because he's the only one who can give it. Nobody else has the right.

I have it if I take it, I said.

No, you don't. All you'd be doing is getting even — that's what Clay did. It's like jumping off a building. Once you go over the edge, that's it, you're on your way, there's no stopping yourself. You've given up to something bigger. Except it'd be worse than that, because you'd be taking everybody with you. Your mom —

Mom's already gone.

And your brother. And me. Don't do that to us.

I shook her loose, pushed her away.

Listen to me, Jesse. I'll say it as clear as I can. I wouldn't want to *be* with someone who'd do that. I *can't* be with someone like that, do you hear? Because the place you're heading? I *live* there.

I put the car in gear and stabbed the gas pedal. My tires spun in the snow on the road's shoulder, then squealed as they caught hold of the tar.

It's me or him, Jesse. You better understand that. Me or him.

Her lips were hot against my ear as I drove. She had hold of my arm with one hand and the inside of my thigh with the other.

Drive us over to church, she said. Mass starts in ten minutes. Please!

I felt ragged inside, knocked off center, but couldn't resist Christine's warmth next to me, her hand kneading my thigh, her mouth on my ear. I drove to the church, where we parked, went inside and sat at the back. This was the second time I'd ever been there — the first had been for Dad's funeral. It was dark and cavernous, the air sweet-smelling and damp. I only half attended to the rituals of the liturgy and half listened to Father Dittmer's words, but knelt with Christine and stood with her, following her lead, trying not to see what my mind kept showing me: the icy green water and my uncle drifting in it, blue-faced. I remembered a Bible verse from a recent sermon of Pastor Lundberg's: *Vengeance is mine. I will repay, says the Lord.*

Christine's sharp elbow brought me back to the service — the congregation's droning recitation of the Lord's Prayer. I joined in — *and forgive us our trespasses, as we forgive those who trespass against us* — but stopped right there and let the prayer go on without me.

Forgive him? I was supposed to forgive him? It wasn't possible, unless forgiveness was something different, something less than

I'd thought it was. There was no way I could forget or pardon or excuse or absolve or overlook my uncle's crime against us. Against Dad. There was no button inside of me that I could reach in and press to soften my hardness toward him, temper my hatred of him, calm the clamor in my blood. And if there was, I wouldn't touch it. I'd rather go straight to the coldest center of the cruelest hell of the most merciless god imaginable.

The organ rose, and around us the people rose too on its soaring major chords. Christine led me toward the front of the altar, above us the raised pulpit, and above that, a bronze Jesus on his wooden cross. Non-Catholics weren't supposed to receive Communion, I knew that — or thought I did — yet Father Dittmer, in his white surplice, caught my eye and smiled. Then, over Christine's shoulder, I saw the gold cup heaped with small white hosts — *the Body of Christ* — and in front of me Christine said *Amen* and leaned forward. I followed her lead, but even as the host softened on my tongue, my stomach contracted and my throat spasmed. With effort, I managed to swallow it and keep it down.

Next came the Blood. What choice did I have? I took a sip from the offered chalice, held the wine in my mouth for a moment or two and forced it down through my clamping throat. The warmth of it traced a thin line from my stomach to my arms, and then out to the tips of my fingers.

Afterward, in the Mercury, Christine tucked herself under my arm and took hold of my hand, gripping my index finger with her left fist and my pinky with her right, as if she owned me. My impulse was to drop her off and go home, bring an end to that interminable day. I didn't want to have to think anymore — about Clay and the plan I had for him, about Christine's ultimatum, about anything. The pressure of it all was too much.

Christine, though, wasn't ready for the night to be over. As we rolled down Main Street, she tugged at my fingers and said, Let's go to Pump's for a while. We need to talk. Besides, I'm hungry.

Except for the bars, Pump's was the only place in Battlepoint that stayed open past eight o'clock, and sometimes on nights when we actually had money, Christine and I would go there for coffee and fries.

Please, she said, and squeezed my fingers harder.

It was quiet inside, a sparse scattering of kids and white hairs. We found an empty booth with a window overlooking the lake and ordered. Country-western music whined from the cheap speakers. The lake's frozen surface was bleak, a moonscape. Normally, Christine sat back and watched me polish off the fries, but tonight she was the one who leaned over the table, dipping them one after another into the little paper cup full of mustard. There was a glow in her eyes, a look on her face that told me she was barely suppressing a secret. It was like she thought she had something on me.

What? I asked, despite myself.

She shook her head, though not to dismiss me — it was the sort of gesture, accompanied by a smile, that may as well have been a nod.

I was just remembering something, she said.

Tell me.

She fixed her eyes on a point in the middle distance. Her smile faded, and she pursed her lips.

When I was little, she started, Mom always made sure I

received Communion. Even summers, working the fields, she made sure we got to church on Sundays. Dad would say, We can't go, we've gotta finish these rows. But we'd go anyway, Mom and I, which usually meant leaving him out there alone. The Body and the Blood, Mom would tell me. They'll save us from ourselves.

Christine's eyes came back to me now and sharpened with a confidence that wrenched my heart. She pushed the rest of her fries to the edge of the table, took a deep breath and said, One day — this was just after my First Communion — I was in the dime store with this friend of mine, Connie, and the old man who owned the place had to go upstairs to help his wife out of the tub. They lived up there, and she was always yelling down at him like that. We'd taken stuff from this guy before. Stolen from him. Never much, a pack of gum, a few suckers, a candy bar. And though it made me feel bad, I didn't feel bad enough, I guess, to stop. Anyway, as soon as he disappeared upstairs, Connie leaned over the counter and grabbed a bag of M&M's and ran for the door. I was right behind her, reaching for a Salted Nut Roll, one of those extra-big ones, but the second I touched it, I felt something hot on the inside of my wrist — it felt like acid burning in my veins. I mean, it hurt so bad I dropped the candy bar. And as soon as I did, the pain was gone. I ran out of the store empty-handed.

Christine's face, flushed, radiant, made me think of a Bible verse I'd delivered at a Christmas pageant when I was in second or third grade. *And wine that maketh glad the heart of man, and oil to make his face to shine.*

I never stole anything again, Christine said.

I laughed at her. So you think that now I'm protected from myself? That I won't be able to do anything God disapproves of?

Hey, I've taken Communion at my church lots of times. Give me a break.

Christine only smiled.

You're not making sense, I said. What about my own free will?

You ate the Body, Jesse. You drank the Blood. You chose.

She shrugged then and gave me a knowing look, complicit, as if my conscience were made of the same indestructible, sensitive material that hers was made of. I wasn't sure if I should pity her innocence or fear the person I'd become. Or maybe she was right. Maybe God wouldn't let me. Maybe he had a hold on me I didn't realize. Or maybe, in all truth, I didn't have the guts I thought I had, and Christine could see it.

I love you, I hope you know that, she said. She was all confidence — she was glowing with it.

I love you too, I told her.

Fifteen minutes later, though, as we pulled up in front of her trailer house, her courage or her faith, whatever it was, had abandoned her, and she began to cry — silent, racking sobs. It's all right, I whispered, it's all right. But she shook her head, dismissing my easy comfort. Then she reached up and grabbed me, pulled my face to hers and held it there, her palms covering my ears. She pressed her nose and cheeks against my own and she ground our faces together, hers warm and slick with tears. Her eyes, wide open, searched mine, and when she took a breath to speak, I knew what she was going to say.

You have to promise me, Jesse. You have to promise me you won't do it.

Shh, I said. It's okay, I promise. Don't worry.

I moved her head to my shoulder and hugged her close, enduring the crash of her heart against my chest. How long we sat there

I don't know, but finally, needing air, I lifted myself away from her. I breathed in deeply and stared up through the windshield of the Mercury.

Above us, the sky, brilliant and densely packed, was like a snowstorm caught on fast film, each star a cold crystal and the moon a bright scythe.

17

At some point that night — home in bed, unable to sleep — I got up and went down into the dark kitchen and opened the fridge. I was standing barefoot on the cold linoleum, trying to choose between orange juice and milk, when I felt a presence. I turned. Mom was at the table, her shoulders and head outlined against the window.

You scared me, I said.

At first she didn't answer. She looked like a spirit sitting there, chrome hair glowing in the starlight, but then she lifted a white cup to her lips and sipped from it, and the familiar sound of that comforted me.

Glad you're home, Jesse, she said. Steam rose from her cup, and the smell told me she'd taken down Dad's bottle of medicinal brandy and added a splash of it to her tea. In the dim light I could see that she was holding the kitten, Lydia, in the crook of her elbow.

I took the carton of orange juice, poured myself a glass and sat down across from her. The previous morning in Clay's kitchen seemed like years ago. Mom watched me. I was a man on trial, a guilty man, my whole life riding on how well I could spin out an alibi. I thought, *All right, I've done this now — it can only get easier.*

I'm sorry, I said to her. I'm really sorry.

You are? Her voice cracked with surprise. She adjusted herself on her chair, and I think she leaned forward a little, though it was hard to tell in the dark.

Yes, I said.

For what?

The whole mess.

Well it's not like you *started* the whole mess.

And it's not like I've done a lot to make it better either, I said.

Mom waited. Her posture seemed tentative, stiff, and I was aware of how vigilantly she listened to me. For as much as I needed to convince her that I'd put all of my suspicion to rest, maybe her own need to *be* convinced was just as great.

It's hard to believe how much I misread it all, I said. I guess I just couldn't accept that Dad could do that to us. Any other explanation seemed better. Anything. It wasn't fair of me, I know, but I wasn't trying to hurt anybody either. I was screwed up.

So, what makes it different tonight? What's changed?

I stopped to think. I had to be shrewd, entirely persuasive, as earnest in my fabrications as I was steadfast in my purpose. But how hard could it be, after my night with Christine?

I guess I'm not sure, I said. Maybe it was sitting there in Clay's kitchen, seeing what I'd done to him. I mean, he looked awful. Or maybe talking to Sheriff Stone afterward.

What did Billy say?

Basically, that there's no evidence. Nothing. I mean, he came about as close as he could to telling me I'm nuts, which I probably was for a while. Oh, and then tonight I saw Christine. Her dad's back.

Oh, Lord, Mom said. Lucky them. You saw him?

I nodded.

He's a piece of work, isn't he? Mom took another sip of her brandy-laced tea. I could tell she was trying to read me, head cocked to the side, the pupils of her eyes merciless pinholes of light, and below them, the kitten's eyes too, smaller but just as sharp.

After you and Billy left, you know what happened? Mom asked. Clay went into the bathroom and threw up. He had the dry heaves. It must have gone on for ten minutes. It sounded like he was hauling up his guts and spitting them out. This is killing him, Jesse. I hope you understand that now. Maybe you're finally getting some clarity. But look, you've got to follow up on it.

I know, Mom. I'm going to.

She sat watching me for a while.

I said, Do you know if Dwayne's called yet?

Mom shook her head. Clay thinks it'll be a few days before he's ready, maybe a week or two. But then he'll drive down and pick him up. You must've given the poor man a real scare, Jesse.

I'm sorry.

I mean, were you putting words in his mouth, or what?

I didn't try to, Mom. Maybe that's how it turned out. You've got to understand, though, it's not like Dwayne didn't have some weird memories from that night.

You've got to accept what's happened, Jesse. You *get* that now, right?

I do, I said, nodding. And I'm going to make up for it, I promise.

Mom sighed, and I thought of going over and giving her a hug to show her my good intentions, but before I could get up she was on her feet and moving. She walked right past me, her arm brushing my shoulder, and when she got to the stairway she stopped and turned. She still had the kitten clutched in her arms. Then for some reason, she leaned down and set it on the floor. It ran straight to me and began to rub against my bare ankle. I wanted to kick it. I wanted to grab it up and pitch it through the kitchen window, but instead I bent over and ran my fingers along the tiny bumps of its spine.

Are you serious about that? she asked.

I'll do anything I can, I said.

All right then. You can start tomorrow. I'm going out to Clay's fish house on Oscar's Bay — he's been begging me to come ever since the contest started, and I'm finally going. You can come along.

18

His Austin sat like a green insect on a spot of bare ice. Magnus and I followed Mom past it and up to his fishing shack, which was made of bright corrugated steel. Gray smoke rose in a straight line from its chimney. Mom rapped smartly on the door, and right away it swung open.

Hey, look what the wind blew in, Clay said, blinking against the sun.

It's not windy, said Magnus.

Clay ignored him and fixed his glare on me — I wondered if Mom had managed to give him a heads-up somehow. He was clearly angry. His forehead was bunched into a cat-and-mouse grid, and he was doing this thing with his hands, stretching his fingers out wide, then clamping them into fists, then stretching them out again, quickly.

We brought you some hot cocoa, I said. Here. For your stomach.

Whether or not Clay was convinced by the conciliatory smile I tried to put on, at least he took the thermos from me and invited us all in. The air was warm and smelled like cold fish and fried bacon. When he closed the door behind us, the darkness was total.

I can't see anything, Mom said.

Give it a minute. You'll adjust.

I heard him twist the top off the thermos and splash warm cocoa into the steel cup. Soon I could make out a dim light seeping up from the lake through the spearing hole in the corner. There was a high loft bed on one wall and a small metal table on the wall across from it, a propane stove, a rack with cooking utensils, a line of clothes on hooks behind the door. He was clearly spending time out here, going for broke, trying to win the contest. He grabbed a kitchen chair for Mom and a plastic bucket each for Magnus and me, then arranged us all in a tight semicircle around the square hole, which must have been at least two by two. Finally, he took his place on a three-legged stool, moving stealthily, as if engaged in consequential, secret work.

Just saw this big one, he said. Before you got here. It came by fast and knocked my lure crooked. First one I've seen today. Twenty pounds, at least.

An admiring noise issued from Mom's throat — or maybe she was only coughing.

I said something like Wow, and nodded.

Magnus sat with his arms crossed over his chest. He'd resisted coming along, but Mom had forced it, and I was more than glad to have him here as a buffer. We all sat for a time, staring down into the water, which I found hypnotic, even inviting. To the far right of what I could see under there, over on the shore side, a forest of spiral plants moved in barely discernible undulations. Eight or ten feet straight down was the pebble-strewn bottom. The occasional bluegill darted into the square of water, attracted by the lure, which Clay controlled with a constant jigging of his left wrist. Finally he shifted on his stool and motioned to my brother. Hey, guy, your turn with the harpoon, he said.

Magnus shrugged him off, but Clay insisted, and soon they'd switched places, Magnus seated on the stool, Clay kneeling beside him and explaining how to hold the spear just so, its five blue steel tines resting motionless in the water so as not to make a splash when thrown.

Don't worry about the first pass, Clay said, because it'll come way too quick. But then, see, she'll come floating back in and put her nose up to your lure and check it out. Wiggle those little side fins. Clay put his hands up near his shoulders and made his fingers move, finlike. *Then* you throw, he said. You throw hard and straight.

We all peered with Magnus into the green square of water. The lure was a wooden, lead-weighted fish painted a brilliant reddish orange, with blue fins and yellow stripes. Clay showed Magnus how to lift and drop the monofilament line to make the lure swim a tight circle. It attracted no predators, though, and after fifteen or twenty minutes Magnus said he'd had enough and stood up from the stool.

Clay offered the spear to Mom, but she wanted nothing of it. It's barbaric! she said, making a face. I couldn't stab something with that. Look at it, it gives me the creeps.

It's a spear. What's it supposed to look like?

And think how it must *feel*. Going in.

They're fish, Genevieve. Not people. Clay glanced my way and laughed, showing his teeth.

You know I've always been squeamish, Mom said. Give it to Jesse. He doesn't mind that stuff.

Clay peered at me sideways, not turning his head, and I shrugged to show him I was willing. He looked back at Mom, paused and said, Hey, did you remember to bring your hibachi? And the coals? He glanced at me again and winked. In case we get a northern. So we can grill it fresh, right here.

Mom set the heel of her hand against her forehead, theatrically. I'm *sorry*. What an idiot! I had it out on the porch, ready to go, and forgot it. We'll run back and pick it up, Magnus and I. It won't take twenty minutes, and by the time we get back, who knows — Jesse's always been lucky with animals, hunting, all those manly, nature things.

She got up, Magnus did too, and just like that, they left me there alone with Clay.

I knew it was prearranged — it couldn't have been more obvious — and I hated her for it. I hated her for everything, for what she'd done to Dad, for what she'd done to me and to our family. I remembered her as she had looked in the sauna, wrapped in a towel, smiling that strange superior smile and refusing to answer my questions, put out with me for getting in the way of her pursuit of love. It was unbelievable. Who did she think she was, flushing my life down the toilet? How would she finally have to account for herself, make up for all she'd helped to destroy? How long could this go on?

Clay sat me down on his stool over the hole, pulled up a bucket across from me, and pushed the spear into my hands. Our knees were a foot apart, our faces about the same. I looked at him and made an assessment. He was taller than I was by an inch, and outweighed me too, but only because of his middle-age paunch.

My build was naturally thin, same as his, but I was in great condition — all the running — and probably stronger in my arms and chest because of the weight lifting we had to do in gym class. If it came to a fight, my chances had to be better than even. Not to mention, I was the one holding the spear. How hard could it be, I wondered, driving it through him? The very thought sent a ripple of joy through my chest. I saw my uncle skewered on his feet, staring at me down the long shaft, trying to speak but choking on his own blood. I imagined his legs going soft, and the growing weight of him at the end of my spear.

When he spoke, his voice startled me. That stunt you pulled yesterday? It was uncalled for, he said.

I looked up. His eyes were dead and flat, like his voice.

I know, I said.

Sure. But you know *everything*, Jesse, don't you?

I didn't say that.

That's the impression you left yesterday.

I'm sorry about yesterday. Really, I am.

Of course you are. Clay scraped his bucket backward on the plywood floor and stood up. I've gotta take a piss, he said, and went to the door and swung it wide and left, slamming it behind him.

As I listened to his boots stomping off in the direction of the shore, it occurred to me that he was on his way to fetch a gun, that in minutes he'd be back to kill me and stuff me down the hole, same as I was planning to do to him. What would he tell Mom when she got back? How would he explain my absence? Or was she in on it too? Had she gone that far? Was she so depraved that every enemy of Clay's had become hers too, even her own son?

In minutes, Clay was back — without a gun. He seemed to

have calmed down a little. He lowered himself onto the bucket, poured out a cup of cocoa from the thermos we'd brought and took a swallow. Look, he said, it's not so much what you did to *me*. But putting ideas in Dwayne's head like that, messing him up — that was terrible. The guy's got it hard enough as it is without somebody screwing with him like that.

I nodded.

He's the sort of guy that believes what you tell him. If you say to him, Here's the way things are, he'll go along with you, because he wants to make you happy. You must understand that, Jesse. What were you thinking?

I didn't respond.

I mean, how'd you dream that story up, anyway? Tell me.

I don't know, I said.

You don't know?

No.

And your mom. Have you considered what this is doing to her? You're putting her through hell.

I nodded, took a firmer grip on the spear.

Not to mention me. Hey, man, I don't care who you are, my nephew or the Prince of goddamn Wales, I'm not going to let you jerk my chain. You understand? You don't just go around accusing somebody of shit like this. Clay reached out suddenly and yanked the spear out of my hand. That's not the way you hold it, he said. Use your fingers, not your fist. We're not boxing here. His eyes were bloodshot and full of hate, and I could feel them bump in my veins.

Clay pushed the shaft of the spear back into my hands and said, Okay now, pay attention.

I adjusted my position over the hole and tried for a gentler grip on the spear's cool shaft, told myself to be patient. His time was coming, but it wasn't now. Below, a school of bluegills zipped past my lure.

My uncle cleared his throat. He said, I can see where you'd be looking for someone to blame, but you've got to remember, this happened to all of us, not just you. It happened to your mom, it happened to me, it happened to Magnus. You know?

I nodded, jigging the lure.

I want to give you the benefit of the doubt here, Jesse, but I have to say, it makes me nervous, seeing what's happening to you. I mean, you're not thinking straight. You need to talk to somebody, get all this bullshit off your chest — somebody down in Bowstring. Your mom could have Dr. Milius set it up.

Bowstring, fifty miles south, was the regional mental hospital, and in our part of the world the name had come to mean crazy, nuts, looney tunes, as in, *You moron, they oughta send you to Bowstring.*

All right? he asked.

I made myself look up at him again. His eyes were trying to pry me open, flicking back and forth, looking for a way in. I imagined his face as the head of a snake and saw myself slamming my heel down on it, pressing with my full weight until it popped. I wondered what he knew — whether anything I'd said to Charlie, for instance, had worked its way around to him.

Okay, I said.

You'll do it?

Yes. I want to put all this behind us, I'll do anything.

Good. That's what I like to hear.

And Clay? I said. I really appreciate this. Thanks.

He watched me carefully, his eyes small and piercing. No problem, he said.

No, really, I mean it. I looked him full in the face until he turned away.

For a few moments he was quiet, then he forced a laugh and reached across and gave me a tap on the shoulder with the back of his knuckles.

When Mom returned with the grill, she was all by herself. Magnus had complained that he wasn't feeling well, and so she'd left him at home. Guess he's not much of a fisherman, is he? she said.

No surprise. His dad wasn't either, said Clay.

Looking up from the hole, I saw Mom's face telling him to be careful. She'd given me the same look a thousand times. Clay didn't seem to mind, though. He tipped his head to her, and one side of his mustache twitched.

I looked back down in time to see the flash of silver knock the wooden fish out of sight and cause the monofilament line to zing out of my fingers.

Hey! I said. The lure came drifting back into view, bent-tailed.

Immediately, Clay was at my shoulder. Watch now! he whispered, his breath warm in my ear. He's coming back. Get ready.

Mom edged closer. Shhh, Clay said. And it wasn't long before the long narrow pike glided in from the direction in which it had disappeared. In the glassy light it looked like a monster out of some preglacial lake, its transparent side fins fluttering like wings. Its snout came to rest exactly at the lure's nose-tip. Clay didn't have to say a word. I thrust downward with all my strength, my fingers releasing and spreading wide. The rope to which the spear was attached snapped tight, and there was a confusion of light and shadow beneath me. The spear wagged off toward the west, toward shore, and I took hold of the rope and hauled on it.

Clay tried to help me, grabbing for the rope, but I shouldered him away and did it myself, pulled the fish out of the hole and laid it out on the floor. I set my foot against its back and yanked the barbed tines free. They made a ripping sound coming out. I hefted the fish by its gills and carried it outside into the sun and laid it on the ice. Right away the green translucent glimmer of its scales began to fade, even as its mouth worked the air for oxygen.

What did I tell you? Clay said, fists on his hips. That's the best fish I've seen all season. It's gotta go twenty pounds! He wasn't looking at me, though, but at Mom, who in turn was watching the suffocating fish. Clay bent down and put his hand on the place where the tines had broken the skin. It seemed like a gesture of sympathy. Then he stood up, and before I knew it he'd touched my cheek with a spot of blood. It felt hot there, sizzling, as if my skin had broken.

That's what you do on the first one, Clay said. Rite of passage. He made a self-deprecating shrug and laughed. He was almost giddy. Sorry, Genevieve, I know it's kind of a nasty business, but I just love the sport of it, I can't help it.

Mom smiled and shook her head. She ran her fingers down through her hair and along the side of her neck, then glanced at me and back again at Clay. Don't worry, I'm not *that* sensitive, she said.

And *you're* going to come back out here, Clay said, turning to me. I've got to have some of that luck. What do you say?

He put out his hand for me to shake.

I didn't have a choice. It felt cold and hard.

Well, I'm going to run this fish into town, get it weighed. In the meantime, you better get that grill going. Clay was looking at Mom again, watching her hard, his eyes going right in. There's nothing like grilled northern, he said. Trick is, you do it real slow, at a nice low heat.

IV

THE HOUNDS OF SPRING

19

Back in September when I started this project, my habit was to write at the kitchen table, from which I could look up and watch the sun move across the north face of the Santa Rosas. I found it difficult, though, to get much done at home. There was always laundry to do, carpets to vacuum and dirty dishes in the sink, not to mention the bottomless pile of student papers waiting to be graded. So now on Fridays — my day off campus — I get up at my usual time and walk down the street to Gladstein's, where they're kind enough to keep a table for me.

On a good day I can do five or six pages of reasonably clean prose, though more often only three or four. It doesn't sound like much, I know, but when you add the two or three pages a week I squeeze out during stolen minutes in bed or in my office, the stack of manuscript grows faster than you might think. I'm beginning to see the end.

This afternoon I was having an espresso and reading over what I'd written, when Magnus walked in. He's a big kid now, bigger than I am, six two at least. Also, he's the one who got Mom's looks. People take notice of him, the hard wedge of his cheekbones, the span of his chest, and of course the white-blond hair, which he slices off at the shoulders. And the nerdy black glasses.

Why the glasses and hair? I asked him once. I mean, you're a jock, they don't fit the image.

That's why, he said.

Of course, he's not only a jock — he'll probably be the only art major on the university baseball team next year. His oils are large in dimension, and the colors he chooses remind me of Minnesota — pine greens and birch whites. Cerulean blues, like the lakes there. I'm dreading September, when he leaves. I can't imagine not having him around to take care of any longer.

What's up? I asked him now. He's never come looking for me at the deli before. What I do in my professional life isn't something he's ever shown much interest in — the articles, conference papers, book reviews. All the reading, all the lecture preparation.

Meyers gave us the night off, he said. We've got that tournament this weekend, remember? Magnus reached across the table and tapped his finger on the open notebook, filled up with my crowded longhand. He said, This is something different, isn't it.

I nodded.

What? Some big secret? Finally trying to write a novel?

Not a novel, I said.

What's it about? he asked.

Me, I guess.

Magnus reached across the table and broke off a big piece of the cinnamon roll I was eating, took nearly half of it and tossed the whole chunk in his mouth.

Get one of your own, I said, and fished a couple dollar bills from my pocket and pushed them across the table.

When do I get to read it? he asked.

Since when are you interested in what I write?

Since you started writing about us.

Us? Is that what I said?

He laughed.

Maybe when I'm finished, I told him.

For a few moments he watched me, then he got up and went over to the pastry counter. He's a sensitive kid — he picks things up in the air. For ten years now I haven't moved an inch from my original story, the one I gave him the morning I helped with his paper route, the one in which Dad's death was an accident. At the time, of course, he heard otherwise, from kids at school, from his teacher, from news accounts we couldn't protect him from. But I always told him, You've got a choice — you can believe them, or you can believe me. And I like to think he believed me. I don't feel guilty for lying to him either. The way I see it, I've done what I had to do in order to give my brother as normal a life as possible. Still, I knew from the start that I'd have to tell him some day, and I've decided sooner is better than later, before he comes to me, accusing.

He returned to my table with his roll, pulled a folded-up piece of paper from the back pocket of his jeans and tossed it down in front of me. Found this on the kitchen counter, he said. You left it out.

I opened it on the table to read. It was a form letter I got in the mail, the invitation to my ten-year class reunion.

Planning to go? Magnus asked.

Why would I do that?

See people, I guess. Catch up on old times. Get the news. You know.

I don't want to catch up on old times, Magnus.

My brother leaned forward and tilted his face, studying me.

Why don't *you* go, I said to him. I'll buy your ticket.

It's not my reunion.

But your class would be graduating.

Magnus leaned back and folded his hands on top of his head. He was wearing a snug gray T-shirt, and his biceps looked like a pair of new baseballs, round and shiny. The smile on his face was sly.

What? I asked.

He shook his head. I'm getting a new puppy, he said. Last night I called Mountain Man Kennels. They told me there'll be a new batch ready to go in June.

Sonny's breeder, I said.

Yup. And they're saving me the alpha male.

It made sense to me then. Ever since last month when we had to put down our old Newf — the second Sonny — Magnus has been dragging around the house. That dog had been a link to the dad he's grown up without, to the place we had to leave, to his first life.

I remember the day Magnus got him.

It was in January, not long after I'd speared the big fish, and I came home from school to find a strange car parked in front of our garage, an old blue van shaped like a fat torpedo. Manitoba plates. Magnus stood next to it, counting out bills to a frail woman who sat in her front seat, door swung open, boots planted on our driveway. Over next to the garage I saw what looked like a bear cub digging in a snowdrift.

As I learned soon enough, Magnus had checked the classifieds of all the newspapers they kept in the school library. In the *Winnipeg Free Press* he'd found an advertisement for a Newfoundland pup: four hundred dollars for an eight-week-old male. He called the number and offered four fifty, delivery included, then went over to the bank with his savings book and laid it down in front of the teller, Bernice Fig. The way Magnus describes it, Bernice looked down along her sharp nose at him and explained that what he had was a joint account. In order to withdraw from his balance, which amounted to five hundred and seventy-six dollars, he would need a countersignature. The money, after all, had been deposited for him by Dad, for college.

My dad is dead, Magnus told her.

Bernice Fig closed her eyes and pursed her lips. She said, Your mother will have to sign for you.

But it's for a birthday present, Magnus countered. Mom can't know about it. I'd like four hundreds and one fifty.

Bernice Fig's narrow body tightened and bent toward him. She screwed up her lean face, unsure of what to do, then finally reached into her cash drawer and pulled out four hundreds and a fifty and counted them into my brother's hand.

And get this, he said to me now, chewing the last bite of his cinnamon roll, his eyes sparkling inside the black rims of his glasses. Sonny'll be this puppy's great, great, great, great, great grandfather. Magnus ticked them off on his fingers. Did I say *great* five times?

I didn't count.

Five greats, anyway.

Couldn't they just ship him out here? We shouldn't have to go clear back there to get him.

They like it a lot better when people come and pick them up. It's more humane.

The kennel's in Winnipeg, though, right? So why Battlepoint?

Magnus watched me for a little while, his face tense with the expression he'd always made when he was trying to get crucial information out of me — about sex, say, or about Dad and Mom, and what they were like together — all those things that have fallen to me.

Here's the deal, Jesse, my brother said. I think *you're* the one who needs to go back there. And this'll be your excuse.

20

Mom wasn't happy about the puppy, especially considering the entrance he made, flopping into the house, big paws scrabbling on the glassy maple floor as he went straight for the kitten, took her by the head and tossed her clear across the kitchen.

He killed her! Mom shouted, and threw herself at the sop-headed kitten, which sprang away and ran straight back to the puppy for more of the same.

That dog can't stay in the house, Mom announced, after she had gathered Lydia into her arms again. He's going to get too big and shed too much hair. He has to stay in the backyard. That's where we kept Sonny, remember?

I'm keeping him in my room, Mom, Magnus told her. He's a baby and needs to be close to me. And his name's Sonny too. Just like Dad's dog.

Mom's mind was busy at work behind her eyes. She lifted her finger to make a point, but the ringing of the phone cut her short. I picked it up and heard the quiet, moderating voice of

Dr. Milius: I was calling for your mother, Jesse, but I can speak with you just as well. I've gone ahead and, um, made an appointment for you — with one of the doctors down at Bowstring.

Oh?

He paused. It was my impression, he said, that you were on board with this. When I spoke with your mother —

No, no, that's fine, I told him. I wrote down the information he had for me, said thanks, and gave the phone to Mom, who was standing next to me with her hand out. She retreated to the living room, speaking in hushed tones and nodding.

I wasn't sure how she had approached Dr. Milius — if she'd done it willingly or at Clay's urging. She had certainly told the doctor about my conversation with Dwayne Primrose, no doubt putting Clay's spin on things. But whatever else she might have said, I couldn't guess. In fact, it was hard for me to tell right now what she thought of me, whether she was concerned about my mental state or saw me as holding out on her, playing some kind of waiting game. Her treatment of me for the last few days had been cautious, as if I were ill. She spoke to me slowly and seemed always to be watching me out the corner of her eye. She questioned my comings and goings as she hadn't since junior high school, and did so in a falsely sweet way that drove me crazy. It was all I could do not to snap at her, scream in her face.

I went to my first session at Bowstring — the only one, as it turned out — with a plan. I would be cooperative, comfortable with myself and honest, but only up to a point, beyond which I would say nothing. I wasn't worried about lines of questioning meant to uncover my feelings toward Clay or my suspicions about him. Those I could deflect. That sore had scabbed over, and I knew exactly how and when I was going to tear it off. I was less sure how I might handle questions about Dad himself — how it felt to be without him, what it was like finding him in the woods, questions that might lead me to say things I had no intention of saying. I was afraid of losing myself in the moment, as I'd come close to doing in Pastor Lundberg's office a couple months before. At least then I'd been speaking to someone I more or less trusted. Now, whatever I said would be used against me.

His name was Dr. Faro, and he was handsome in a feline sort of way: small nose, small teeth, light green eyes, a wispy growth of whiskers around his mouth. His hair was mussed up and dampened with gel. He wore frameless lenses, and he smiled with more sincerity than I'd expected. When his eyes clamped down on me, the skin around them quickened in a radius of tiny arrows. His first questions were straightforward, designed to put me at ease — questions about my living situation, my mom and brother, my experience at school, my interests. He seemed genuinely interested and probed me for details I wouldn't have thought mattered. What did I like about running, about playing the trumpet? Which class at school was my favorite? What was my favorite novel? Why? Who were my best friends? What sorts of food did I like? Sometimes he'd offer some bit of material from his own life, and every so often interrupted himself or me to say something completely off topic.

Once, he pointed out the window at a large crow sitting on top of a telephone pole and said, Did you know that crows can be taught to speak? Yes, their potential for language is greater than that of the parrot.

We spent most of the hour in this way — getting acquainted, I guess you'd call it, and finally, with ten minutes remaining, he glanced down at the file in his lap and said, almost offhand, Since your dad's death, have you had any unusual experiences? I mean, have you seen or heard anything that seemed odd, that you might have difficulty explaining to someone else?

Automatically I shook my head no.

No? he asked.

I ransacked my mind for something that would satisfy him, make him stop frowning, some experience that would qualify as strange but lead him nowhere. Sometimes, I said, I wake up and forget he's gone. In the morning. That's the hardest part — not remembering and then having it all come back again.

Dr. Faro nodded and tilted his head. I allowed myself a glance at his eyes and immediately felt a tug inside my gut, as if he were trying to draw something out of me with an invisible line. I felt the urge to spill it, tell him everything I knew and feared and wanted, everything I wondered about, as I'd been able to do only with Christine. I wanted to describe my visits with Dad and ask him, did he think I'd dreamed them up on my own, or were they messages from purgatory or a place that was even worse? To protect myself, I tensed hard, tried to transform my stomach into a grid of steel.

Nothing has happened in the last couple of months that other people might have trouble believing? Dr. Faro asked.

For a few moments his voice roamed inside my head. I could hear the golden sound of it, the compassion, the gently drawn-out syllables.

No, I said to him.

He watched me harder now, his eyes darker, lips glistening at the corners. I felt the blood go out of my hands and resisted the urge to sit on them, warm them up.

Jesse, does it ever feel like it's hard to go on? Dr. Faro asked.

What do you mean?

Do you ever think of suicide? It wouldn't be strange if you did, considering what you've been through.

I looked down at my hands, resting palms up on my lap, and couldn't help but remember the night by the double bridge, the poem by Frost.

Not really, I said. No.

And you don't believe your father took his own life, do you?

I don't.

Why not?

Because I can't imagine it.

Even though all the evidence points that way?

That's right.

Dr. Faro nodded. He lifted one hand and slid it precisely through the air as if he were a mime trying to demonstrate the presence of a wall between us. He said, The two of you were close, right? You did a lot of things together. You understood each other.

Yes.

And knowing him as you did, you can't believe he would have killed himself.

I nodded.

Do you think it was an accident then?

It wasn't an accident, I said. It wasn't that kind of a wound.

Then you must believe that someone *took* his life. That he was murdered. Dr. Faro's eyes came open wide behind the small lenses.

No, I lied. I'd like to believe that, but I can't. There's no facts to back it up. My dad wasn't murdered.

Dr. Faro looked up at the ceiling, pursed his lips and began to hum quietly, as if he were making calculations in his head. So, he said. It wasn't an accident — and yet I'm to understand that you don't believe he killed himself or was killed by someone else.

I shrugged and made sure not to move my hands — not to touch them to each other or wring them or lift them to my mouth. Inside my head I screamed, *I'm done now! Leave me alone!*

Silence hung between us for a while. Then Dr. Faro, smiling, said, It's one of those strange things, Jesse, but the human mind is flexible enough to hold, at the same time, separate opinions that logic tells us should cancel each other out. In fact, it may even be *necessary* to do so. Healthy. He laughed, and added, Sort of like one person living two lives, hmm?

Dr. Faro was smarter than he knew.

At home with Mom I was unswervingly apologetic. I went out of my way to be helpful around the house and at every chance expressed regret for having caused her to suffer more than she'd already had to. I reassured her that my mind had cleared, that I'd accepted Dad's death for what it was. With Clay, I made a display of my good intentions, twice spending an evening with him in his fish house, once showing up at the Galaxy to hear his band. I even strategized with him on how he might persuade Mom to reopen the Valhalla — that's what he seemed to want.

Tell her to hire a manager, I said. That'll do the trick. It's what she always told Dad. She never liked being tied down to the place.

He nodded and ran his tongue along his bottom lip. He raised his eyes from the spearing hole and winked, complicit.

That was one life.

Meanwhile I was giving myself wholesale to the storm that blew and drifted through me. Hate ran in my veins like a river of ice. I made plans. According to the *Physicians' Desk Reference*, as little as two milligrams of Halcion could bring on overdose symptoms, including confusion, slurred speech, problems in coordination, somnolence and even coma. The fourteen tablets I'd confiscated from Mom's bottle in the medicine cabinet — she'd stopped taking them after about a week — would be more than adequate. Each was a quarter of a milligram. I chose a date that offered me an alibi. February 8, a Friday. The university in Duluth had invited high school seniors to visit campus that weekend, and Mom was encouraging me to go. Registration began at five p.m. and lasted until ten. February 8 also happened to be the day the spearing contest ended, and Clay, of course, would stay in his fish house until the last daylight had faded in the west — until at least six. I intended to show up with my thermos of cocoa about four thirty. Within an hour I'd be finished and gone. By nine o'clock I'd be in Duluth, at the university. Clay wouldn't turn up missing until the next morning. It was perfect.

Sure, they might be able to trace the Halcion in Clay's blood, but how hard was it to score a handful of sleeping pills? And anyway, his reputation for hard living would make the nature of his death seem almost fated.

What else do I need to say about those weeks?

I heard nothing from Sheriff Stone — or at least nothing new. He told me that he'd finally spoken with everyone who lived within a mile of our deer stands and that nobody had seen or heard anything unusual on the day my dad died.

Dwayne Primrose stayed gone. I had a dream about him in which he was standing across the street from our house, at night, watching me through the window. He wore his pink mittens. I went out to talk with him, but he turned and walked away.

Between Christine and me things were uneasy. After our night at Mass we began to pull away from each other. We grew cautious, skittish, afraid. I felt her eyes on me, judging and guessing, trying to find a way to connect, but she didn't bring up the conversation we'd had — it was like she'd blocked it out. She didn't invite me to her trailer house anymore either, and when I asked how things were going, she claimed her dad was doing well, better than she'd ever guessed he would. He had gotten a job at an auto-body shop and liked it, she said. I saw him once, at the hardware store. I was at the counter buying a rubber washer for the leaky faucet in our bathroom, and when I turned to leave, there he was, right next to me. I said hi, but he turned his face and lifted a hand to cover up the scar.

He seems to be working through it all, Christine said to me. And they're getting along, he and Mom, she added.

Seriously? I asked.

Really, Jesse. It's not so bad.

I knew she was lying, but I didn't push because I didn't want her to push back. It was a scrupulous dance we performed, circling each other, keeping our distance. Which isn't to say we didn't spend time together. We did. But people can soak up only so much trouble, and we were both saturated with it. And so by silent agreement we chose to pretend that all was well, that we came from happy, normal families. Instead of hanging out at her place as we had before — studying, watching Renata and talking — we looked for solace in the blind, hot refuge of our bodies. We'd steal into my basement and make use of Dad's big desk down there in his old office, a six-foot monstrosity he'd bought at a yard sale, Mediterranean oak, with Italian leather inset into the top. Or else we'd drive the Mercury into the country somewhere and park.

One night, though, she finally talked — or tried to get *me* to. The temperature was twenty below zero, and the heater was going full bore but still not keeping the cold away. My feet were like blocks of wood. Our breath steamed up the air around us and frosted the windows. We were parked on a dead-end road that led to a sandpit in the woods. My fingers were freezing, and beneath them Christine's smooth bare skin felt miraculously warm. Suddenly she pulled away, slapping at my hands.

How are you going to do it? she asked me.

Do what?

You know what I mean.

I told you, I said. Remember? You don't have to worry.

She buttoned up and rezipped, breathing hard, angry. If you won't answer me, then take me home, she said. Right now.

I gave you my word, I said.

Christine sat with her arms crossed in front of her, staring ahead. Take me home, she said. And don't bother calling anymore. You hear? Either you tell me right now, or I don't want to see you again.

I put the car in gear, backed up to the main road and drove her to the trailer park. The next day, though, she seemed to have forgotten all about it, acted like nothing had happened. In fact she seemed almost cheerful. Her birthday was ten days off, and she wanted to make plans. She was animated, excited. The last couple of weeks she'd been less steady, her moods unpredictable.

It's got to be special, she said. They were always special. My birthdays, I mean, before we moved up here.

What do you want to do? I asked.

I don't know.

We could go to Paradiso, I said. It was a restaurant in Opportunity, an hour's drive away, and people liked to say it had the best Mexican food in our part of the state.

You don't have that kind of money, Jesse.

I could raid my college account, like Magnus did.

Christine turned away. Her shoulders collapsed in self-pity. She said, It was always the time of year when the rains let up, and it started getting warm. It wasn't winter anymore, and I used to think it was because of me somehow. Because it was my birthday. Pretty stupid, huh?

Maybe it *was* because of you.

Right. And this one time it was a hundred degrees, and we played hide-and-seek in this field behind my grandparents' place. I hid in a culvert, and no one could find me. I didn't want to come out because it was so cool in there. This was before Grandma died, and I remember she made lemonade and Grandpa put on a sprinkler and we all ran through it. It was so hot. That's what I want for my birthday, Jesse. I want it to be hot.

All right, I said.

You'll do that for me? Make winter go away? Make it hot?

Of course. Anything.

Promise? she asked.

Promise, I said.

And the strange thing is, I pulled it off. A couple of days later the snow clouds blew away, the sun came blazing out of the south, and our snow began to melt. It might not be accurate to say that such a thing had never happened before, but it was rare. They call it a false spring. Except this time it wasn't false. The weather held, and the snow left. All of it. Buds popped out on the trees. The grass turned green. It was April two months early, and delirium reigned in Battlepoint. White-haired ladies lifted their dresses above their knees and forded sidewalk puddles barefoot. Kids dragged their bikes out of the garage and rode splashing and screaming through the streets. Bascom brought our English class outside one day, marched us down to the lake, out onto a wooden pier, and read poems about spring by Frost, Wordsworth and William Carlos Williams.

There was a problem, though. As the lake ice blackened and honeycombed, the department of natural resources ordered every fish house off the ice by sundown on February 5 — three days before my target date. Then the Sons of Norway announced that their spearing contest would have to wrap up at midnight on February 4 — Christine's birthday. I had no choice but to change my plans.

21

The weather was more seasonal that day, still fairly mild, but blustery, snow in the air. At about four fifteen I took milk from the fridge and heated a quart of it in the microwave, then poured it into Dad's steel thermos — an old battered one wrapped in duct tape — and added enough chocolate syrup to make the milk dark. In my bedroom I found the fourteen Halcion tablets I'd squirreled away in a sock in my bottom drawer and brought them down to the kitchen and ground them up with a spoon in a cereal bowl. I ground them up fine, like you would espresso beans, and mixed the blue dust into the hot cocoa. I felt clearheaded and calm, so confident, in fact, that I still surprise myself every time I remember it. All those weeks of uncertainty — of waiting, wondering, reacting — but now, finally, I was *doing* something, making things happen. It felt good.

That afternoon at school I had asked Christine if I could pick her up at seven thirty instead of at six o'clock, as we had arranged.

Magnus needed a ride to the school carnival, I explained, and Mom had to be at a meeting at church and couldn't take him.

She watched me for a beat, eyes narrowing, her long black lashes coming down like a veil. She knew me well enough to know that I didn't appreciate last-minute changes in plans. I was nothing if not dependable and prompt. Cautious. Responsible. Inflexible too, I suppose. I guess I'm still like that.

All right, she said, frowning.

Are you sure?

We won't get to the restaurant till what then, eight thirty? We won't eat until at least nine.

I know. But they're open till eleven. I called to make sure.

Okay, seven thirty, she agreed.

I'm sorry.

No, it's fine, she said. It's okay.

By the time I left the house, a spring squall had arrived, huge wet flakes driven by a south wind. Another degree or two and it would have been raining instead of snowing. The roads were fine — everything melted as it hit the ground — but visibility was terrible, the beam of my headlights a kaleidoscope of swirling white. Top speed, twenty miles an hour. At Oscar's Bay I turned in at the walleye-shaped mailbox and pulled up next to the log building that served, summers, as the office and grocery store for Paulson's Resort. Clay's Austin was already there. I got out and walked down to the edge of the lake, where a plank had been laid to span the water separating the rocky shoreline from the pack ice. I stood there searching for the outline of Clay's fish house but couldn't see a thing. I looked to the right and then to the left of where it should have been, to trick my eyes into giving it to me — and then the image darkened. In the gauze of wet snow I could just make out its square shape. Then the wind slacked off, and I could see it fine, not more than forty yards from where I stood. I crossed the plank and moved along the ice, which sounded hollow and squeaky under my boots, like Styrofoam.

Wisps of smoke blew from the chimney of Clay's shack. Before knocking, I took a breath to calm myself. The confidence I'd felt earlier was gone. My armpits were dripping, and I could feel the quick pulse of my heartbeat in the tips of my fingers. I turned around to reassure myself the shoreline was still there, within sight, but then, with the sound of a million birds taking flight, the wind picked up, and all I could see was horizontal snow.

I knocked.

Clay didn't seem especially surprised, though I could tell he hadn't expected me either. His long handsome face had a quality about it tonight that made me think of a well-bred hound dog, alert to whatever might be in the air. He said, Judas Priest, Jesse. What kind of weather did you order? And where's your car?

I pointed back toward shore, nothing to see there but the faint image of dark pines in the storm, like sweaty handprints on a white wall.

Thought I'd bring you this, I said, holding up Dad's thermos.

Hey, thanks.

You think the ice'll last the night? I asked.

He shrugged. If this shit turns to rain, we'll have until about noon tomorrow. The ice'll go like butter in a frying pan.

He brought me in, grabbed a plastic bucket, flipped it over and set it down next to his stool by the spearing hole, which drew his eyes — mine too — like a bright window on a gray day. The sun may have been gone and the sky clogged with snow, but somehow the lake still had light to give, as if light, like heat, could be stored up and given back over time. Clay sat down and bent over the water. His face, lit from below, looked greenish yellow, unhealthy.

Mom was worried about your stomach, I said. I spun off the top of the thermos and set it on top of the propane stove and poured it full. My uncle glanced up at me and then back down.

Any luck?

He shook his head. Getting too dark. Another half hour, forty-five minutes, and I'll have to call it quits. Maybe I'll get some last-minute luck out of you.

Hope so, I said. So far, each time I'd come out here I'd managed to bring in a fish for him, none as large as the first one, but good size nonetheless, all of them.

Any idea where you stand? I asked.

Huh?

In the contest. The thousand bucks.

He looked up at me and made a face. He said, Bull Foss is talking big, but who knows. Spearing guys — the old-timers — they hold their tongues. They don't say a lot. You gotta watch out for the retired farmers who live in their shacks and don't take their eyes off that hole. You know?

What'll you do with the money if you win?

Clay laughed and then passed a hand over his face. God knows I'm going to need it, come summer. What I'd *like* to do is put a new tranny in the Austin. Buy some alloy wheels, give her a new paint job. Get her all fixed up. She's been nickel-and-diming me to death.

I handed him the cup full of cocoa, a third of what the thermos held, and at least a milligram of Halcion — four times the recommended dosage — in that single cup. He accepted it from me and took a long slug of it. Thanks, he said, and took another swallow, sniffed at it, nodded, set it down on the floor beneath his stool. Then his eyes flicked sideways and his head followed. His fingers grabbed the spear, and he eased the five tines into the water, coiled himself over the hole.

She's coming back, he whispered. I can feel it. Shhh.

I sat watching him and prayed. *Stay away, please, God.*

A whale, Clay hissed. God, Jesse, why the hell haven't you been out here every night? I'd have this thing wrapped up.

He sat there five minutes, one hand on the shaft of the spear, the other jigging the lure. Then suddenly he pulled his weapon up and shifted around on his seat to face me.

Damn, he said.

I reached down beneath his stool and handed him his cocoa. He took a big swallow, raising the cup past horizontal. The cocoa must have cooled — no need to sip any longer. He drank the whole thing off, and I took the cup from him and refilled it. He resettled himself, watching the hole.

Want me to take the lure for a while? I asked.

Help yourself.

I took hold of the monofilament line and eased it up, then let it down — I found a rhythm for myself. Two feet below us the wooden fish performed its circular jump and dip.

Come on, you mother, Clay said. Come on now.

As he worked through his second cup of cocoa, I watched his hands. They seemed steady. His face remained focused and set. He kept his shoulders squared off and his feet planted firmly beneath his knees. Maybe the pills were no good. Maybe Clay, for whatever reason, was immune to their effects.

It's hard to explain, he said after a long silence. Hard to explain,

Jesse, but it's like I'm closer to him now. My uncle ran his tongue over his chapped lips and rubbed his stubbly jawline with a finger. His tongue came out and stabbed at the tip of his mustache.

Closer to who?

Your dad. Through Genevieve. *Comprende?* He moved his face toward me and then pulled back, blinking. It was like he couldn't get me in focus.

Not really, I said.

He squinted, leaned ahead, almost tipped but caught himself. Then he smiled like a kid who wants to be liked but knows better. He lifted the cup of cocoa and finished it off, tilting his head way back, then he leaned over and set it on the floor beside his feet. I picked it up and poured in what was left in the thermos. Clay sat watching me, his eyes slower now, as if he were trying to catch up to some lightning-fast command from his brain. He glanced toward the faint glow of the hole and then back up at me. He seemed preoccupied, his thoughts far off.

Your mom and I dated in high school, he said.

I know that, Clay. I've always known that.

He chuckled, his shoulders jerking, pleased with himself. Then he took a long swallow, lowered the cup and peered into it, raised it again and drained it.

What? I asked.

There's something you *don't* know.

What's that?

He reached out and grabbed the empty thermos and tried to pour himself more cocoa, shook his head at the few drops that fell.

Shouldn't tell you, he said, but she's the one that asked me out first. To prom. Nothing personal, Jesse, but — your mom and dad? I don't know. I don't know. People make mistakes, of course.

For an uncomfortably long moment Clay stared past me, eyes caught on something that made his smile fade and flatten out. Then he shook his head, coming back to himself, and gave me a look I could feel, like tainted food in the very bottom of my guts.

Something else too, he said. The way he did it. Your dad. The way he took her away. You ever hear about that?

I didn't answer him, but I was curious.

We went to a movie, Genevieve and me. Your mom. All right? Clay blinked, shook his head, rubbed his face. So I've got my rusted-out shit stain of an Oldsmobile. And afterward it won't start, so I call home and he says — your *dad* says — Sure, I'll come and get you. My big brother, back from the army, right? Got himself a Mustang. So he shows up, and we climb in, Genevieve and me. He drives straight to our place, drops *me* off, and the two of *them* drive away. And she's *my* date! He doesn't come back for two hours! End of goddamned story. She never went out with me again.

Clay lowered his face into his hands, and he cried a little, just a few pathetic squeaks and moans. I caught an image of him staring cold and wide-eyed in the water beneath the ice, his long body rolling like a log, a bit of lake weed wrapped about his neck like a green tie. I willed him to topple over, to hit the floor, loose and rubbery. I had to be rid of him now. The world had to be rid of him. I saw Mom on the bed she had shared with my dad, Clay on top of her, and a surge of energy flowed up from the place where my legs joined, a wave of nausea that rose through my bowels and into my stomach and throat. I stood up and rushed the door, hit it on the run and sprawled outside. I vomited on the black ice.

Jesse! Clay shouted.

I turned and looked up at him through the falling snow. He

was on his hands and knees in the doorway of the shack, kneading his forehead with his fingertips.

What's wrong? he asked.

You're what's wrong, I said.

He grabbed hold of the door frame and pulled himself up, inch by inch, it seemed, then leaned forward and offered me a hand. It trembled. A line of saliva hung from the tip of his mustache. I didn't move. He stumbled over and grabbed me awkwardly by the armpits and helped me back inside, patted my shoulder as I sat down again on the bucket.

God, I'm tired, he said. He moaned, sprawling humpbacked on his stool, legs spread, the heels of his boots propped on either side of the spearing hole. Then suddenly, as if somebody had slapped the back of his head, his face jerked forward. Judas Priest, he said, and his eyelids flickered.

If I had kept my mouth shut, he would have dropped off then. He looked about ready to turn inside out, eyes crossed, elbows tucked in close like chicken wings, chin on his chest. But here's the thing: I didn't want him to leave before he knew *why* he was leaving. This was something I hadn't considered — how I'd feel when the moment arrived.

You killed my dad, I said to him quietly. And now I'm going to kill you. I'm going to put you under the ice.

My words registered, *puk*, like a stone dropping into calm water. They woke him up. His body stiffened, and his eyes flicked open again. Unaccountably, he threw his head back and laughed, not for long, just one big hoot, showing me that dangly pink thing at the back of the throat.

Huh? he said. Huh. Love it. Smart boy, Jesse. Tell me, though. Was it you that wrote that letter?

I nodded.

God! Scared the shit outta me. Didn't hardly dare leave my house for a month. But yeah, I thought it was you.

Clay nodded, rocking himself, then stood up fast and for a few moments wobbled there before coming down in slow motion to his knees, one arm stretching out to the wall for support. His face, on a level with mine — no more than a foot and a half away — seemed distant, unreachable.

Did you come up from behind him? I asked.

He screwed his face into a grimace, as if I had put a blade in his stomach and turned it. He said, Yeah. He didn't see it coming. Wasn't paying attention.

And you threw the rifle in the lake.

The one I used, yeah. Not the other one.

Did you kill Dwayne too?

Clay blinked hard, forehead squeezing down against his eyes, cheeks lifting. He laughed again, same as before, then shook his head, forcefully — though I couldn't tell if that meant no, or if he was just trying to shake things clear inside his brain. Dwayne'll turn up soon enough, he said. And I doubt if he'll have much to say.

My uncle went lax then, head falling to one shoulder, fingers going limp between his knees. He took a deep breath and let it out in a long, humming, vaguely rhythmic monotone, as if he were trying to recall a tune. I stood and backed up to the door, opened it and took a peek outside toward the shoreline, barely visible through the falling snow.

We were alone still, all by ourselves.

The door squeaked when I closed it, and Clay's eye rolled open. His face crumpled up, and he gave a big dramatic heave. He hauled himself to his feet and pawed at the two-by-four leg of the loft bed against the wall. I watched him fight to command his arms and legs, his electrical circuits all twisted and rearranged. The wooden ladder leading to the sleeping platform had four rungs, and he managed the first three before his body seized up on him. It simply froze. If he had leaned forward, his weight would have carried him over the guardrail to the mattress, but he didn't do that. Instead he raised his arms and placed his palms flat against the ceiling. He glanced down at the floor behind him, then over one shoulder at the green hole — plenty wide to admit his shoulders — and uttered a cry. It sounded like a question: *Huh?* Then he fell backward, hands gripping the top of his head, and landed square on his back and rump. He bounced once on the plywood floor and settled there, all stretched out, mouth open in a small circle, like a fish. I couldn't tell if he was breathing or not.

I stepped over and laid a hand on his heart. He didn't move or register my touch. His face was placid, eyelids smooth, the corners of his lips turned up. I tried his neck with my fingers and found a pulse there, steady and strong. A spasm went through him, and he hauled in a lungful of air and blew it out, sputtering like a bad faucet. He wiggled his hips and shoulders, as if trying to work himself into the fabric of a mattress. Seeing that, I had an impulse to smash him, crush his nose with my heel, kick him in the head. But I held myself back and considered instead whether to put him down the hole headfirst like a birthing fetus or feetfirst, breech.

I would have done it then — I was ready and able — but that's when the door latch rattled and the hinges yelped, and there against the mosaic of snow I saw a familiar silhouette.

You lied to me, Christine said.

I didn't move or speak. Clay, next to me, breathed steadily now. *Damn it,* I thought. *Give me five more minutes.*

I could tell by your voice, she said. I knew it right away. I called your house and talked to Magnus. He was on his way to school. Your mom was taking him. I knew something was up.

I moved around to Clay's head, and I leaned down and took hold of him by the shoulders and lifted. I hadn't expected him to be so heavy. Maybe you could give me a hand, I said.

Is he dead?

Not yet.

Then why is he like that?

I explained about the cocoa, the Halcion. As I spoke to her, I was bent over double, holding the top half of my uncle's body off the floor.

Have you got a lamp in here? Christine asked. I've got to show you something.

The steel in her voice, the hard ring of it, made me drop Clay's shoulders, move to the corner where the kerosene lamp hung and take matches from the old cupboard and light it. The room took shape around us. Christine turned away to shut the door. When she turned back I saw the bruises on her face — tattoo-colored bruises, greenish blue, two of them. One darkened a cheekbone, a big knot there. The other, on the opposite side, had marred the straight line of her jaw. She'd been hit hard at least twice, and her face was out of true. My stomach clenched. Acid stung my jaw and coursed into the back of my throat.

I'll kill him, I said.

Christine moaned, but not from pain.

I will, I said. I'll kill him.

She looked down at Clay's long body on the floor, all stretched out, and then back at me and shook her head. You're not killing anybody, she told me.

To prove her wrong, I bent down and got hold of my uncle by the shoulders again, and lifted. He sighed as if he'd been caressed. Christine moved straight to his feet and grabbed his ankles. We looked at each other across the length of him. When I pulled, leaning back with all my weight, she pulled too, one knee braced against a bedpost. My boots slipped on the plywood.

You're not doing this, Jesse. Forget it.

The pressure went out of me, and I dropped Clay's shoulders and lowered myself to the floor beside him. I peered into his face, upside down. His smile was gone, but his expression was benign, almost peaceful. He might have been getting some rest after a good day's work.

You shouldn't have come out here, I said.

No?

No.

I should've let you throw your life away?

It's gone already. How did you know where I was?

Where else would you be? She scooted over and laid a hand on Clay's chest and held it there, listening. She bent over and put her ear up close to his nostrils.

He's breathing good, she said. I bet he'll sleep it off.

Do you realize what's going to happen when he comes to?

Maybe he won't remember anything.

Oh, he'll remember. You must want to see me locked up, I said.

Christine brought her fingers to her face and explored the bruise on her jaw. My life's gone too, she said.

I asked her to tell me what happened, and she sighed and let her head fall back and loll from one shoulder to the other. She closed her eyes as if to collect her thoughts.

He's been drinking again, she said, but I'm sure you knew that.

Pushing Mom around. Hitting her. I got tired of tiptoeing around him all the time, nodding at everything he said, all his pissing and moaning. How much better he was than his teammates who made it to the majors, and how it's Mom's fault that he never tried. How everybody in this town hates his guts, which is probably true. Anyway, I couldn't take it anymore, and tonight I finally told him to shut the hell up. Look at me, Jesse. You see this? You think I don't know what it's like to hate somebody? You think I don't want to kill him?

I'm sure you do, I said.

But I'm not going to. And *you're* not going to. And you're not going to. And you're not doing this either, she said, nodding at Clay. God, you're crazy!

Kneeling there on the other side of my uncle and sitting back on her feet, Christine pushed her glistening hair away from her face and smoothed her hands down across her tight-fitting jeans, her lovely thighs. Her hands looked small and capable, each finger interesting beyond all reason — a little silver ring on one pinky, no other jewelry, her nails polished the color of her generous, curving lips. She loosened her coat and laid it open. Her V-neck sweater showed the smooth dark valley between her breasts. The propane stove huffed away. The shack was almost hot.

You're gorgeous, I said.

So what if I am.

I'm just saying. Wow.

Saying what? This is insane.

I've tried everything else, I said.

No you haven't. You could *leave*. That's what I'm doing. If Mom wants to stay here and take it, fine, but not me. Screw it, I'm out of here.

You're leaving? I asked.

Leaving, yes. Tonight. I have a cousin in Texas. Come with me, Jesse.

She was serious, her face composed and resolute, her voice nonchalant, as if she were announcing a trip to the grocery store for milk, and I knew then that everything I admired about her — her beauty, her steadfastness, her strength — was real and permanent, that she had substance beyond anyone's reckoning, especially mine, and that I didn't deserve her.

Your life here is over, she whispered. You said as much yourself.

She reached over and laid the palm of her hand on my chest and pressed it there, as if to remind me who I was or who I might become — as if we had already reached an understanding.

Which indeed we had.

As the snow turned to rain and rattled against the roof, we sat talking and drowsing and monitoring Clay's breathing. It remained steady. I knew that when he woke up he'd be fine — tired maybe, and sick or hungover, but fine. I knew also that between the two of us, Christine and me, she was the one with a clear picture of where to go from here and that I could do a lot worse than to follow her, that in fact I had no notion at all about what should come next, where I should go, what I should do. Nothing.

At midnight Clay began to stir, and that's when we took our leave. We tiptoed out of there, shut the door on him, walked across the honeycombed ice and through the rain to shore, then drove our vehicles into town, having decided to make the trip in her dad's yellow truck.

He's got to realize who he's messing with, she said. I want him to understand there's a price to pay.

We had agreed to drive only as far as Minneapolis tonight and stay there with one of her mom's sisters, lay low for a day or two before going on. It was hard to tell who might be out looking for us. We had to be careful.

At my place she waited in the truck while I went inside and crept upstairs and put a few things together, same as I had that night more than a month ago when I'd slept at the Valhalla — some clothes in a duffel bag, my toothbrush and razor, my trumpet. Before coming back down, I went into Magnus's bedroom. He was breathing easily, with the same drugged calm, it seemed to me, as Clay had been earlier in his fish house. I touched his warm shoulder, though not to wake him.

Good boy, good boy, my brother said out of his sleep, smiling. Come back now.

22

What there is to tell about the rest of the night and the morning that followed won't take long, because in truth I remember little. I was tired and deeply perplexed. The snow had turned to rain, as I've said, and the rain fell hard. It beat upon the windshield in hammerbursts. I drove. For the first thirty miles we passed through heavy forest and twice had to brake for deer, one a buck with a gleaming wet rack that looked like a chandelier tipped upside down. He stood silver-eyed in our high beams as we came on, then jumped clear as we slid toward him, wheels locked. Minutes later we left the woods and entered the rolling prairie of that part of the state. The rain persisted. The truck's crackly AM radio told us we were in for a long night of it. I remember Christine leaning forward on the seat, both hands on the dash, and peering at the road through the flapping wiper blades. Her rosary beads threaded through her fingers.

I tried to imagine what it was going to be like, this flight of ours, saw the two of us passing south through a land greening up with spring. I imagined the towns along the way, prairie towns and river towns — and cities too, with glass and steel towers. I saw the grocery stores in which we'd buy cheese and bread, and heartland cafés with names like Mom's Kitchen and Kountry Korner. I wondered what they would think, the people who saw us, how we'd look to them: Christine, small and dark, elegant in how she moved and held herself, and gangly me beside her, my hair almost as chrome blond then as Mom's was — and as Magnus's still is. We'd be noticed, I knew that much. Two kids running from trouble.

When I tried to think beyond the trip, I drew a blank. I couldn't picture the buildings in that part of the world, or the trees, the sky or the landscape. I couldn't conjure the place or the smell of it. Not only that, but as crazy as I was for Christine, I couldn't see the two of us together, day in and day out, getting up and going off to work somewhere and coming back at night to an apartment occupied by the two of us. Or three of us. Were we going to stay with her cousin? Was that the plan? We hadn't gotten that far yet in our thinking, or at least hadn't talked it over. We had given ourselves only to the idea of leaving, a plenty big decision all by itself — so big in fact that we left it alone as we drove through the rain. For a few hours we said almost nothing. We were as quiet together as we had ever been.

Her aunt Clara lived on the south side of the city, where she rented the first floor of an old Victorian on a brick-paved street lined with naked, dripping elm trees. On her front porch she gave her niece a suffocating hug, then turned and offered me a cool dry hand. It was three forty-five a.m., dark. An hour ago we'd stopped at a wooden phone booth on the desolate corner of a dying town, and Christine had called to tell her we were coming.

You better put that car in the alley, Clara said. In fact, you'll want to pull it into the garage.

She stepped back and made a careful assessment of me, drawing hard on a long dark cigarette. I held her eyes, which she'd taken pains to beautify, the lashes thick with mascara, her lids shaded in royal purple. She was not pretty so much as handsome, larger and older than Christine's mother but still narrow at the waist and slender-limbed. She wore a loose skirt with a bright flower print and a furry lavender sweater.

Thanks again, said Christine. Her hair hung in wet ropes on her shoulders from the quick run up the sidewalk. It was raining that hard.

Her aunt shook her head and narrowed her eyes to slits, touched Christine's bruised face. Too bad they ever let the bastard out, she said.

Whether Christine got a chance to explain what must have seemed to Clara as my unlikely presence, I don't know. My guess is that she did, though I suppose it doesn't matter. Instead of sitting up with them over coffee, I excused myself to the living room and lay down on the crushed-velvet couch, its cushions smelling of dust and cigarettes and sweet perfume, and went immediately to sleep, fell straight off the cliff.

I came to the dream with no memory of Dad's death, my heart in that sense unburdened. I was in the backyard of our Battlepoint house and looking out at Crow Lake. Nighttime, no light visible in the pines to the east, the moon half full, the air cool. I walked down across the crinkly dead grass to our boathouse and there found Dad, standing inside the maple hull of his Chris-Craft, which was propped up on blocks. The scent of drying varnish stung my nostrils. He was up in the cockpit, applying a black leather wrap to the steering wheel and wearing nothing but a white T-shirt and a pair of white boxers. With a start, I saw that the dome of his head was gone, blown clear off, and that his left eye socket was empty.

What happened? I asked him.

He ignored me, intent on what he was doing, didn't even glance my way, and I wondered how I could have fallen so far in his affections. There had to be an explanation for the ruined condition of his head, I was sure of it, but none came to me. He tied off the cord on the leather steering-wheel wrap, picked up a spray bottle, squirted some kind of polish on the teak dashboard and began to rub it down with a rag. I stepped closer and peeked into the cockpit. A candy bar, half eaten, lay on the driver's seat. I wished Dad would offer to share it with me, but his mind was clearly elsewhere. He kept looking up through the boathouse door at the lake, still ice covered, though ringed at the edge with a few yards of open water.

What kind of candy bar is that? I asked.

Nothing you can buy in this town, Jesse. He tucked the rest of the bar into its wrapper and placed it in the cubbyhole set into the dash, then climbed out of the cockpit onto the boat's prow and went after the outside of the windshield, blasting it with spray and scrubbing away with the rag. I noticed that he'd stowed his old matched pair of hard-sided suitcases — the brown ones, embossed to look like alligator skin — next to the gunwale. There was a sleeping bag also, and a duffel.

Dad was packed for a trip.

Going someplace? I asked.

No answer. He continued squirting with his bottle and polishing with the rag, scowling, hands moving fast. He seemed troubled.

Does Mom know? I persisted. Have you told her you're going?

He hopped down from the prow and padded to the stern.

Dad! I said, alarmed. What about Mom and Magnus? You can't just leave them like this.

He spun around and pinned me with his eye. And you *can?* he asked, aiming his bottle at me. He pulled the trigger again, but this time the spray ignited in a burst of orange flame, and I woke in a sweat, drooling on the dusty cushion. Someone had covered me up with a scratchy wool blanket. Christine was sitting Indian-style on the floor next to me, watching a morning news program on the TV.

What time is it? I asked.

Shh! She held up her hand to silence me.

With a maddening smirk the local news anchor described the unusual weather and its consequences: lake ice breaking up two months early, unprecedented flooding in river valleys, waterfowl heading north, confused. His tone and glimmering eyes suggested that none of this surprised him, that foreknowledge of momentous events was part of his job description.

And in Fatwater County, he said, near the town of Battlepoint, a body has been pulled from Crow Lake. Authorities say it's too soon to blame the death on this freak rainstorm. No identification has yet been made.

Christine turned and looked at me, horrified. That can't be, she said. He was coming to, wasn't he? He was coming to. I know he was.

In my chest something light and sweet rose up — vindication. Maybe there was justice in the world after all. Christine crawled up on the couch and curled next to me, buried her face in my chest, reached her arms around me and squeezed so hard she almost cut off my air.

Don't go back, she whispered. Please.

As we lay there holding each other on her aunt Clara's couch, an odd thing happened — or probably it wasn't so odd. My sense of triumph leaked away, it abandoned me entirely. I remembered the first deer I'd shot and how, with Dad's help, I'd slit its belly open and scooped out the hot, slippery coils of purple life, remembered how sickened I had been by the smell. I felt the word *gutted* on the roof of my mouth, on the tip of my tongue, and it struck me that Clay had robbed me again. He'd taken my dad, dirtied my mother, swallowed me down and shat me out. And now he'd simply waltzed away. My stomach burned with hate. I wished I'd done it myself, shoved him down the hole before Christine found us. Then I wouldn't have had to cut and run. I thought of Magnus waking this morning, going out on his route in the rain, coming back soaked and then eating his cereal, alone in the kitchen.

Please, Christine said. Stay. Don't you see? I can't go back with you.

I know. But it won't be for long. I just have to let them know what's going on. With us, I mean. I can't just disappear like this. Mom might deserve it, but not Magnus. I can't do that to him.

She didn't argue with me. I think she understood — I could tell by the way she hung on to me, her arms full of an urgency that would soon spend itself. And when it did, when she finally let go and sat up, she slid over to the other side of the couch and refused to look at me.

Do you know where the phone book is? I asked. I'm going to call Greyhound.

She leaned back against the couch and looked straight up at the ceiling, as if trying to stare a hole in it. Outside, an unmuffled car drove past. I watched the weatherman trace the east-moving trajectory of the storm with his hand. Then I turned and noticed on the side of Christine's face, just in front of her right ear, a small mark in the shape of a water drop, not dark. It was vaguely reddish in color and no larger than a pea. I reached over and touched it, amazed I'd never been aware of it before.

What *is* that? I asked.

She looked at me sideways, frowning. A birthmark. You never noticed?

No, I said, and at once I was aware of all the things about her I wanted to learn — her morning rituals and sleeping habits, the changes in her face and body as she aged, the dreams that would keep her young or break her, the children she would have and the ways in which they would turn out like her.

You'll be back, right? she asked. Because I don't want to drive down there alone.

Don't worry, I said.

She didn't ask for any more assurances, didn't say anything more at all, but simply got up and went into the kitchen and came back with the phone book, which she dropped next to me on the couch.

At the depot we sat together on a plastic bench and watched morning rush hour through the window. Rain continued falling. Heavy, blue-black clouds shouldered their way, unrepentant, through the city. Thunder cracked and rumbled and cleared its throat. Cars honked. Pedestrians scurried by with umbrellas. Across the street, beneath an awning that bulged with water, a man stood with his hand out for change. Neither Christine nor I knew what to say.

As the time to leave neared, she seemed to grow smaller next to me, less distinct, and I had the sensation of some border closing in around us, of the light dimming. Outside, a pair of lovers older than us by a few years came walking by, holding hands, leaning into each other, not seeming to mind the rain. There must have been something compelling about the sight of Christine and me, because they stopped and stared through the window — the young woman beautiful, straw blond hair plastered to her shoulders, slanting eyes, a strong delicate nose, the man tall and curly-haired, with glasses. They regarded us gravely for a few moments and then hurried on through the storm. I was ashamed of how much I envied them.

We're supposed to be together, Christine said to me. I knew it from the start.

There's no way to just know something like that, I said.

Sure there is. If something's supposed to be, there's nothing you can do about it. It'll happen.

I laughed and put my arm around her, surprised by how compact she was, by what a small package she made.

Remember, I'm coming back, I said, but I doubt she heard me, because just then the bus rolled in and wheezed to a stop on the street in front of us, and the folding doors clapped open, throwing water. The driver, frail and wild-eyed, stepped down onto the curb, rushed past us and disappeared into the men's room. When he came back out, I gave him the ticket I'd purchased for thirty-seven dollars and handed him my duffel bag and trumpet case, which he stowed in the belly of the bus.

On the sidewalk in the pouring rain, Christine kissed me unsatisfactorily and turned me loose to board — pushed me away from her, is more like it. Halfway up the steps, though, I felt her fingers grab at the back of my jacket, and I allowed myself to be pulled back down. This time her lips were tender and firm, soft yet adamant. This kiss I felt in the roots of my soul.

23

Everybody was sick. Across the aisle a kid with a tremendous overbite coughed unremittingly and spit into a soup can. The old woman behind me moaned each time the bus jounced on a frostheave or clunked through a pothole. On several occasions the driver pulled over to the side of the road and hustled down the aisle in order to make loud, gaudy use of the toilet at the back. Nevertheless, by twelve thirty that afternoon I was deboarding at Warner's Amoco in Battlepoint. Thunder rattled and boomed. The wind blew the rain in all directions.

Home was seven blocks through the heart of town, and I kept a low profile, head down against the driving rain, staying to the alleys and backstreets in case Mom had reported my absence. I had no idea what I would say to her — or rather, I *knew* but wasn't sure how I'd say it. I hadn't forgiven her and doubted I ever could. In fact, I looked forward to being a witness to her pain. She had it coming. Maybe, though, with Clay gone we'd find it possible — Mom, Magnus and I — to start over again together, or at least begin going through the motions, so that someday it wouldn't seem like we were only pretending. Maybe we'd be that lucky.

Except I wasn't staying around, was I? Christine was expecting me back.

As I stood hunched in the dry cleft between the Sons of Norway building and Bob's Grocery, waiting to cross Main — duffel in one hand, trumpet case in the other — Battlepoint's undertaker, Jack Runion, came by in his hearse, wipers beating. Half a block away he pulled up in front of the Valhalla, in front of Dwayne Primrose's apartment door, actually, and parked diagonally on the street. His door popped open, and out came a red umbrella, which rose into the air, Jack rising beneath it. He was tall, a good head taller than anyone else in town. Without thinking, I set my luggage down and moved toward him. He seemed to hear me and turned, one hand resting on the wet shiny roof of the hearse. Today instead of his usual black suit, he wore a yellow fleece and a pair of faded jeans. We eyed each other, his face quizzical, mine, I'm sure, pale with dread — because I was thinking fast, in the way you do sometimes when the present and past click together just so. What was he doing here, in front of Dwayne's place? I thought of Clay in his fish house, half conscious on his stool and laughing, showing me his tonsils and that pink dangly thing at the back of his throat. And I remembered his words: *Dwayne'll turn up soon enough. And I doubt if he'll have much to say.*

I'd made a mistake, I realized now. The body we'd heard about on the news wasn't Clay's after all.

Jack glanced over at Dwayne's door and then back at me. He was a thoughtful man whose eyes told you he'd seen too much pain to want to cause any more of it. Sometimes he read the scripture lesson for Pastor Lundberg's sermons, and the softness of his voice had always surprised me.

You're going up there? I asked, motioning toward the broken-paned door that led to Dwayne's stairwell.

He nodded. His eyes caught at mine, then jumped away.

I said, Tell me why.

I guess you haven't talked to your uncle today, Jack said. I was just out there. He gave me Dwayne's key.

You saw Clay *today*? This morning?

Jack watched me for a moment. He nodded. I saw your mom too, he said.

I waited for him to go on, explain himself, put into words what I knew and didn't want to hear, but he was quiet now, his long face somber as he looked me up and down. A hard buzzing started up in the pit of my stomach, and radiating out from it, a creeping numbness. Rain pounded the top of my head and ran down my face. Then the muscles in my legs loosened and gave out, and next thing I knew I was sitting on the cool wet sidewalk, Jack Runion kneeling beside me, one hand on my chest and the other on my back, holding me up that way. I wondered how Clay had explained things this time — assuming he'd even been asked to. I wondered if Mom had finally been tempted to consider Dwayne's version of that night, as he had described it to me. What more was it going to take?

Are you all right, Jesse? Do you need a ride home?

I managed to get my feet underneath myself and with some help, stand up. Jack kept a hand on my shoulder as if I might go down again. I looked over at Dwayne's stairwell door and remembered the look on his face the night we had talked, his trembling lips, purple, starved for blood. His cadaverous face. I remembered the cabbage smell of his apartment.

Tell me what happened to him, I said to Jack.

Here. Maybe you ought to sit down for a minute, get out of the rain. He reached over and opened the driver's door and tried to move me in that direction. I stayed put. He cleared his throat. They found him last night, he said. Some kids did, down under the railroad tracks at the double bridge. You know the place.

Where he always walked, I said.

Right. Apparently he fell into the rocks, those big ones on the east shore. He'd been there a while. At least a couple of weeks, according to Doc Milius. And it's lucky they spotted him. With the fast melt, the river was rising fast. Another half an hour and he would've been carried way out into the lake.

Did anybody ask when he got back from Minneapolis? I asked.

What do you mean?

Never mind, I said.

He tried to move me toward the hearse again, but I shrugged his hand away. Are they sending Dwayne's body to St. Paul? I asked. To the state coroner?

Jack shrugged. No, Doc made the call, he took care of everything. Accidental death, he says. It's all wrapped. We just released his name to the media an hour ago, and I'm going to go up and get a few things for the memorial service. His horn, maybe some photos, if I can find any. It's Clay's idea. You sure you don't need a ride home? You don't look well, Jesse.

I stared past him into the open door of the hearse, and a smell came to me — sour, chemically rank. I tried to see beyond the high front seats into that dark hold, but I couldn't make anything out.

Do you have him in there? I asked. In the back?

Jack turned around to look, as if he wasn't sure himself, then turned back to me. He wiped rain from his face, pushed a thin stripe of hair from his forehead and nodded. Picked him up this morning, yes, he said. From the hospital morgue.

My impulse was to climb inside, pry open Dwayne's box or bag or whatever he'd been stuffed into, and have a last look at him. I wanted to know what his face might tell me about his death. I wanted to touch him, let him know that he mattered — let him know that I understood he was more than the honest, loyal, gentle fool no one in Battlepoint had ever paid any mind to.

This is a terrible day, I said to Jack Runion.

He nodded. I know.

I doubt if you do, I said. And then it was like a motor started up inside my brain, humming along, fast and warm. I felt hot shame at running off as I had and leaving Magnus behind with Clay. And more than that, I felt capable of doing whatever needed doing. I've got to leave, I told Jack, and hurried back for my bag and trumpet case, both still resting on the sidewalk in the rain.

24

I dropped my things in the entry and made a beeline to the bathroom off the kitchen. For hours I'd been clamping down hard on my bladder, which felt like it was filled with lead. I had to stand there breathing deeply, eyes closed, leaning stiff-armed against the wall above the toilet, until I was relaxed enough to pee. From the basement came the sound of Sonny's patient whining, and though I was sympathetic to his need — he probably had to go as badly as I did — I told myself he'd just have to hold on a little while longer, until after I'd talked to Mom. Because that *couldn't* wait.

Before heading upstairs I went to the basement door and spoke to him softly. It's okay, boy. Give me half an hour. Just hold on.

Sonny quieted.

I crossed through the kitchen and started up the steps, thinking Mom must be in her room — I could hear the radio going. Magnus, of course, was at school. My watch said one o'clock. As I made the turn at the top of the stairs, lightning struck close by, a concussive jolt that sped like a zipper up my spine. Sonny yipped.

The stairway light blinked and went out, flickered and came back on — along with it, Mom's radio, Led Zeppelin's rousing Stairway to Heaven, the volume turned louder than she normally had it. Then six feet in front of me Clay materialized out of the bathroom. He was naked and moving like a dancer on a stage, one arm extended for balance, an orange washcloth fluttering from his fingertips. He saw me and stopped short, snapped the washcloth in front of himself and opened his pink lips in a stupid grin. I was hyperlucid, every detail coming with painful clarity. The amber light fixture centered above Clay's head, halolike. His concave chest that looked as if someone had stomped it, dark hair growing like weeds around his nipples. The corded, stringy muscles in his hams. His pointed kneecaps and his veiny feet, which straddled a dark knot in the maple floor.

For a few moments we stood frozen, each waiting for the other to make a move. I thought at first that Clay was embarrassed — his eyes came at me from beneath their lids and glanced away. But then I saw the muscles quivering in his belly and noticed the twitching at the corners of his lips, and I knew that he was trying not to laugh.

Genevieve? he called.

He looked past me toward the door he'd been heading for. I couldn't decide whether to go forward toward my bedroom or back toward the stairs, but then I heard the bedspring creak and the squeal of Mom's door on its hinges. I turned. The top third of her leaned into the hallway — her face, a shoulder and a pale breast.

Jesse, go into your room for a minute. Clay, you better come back and get your clothes on.

Her voice rang in my ears, metallic. It was the voice she'd used when she emerged from her room after a day or two of hiding out, a voice meant to prove she was still a force to be reckoned with. Warily, like strangers meeting on a narrow sidewalk, Clay and I stepped forward, but we moved instinctively to the same side and my shoe touched his bare toes. We both recoiled, then tried again, this time sliding on past each other. My mind told me, *Don't look back* — but ducking for my door I looked anyway and saw the narrow white clutch of his buttocks.

Pressure built inside my head, and I tried to contain it, pressing my palms against my ears. My chest felt unnaturally light. I focused on my breathing, drawing long even lungfuls, imagining the oxygen ascending in soothing bubbles to my brain. Then Clay's voice came to me through the wall, his tone low and teasing.

What he said was, Can you believe our luck?

I couldn't make out her response, but he laughed then, which brought to mind his fingers and the way he'd held the washcloth almost daintily in front of himself. I imagined Mom in her bed, bare feet keeping time to Led Zeppelin, and the kitten, Lydia, squirming in her arms. I saw Clay threading his white legs into a pair of pants.

From the bottom drawer of my dresser I plucked two brass .30-30 cartridges. They were long and sleek and felt cool in my fingers. I went to my closet, lifted my rifle from its place in the corner and thumbed the shells into the magazine, then levered into the chamber the round I intended for Clay.

I stepped into the hall and shouldered the rifle. Blood roared in my ears.

Almost immediately Clay emerged. He was backing into the hallway, tucking his blue denim shirt into his jeans and mouthing something to Mom. Then he glanced over his shoulder, saw me and swung around. His expression turned from playful to dead serious, as if he'd been instantly infused with every bitter drop of spite I had for him. He looked like a dog that's been caught chewing on a table leg and knows what he's going to get. He put his hands up in front of his face, palms flat, fingers spread wide, and peeked at me through them, his eyes squinched, readying for the blast.

It's a film clip that comes to me at any time, night or day, usually when I least expect it, and when it happens, I have to stop what I'm doing until it passes. I might be eating, walking, reading or driving — it doesn't matter. I might be standing at the front of my class, explaining an assignment or offering some bit of advice about how to sharpen a thesis or read a poem, and I simply have to stop and close my eyes, facilitate the dream, let it roll on over me — Clay standing there peeking at me through his fingers, as if that might protect him.

To his credit, he didn't run or cower — I think because he knew he had it coming. I could see in the set of his face that he understood: now he was going to die. Mom's in the picture too, at the very edge, holding a bedsheet around herself as I get ready to put down her new man, and she's taking the time to tuck and fold it just so, like it's some kind of a sarong. The kitten skitters from the room and disappears down the stairs. Sonny's howling in the basement. I line up the bastard in my sights, my uncle, take a bead in the middle of his forehead, just above the line of his brow, dead center. My heart flutters. Remembering Dad's advice, I tell myself, *Okay, just reach out and touch him with your finger.* I'm calm, same as when I shot the spike buck on that first morning that I carried a gun into the woods. Dispassionate, as a hunter is supposed to be. I want to kill him. I have no misgivings. I can feel the cool metal kiss of the trigger on my finger as I start to squeeze.

Except something happened then that I didn't expect. The image changed, like on one of those hologram pictures, a baseball card, for instance, where the batter swings as you shift your angle of vision. Suddenly, I wasn't looking down the barrel at Clay anymore, I was aiming at myself instead. It was *my* face in the iron sights, a little of Dad's rugged fat maleness and less of Mom's good looks, but *something* anyway that Christine must have seen, some potential — me — and it made me want to cry. She'd been right in what she'd said. I'd be killing myself too, at least the part of me she had decided for, the part that lived in her. I remembered her words to me in the car as we headed for Mass — *I wouldn't want to be with someone who'd do that* — imagined her standing now in Mom's place and watching the bullet explode through my skull and spray the wall behind me, my body folding up and dropping like an empty suit of clothes. And so to save myself — to save myself for her — I put down the rifle, dropped it alongside me and let the butt of its stock come to rest on the floor.

Here's what I wish had happened next, the way I'd write it now if I were making it up. I wish I'd held off. I wish I had let Mom come over and take the rifle out of my hands, level it at Clay and shoot him dead. I wish she'd been capable of doing that. In a single moment she could have saved me the burden of killing him and laid it on herself instead, thereby achieving at least a measure of dignity. There would have been symmetry in that — justice, poetry.

But that's not how it happened, because when I lowered my rifle, Clay's expression turned, just like that, from fear to insolence. He straightened up and puffed out his chest. He sniffed the air and curled his nose as if disgusted by some smell. He seemed to forget himself, forget his act, and stood transparent before us, the skull beneath the flesh. Mom watched him, transfixed. She stood there, her mouth half open, like one of the blind beggars newly healed by Christ.

Mom, I said. He killed Dwayne too. Don't you see?

I could tell that she did by the way she turned and blinked at me.

Clay, meanwhile, couldn't seem to move. He looked stuck in time. He stared straight into my eyes, and his lips worked the air. Finally he spoke. He said, You son of a bitch. I told her what you did last night, what you tried to do. She knows about you. She knows.

Tell me, I said to him. Did you kill Dwayne too?

He shook his head. No, I swear to God, he said. He jumped. Loyal as a goddamn dog, you know that. He never would've crossed me.

Mom shuddered and broke loose then. She came over and touched my shoulder, put her face right up to mine. She wanted to speak, but there wasn't time. I pushed her away and lifted my rifle. It was still ready to fire, the safety button showing red.

I shot him without taking aim, the sound of the blast blowing everything into gray silence, and Clay lowered himself under his own power, after first looking down at the entrance hole between his sternum and left shoulder — a dazzling red spot on his shirt — then turning and glancing behind as if to see where the bullet had gone next. That's when I saw the exit wound in his upper back, larger than the spot in front, and messier. But like I said, he went to the floor, first to his knees and then backward on his butt. And the blood came fast. When he tried to breathe, he made the sound of a straw sucking up the dregs from the bottom of a paper cup.

What I remember next is the certainty of knowing what I had to do. Disinterested lucidity settled down on me like some kind of bewitching dust. The air almost sparkled. I brought Mom into her room, wrapped her up in her heavy corduroy robe, then took her downstairs into the kitchen — she allowed herself to be led — and sat her at the table. Then I went outside and started the Mercury. I backed it up on the sidewalk to the rear of the house, like Mom did when she unloaded groceries. Only a foot or two separated the trunk — which I opened now — from the porch door. The rain fell steady and hard even as the latest round of thunder moved east. It wasn't yet two in the afternoon but the sky was almost as dark as night, and green tinted. Upstairs I found Clay as I had left him, lying on his back and staring at the ceiling. Except now he was silent. I nudged his foot with mine. I bent over and waved a hand in front of his eyes. He didn't flinch or blink. I don't remember having any trouble at all as I hoisted him up and over my shoulder. His head bounced against my lower back and his legs stuck out front as I carried him down the steps and through the kitchen to the back porch.

At the table, Mom hid her face, lifting a hand like a blinder.

On the porch, with Clay draped over me, I looked to the right and left — to one side, our garage, to the other a stand of spruce trees walling us off from the neighbors. And straight ahead, of course, Crow Lake, choppy today and green like the sky. I kicked open the door, negotiated the steps and dropped my uncle's body into the Mercury's roomy trunk. Somehow one of his silver-toed boots caught on the trunk's latch and, impossibly, sprang free and landed in the yard. I scrambled for it, pounced as if it were a living thing trying to get away, and wrestled it back on his foot before slamming the trunk lid down.

It all sounds terrible, I know, and there is worse to come.

At the front closet I stopped for a pair of light cotton gloves, put them on, then sprinted back upstairs to my room and took from my dresser several more .30-30 cartridges. I drove out to Clay's place, headlights on, wipers going, and turned in at the birch grove. I met no cars on the way, or none I recognized. It was hard to see with the rain and the low dark clouds. As I drove, I went through in my head the phone call I'd have to make that night, the one in which I'd tell Christine what I'd done and then listen to her silence as she absorbed the news and recognized what it meant to her — as she hardened herself for the future. Regret lay on my heart like a cold hand.

In Clay's gravel driveway I parked and unloaded him, lugged his stiffening body to the lawn beneath the giant cottonwood. The bleeding had more or less stopped. I laid him out in the grass and arranged him there, fifty feet from his front door, faceup, as if he'd been looking toward the house when shot, and fallen backward. Then I walked inside — it was unlocked — and went down in the basement and found the bolt-action .30-30 he'd showed us: his alibi gun, the rusty one. It was leaning against an old wardrobe, in plain sight. I put two cartridges in the magazine and jacked one into the chamber, hoping the old thing actually worked, and then walked out to the barn.

There were cats in there, six or seven of them, what Clay would have called barn cats, in various combinations of orange, white and black. I picked one out and shot it, same as I'd seen him do that time on the Fourth of July. I ejected the spent shell, stuck it in my pocket, fired the gun once more and left the empty shell from the second shot in the rifle's chamber. I picked up the dead cat by one leg and carried it outside and laid it next to Clay beneath the cottonwood.

Then I brought the rifle to Clay's front stoop and leaned it up against the metal handrail, steel barrel against slick metal pipe. I did this carelessly, as if I were Clay having just murdered a cat beneath my tree and about to pick it up now and toss it in the lake. I leaned the rifle against the railing and then nudged it forward, toward Clay's body, so that it clattered down hard against the wet concrete steps, hard enough to jar the trigger had the gun been cocked. Finally, I took the spent shell from my pocket, the one left from the round I'd used on the cat, and tossed it into the grass beside the stoop for someone to find. I stood back and surveyed my work:

Barn cat beneath the dripping cottonwood, head mangled.

Ejected shell in the grass beside the stoop.

Clay on his back, chest-shot, eyes open to the rain, lying beside the cat.

Fallen rifle with spent cartridge in the chamber.

And I thought, *It will do. It will have to do.*

At home Mom had been cleaning. She'd scrubbed the blood from the floor and was pouring a bucket of water into the toilet, flushing it away. I located the bullet in the wall — in the corner near the door to the attic sauna — and dug it out and filled the hole with toothpaste. The empty cartridge was still in the rifle, which she had laid on my bed. I ejected the shell and placed the rifle back in my closet. My clothes were bloody, and so I took them off and cut them into rags no larger than baby socks and put them in a grocery bag and burned them, along with a month's worth of newspapers, in the burning barrel down by the lake. I drove the Mercury into the garage and scrubbed out the trunk.

By the time Magnus arrived home from school that afternoon, Mom and I, speaking to each other matter-of-factly as we'd grown accustomed to doing, had planned our future: the auctioning off of the restaurant equipment as soon as possible, the sale of the Valhalla and the house and a move that summer to California, a place that sounded as likely as any other — plans we ended up following to the letter. What we didn't anticipate, at least I didn't, was the reoccurrence of her heart ailment and her death within the year.

But I've gotten ahead of myself.

I should tell you that Clay's death *was* ruled an accident. The *Battlepoint Observer* described the scene — and the most likely explanation for it — in exactly the way I'd hoped they would, in exactly the way Sheriff Stone described it to us the next day, standing at our front door, hands stuffed in the pockets of his pants, the knees of which were grass stained and wet, alcohol on his breath.

Can I come in? he asked. There's something I've got to tell you, but I think we ought to sit down first.

Tell us right here, Mom said to him.

And so he did, his eyes fixed on a spot somewhere above and beyond us. Clay, he explained, had been discovered that morning by the mailman, who thought at first that he was taking a nap beneath the tree. It appeared that my uncle had plunked another of his barn cats, doing this from the front steps. Then he leaned the rifle against the railing before walking over to dispense with the carcass. As far as could be determined, the rifle must have fallen on the concrete steps and discharged, killing Clay. Crazy is what it was. Freakish. A stupid gun accident.

Anyway, look, Sheriff Stone said. He didn't suffer much. Doc says the bullet clipped his heart. Didn't live long.

He reached out and put a hand on Mom's shoulder.

At the time I wanted to think of Sheriff Stone as an ally who, if he knew the whole story, would understand what I had done, sympathize. During the months leading up to our move, however, I had trouble meeting his eyes when I saw him on the street, half expecting a wink or, worse, some probing question. I can't help but wonder if he was simply unwilling to look at those things I hoped he wouldn't see. If he consciously spared me. I can't help but wonder if I'm in debt to him for the life I've been able to live. It troubles me, not knowing, haunts me in ways you can't imagine — and in fact remains a mystery almost as compelling as the one presented by my mother. That would fill another book.

What *had* Clay meant to her? How much, if anything, had she known about Dad's death? How far had she gone to rationalize Clay's innocence? Would she ever, with time, have been able to forgive herself? *Is* there such a thing as forgiveness, this side of the grave?

I don't know. I can say that Mom never confided in me and never submitted to my questions. I often think it would have been better if she had grabbed hold of the rifle, once Clay was down, and turned it on herself — because after that day she retreated farther into herself than even I thought possible. Practically overnight, her beauty vanished. Her chrome hair lost its luster, her blue eyes faded and her skin turned gray. Her bones seemed to melt. She began staying up nights, refusing sleep, as if to punish herself. She stopped listening to music. Stopped speaking, except to convey information. Stopped smiling. She flinched at any touch, even Magnus's, and as far as I could tell never ate more than a few bites at a time. She gave herself up wholly to packing our things and moving us west — maintained her energy for that, at least. Then, once we were more or less settled out here, she got sick. It was the same arrhythmic condition she'd had before, but this time she didn't fight it. I doubt she bothered to take her meds. Even the doctor described her progress toward death that December as a headlong capitulation.

Finally, for me, it was easier to watch her die than to imagine her living on as she had been: uninterested, blank, hollow, voiceless.

But I still haven't described the hardest thing.

Three days after Sheriff Stone's visit I drove down to Minneapolis in the Mercury. I'd repeatedly tried calling Christine, but there had been no answer at her aunt's house. I was frightened by how much I missed her, but more frightened by the prospect of seeing her again.

The sun was shining at last, the sky a deep spring blue that day, and when I got there, I drove first through the alley behind the house and took a quick peek in the window of the garage. Then I drove around to the front and parked in the street. Her aunt Clara met me at the door, arms crossed at her breasts.

Gone, she said.

Then why's her truck out back?

Clara glared at me so hard my scalp tightened. You'll have to speak with her here, she said, and backed into the house, never removing her gaze from my face as I followed her inside, where all the shades were pulled. It was dark and close.

Christine was in the living room, sitting on the couch where I'd had my dream about Dad, watching the same TV on which we'd seen the report about the body in Crow Lake. She looked older, drawn, her olive skin yellow and dull, her hair lying flat. She wore gray sweatpants and a gray sweatshirt, both too large for her — they must have been her aunt's. Her eyes didn't brighten when she looked at me. She didn't say hi. She didn't nod.

I sat down in the chair next to her, and Clara stood to my left, watching, fingers knotted together at her waist.

I told you I'd come back, I said.

You're not back.

We have to talk, I said.

We do?

Can't we go for a walk or something? It's nice outside. You can actually see the sun.

Next to me, Clara shook her head. You can talk right here! she hissed.

Christine, never one to take orders, popped to her feet, grabbed my arm and pushed me toward the door. Behind us, Clara sighed, then gave up.

For the first few blocks Christine was silent, and though I took that as an opening, a chance to make a case for myself, I couldn't speak. On the drive down I'd rehearsed it all — my demeanor, my tone and especially my lines: Clay, dead of an accident, just like they'd said on the news. I'd made an assessment of my soul and was certain I could carry the lie — at least for Magnus I could. Already I had begun to dig the hole that would hide it, a hole so deep I would forget it was there. Or so I told myself.

But Christine — I could see this already — she was another matter.

We came to a dead-end street, stiff brown weeds standing shoulder high in a vacant lot, a sign that said NO TRESPASSING, a chain-link fence blocking our way, the sound of water moving. A lot of water.

Right here, Christine said, and led me through a rip in the fence. We hacked our way through the weeds and came out on the surface of an old rail bed — ahead of us a bridge, and beneath it the Mississippi, wide, blue gray and shimmering. We walked out over it. To the south was a curving falls, and off on the other side of the channel a system of locks. Concrete piers and low steel buildings. The western shore was steep and heavily treed. Gulls wheeled above us. One set its wings and dropped down to perch on the rock-and-mortar wall of the bridge and commenced barking at us like a dog, before turning and diving out of sight. I imagined jumping up on the wall and releasing myself toward the invisible spot where the gull had disappeared.

Are you here to tell me you didn't do it? Christine asked. She had to lift her voice above the sound of the falls. That I'm supposed to believe what they said on TV?

I thought of that — but no, I said.

Then what are you here for? What do you have to say?

Christine pushed a rope of unwashed hair out of her face and tucked it behind an ear. I wanted to pull her close to me and squeeze her until she softened — but she was radiating a kind of magnetic force field, a repellent I couldn't overcome.

I said, Doesn't it matter how it happened? Don't the circumstances count for anything?

Listen to yourself, Christine said.

We were standing a foot or so apart, but now she stepped away and looked up at me as if to get a better look. Her face told me how disappointed she was with what she saw.

She said, First you come here intending to lie to me, and now you're talking about *circumstances*.

I'm here, though, aren't I?

You want me to congratulate you for that?

Look, when I left you at the depot, I didn't know what I was going back to. We thought he was dead, remember?

Fine. So tell me all about it, get it off your chest. Make *me* live with it too, that's just what I need.

In the days since I'd seen her, the bruises on her face had darkened. They were nearly black at the center now, then purple farther out and yellow at the edges, like the circle that surrounds the sun in a cold winter sky. The swelling was down, though — he hadn't done any lasting damage to her perfect lines.

She said, Can't you see? I pulled you out of that mess you were in. Or tried. As soon as you're free of me, look what happens. You think that's my calling? To keep you in check?

I pleaded with her, my stomach clenching like a fist. I said, Hey, nothing like this is ever going to happen again, and you know it.

That's not the point, Jesse. The point is, it happened, and you can't change it. I'm sorry.

I thought you loved me, I said.

I do love you. I'll always love you.

But you won't forgive me.

I *can't* forgive you, Jesse. There's a difference. Maybe if I came from someplace that was half normal I could deal with it. But I don't. I'm broken, and you're not the one who can fix me, because you are too.

I thought of the night in the Mercury, after we'd received Communion together, and how I'd wondered for how much longer I'd be able to convince her that I was the one who could give her what she needed for a happy life. I stepped back now and tried to absorb who she was, the beauty and goodness of her. Her weary eyes. Her lips, which, if only she would allow them to, could speak every word I needed to hear. I remembered the way she kissed, always tentative at first, shy before warming to me, and how her teeth always felt smooth and clean. I remembered the black-olive taste of her.

There was no reason to draw out the pain. We walked back across the bridge, traversed the high weeds, slipped the gap in the fence and followed the streets back to Clara's house. On the sidewalk next to the Mercury, with her aunt watching from the porch, Christine and I said good-bye, pressing against each other, chest to chest, waist to waist and knee to knee, trembling — at least I was — and crying, until I found the hardness it took to pull myself away from her, the steel I would need for the years ahead.

Driving off, I didn't look back.

V

UNDISCOVERED
COUNTRY

25

Whenever I'm sitting in a restaurant or shopping for groceries or, for that matter, teaching the first class of a semester, I find myself scanning faces for telltale signs: premature lines in the forehead, a mouth set against loss, eyes that look as if they've grown a protective film. Careful eyes. When I find them, a charge goes off inside me, and I have to wonder: What has *he* done that obligates him to guard his secrets so closely? Who has he killed, and for what good or terrible reasons? How deep are the holes he's dug? I wonder if his body out of some visceral urge to justice will betray him. I wonder who it is he's had to protect and what he has lost in the process. I wonder if he'll ever forgive himself. I wonder if he'll ever just give up.

It's a temptation, I know — one, over the years, I might have succumbed to if not for my brother, who needs me.

Magnus and I flew into Minneapolis yesterday and drove up in a rented car. Summer's exploding here: every imaginable shade of green, the smell of growing things bursting up out of the black soil, shining lakes scattered all around like imitation heavens. What my memory failed to hold is the prominence and persistence of the trees, the pines and birches and maples, but especially the pines, which surround the lake and stretch away from town's edge in every direction. There's a feeling I get of the forest pushing in and wanting to reassert itself, take root in the gutters of the roofs and the cracks in the sidewalks, infiltrate the buildings and pop up through the streets. It's easy to imagine this place a few hundred years hence, buried under layers of brown needles, decayed ferns and a sandy, acidic topsoil — all beneath the vault of the trees.

Battlepoint is still Battlepoint, we're finding. It hasn't changed much. Our old Lake Street house looks comfortable and solid with its rock-and-timber sides and shake roof. Part of me would like to knock on the door and ask whoever lives there to please let me have a peek inside. The part of me I've learned to listen to, though, is saying, No — forget it. The Valhalla building, still being used as a restaurant, has a new, stucco facade and also a Spanish name. Next to it, the door leading up to Dwayne Primrose's old apartment is hanging aslant and needs paint. Little Mexico, of course, is gone — at least the trailer houses are. In their place stands an orderly rank of bilevel homes, two streets deep, all of a single design, most painted in earth tones: brown, gray or green. A pleasant enough neighborhood, with picket fences and swing sets and lilac hedges. Bicycles and barbecue grills. On the mailboxes are names like Soto, Rodriguez, Ortiz, Gonzales, Diaz, Villareal. Also, Peterson, Smith, Hall and Fraser. I didn't see the name Montez.

Anyway, I think Dad would be pleased.

Magnus and I are staying in a cheap new motel on the strip south of town, where I'd reserved a suite with two rooms. Tomorrow we drive north to Winnipeg to pick up Magnus's new puppy, but in the meantime there's the matter of my class reunion: a picnic this afternoon and a dinner and reception at the VFW tonight. I'm not looking forward to it. In the booklet I was sent last month there's an entry from nearly everyone. Most of my former classmates composed a paragraph or two, a small gloat list: who they married, how many kids they have, what they've achieved in their short careers, that kind of thing. Exotic hobbies and trips, names of pets. I mentioned my teaching job but couldn't come up with anything else. I would have bragged about Magnus but thought it might sound strange. Christine had an entry too, even though she didn't end up graduating with the rest of us. She offered only an address and phone number in Minneapolis.

For two weeks I was distracted. Hadn't she ever gone on to Texas? Was she still living with the aunt I'd met? And what about her dad? Had she reconciled with him? Had her parents managed to stay together? What had she been doing with herself all this time? Her name was still Montez — hadn't she ever married?

Finally, though, I allowed myself that most careless of all indulgences, hope, and worked up the courage to write her a letter. Two days ago I got one back. It turns out she won't be here for the reunion. She's taking courses at the university, and final exams are scheduled for this week. She didn't say what she was studying, didn't say much of anything about her life. Not a word about her dad or mom. Nothing about Renata. She did include a picture, though, to show me, I suppose, what I lost — or what I would have gained through the act of grace I couldn't summon. She's standing in front of her pickup truck, the same one, though its body is smooth and covered over in a bright new skin of yellow paint. She looks smaller than I remembered, and her hair is short now, in bangs that cut straight across the top of her eyebrows. She's wearing a pair of glasses, nerdy ones, the same as Magnus wears — but her eyes haven't changed. I can still see a glow there, a light I can't help but feel is aimed at me.

I hope you'll consider coming to visit, she wrote. *But only if you think it's a good idea.*

I'm not sure if it is. Instinct tells me I'd be a fool to believe there was ever anything between us that would have lasted beyond the troubles we were caught up in. On the other hand, I might just kiss off my instinct. It's been good for me, having contact with Christine again. Hearing her voice, even on the page, soothes me. *I said a lot of things I'd like to take back*, she wrote — and I wonder if she can possibly know how her words, simple as they are, have thrown me off balance, caused me for the first time in memory to look ahead instead of back.

This morning as I write these words, the sun has already cleared the treetops. Soon it will heat up the asphalt of the parking lot outside my window, make it shimmer and wave. It's early, six thirty, and Magnus is still in bed. He's not sleeping, though — he's reading. Last night I gave him the manuscript, the whole stack of it, every page I've finished up until now, and through most of the night I sat right here on this couch listening through his closed door for any sound that might tell me what it feels like for him to learn at last what the source is of the sadness we've lived with, the silence that separated what I knew from what I told him. Every so often I heard papers shuffling. Once in a while a cough. About four o'clock, I fell asleep.

It wouldn't surprise me if Magnus has already figured out much of the truth about our story for himself. That would explain why he's been so quiet lately, so thoughtful. Why he gave me a hug last week for no reason. Why he sat hunched over his breakfast cereal yesterday morning, tears in his eyes, before we left to catch our flight.

In any case, I'm grateful to him for dragging me back here again. I have him to thank, in large part, for the dream that followed me to the surface half an hour ago and broke there like a buoy released from deep under water. I was standing waist high in a meadow of wildflowers and looking down toward a lake whose opposite shore was lost in blue haze. It may have been Crow Lake, it may have been the North Sea, I don't know. But a ship rested in quiet water down at the edge of it — a Viking boat half in and half out of the shade cast by a line of pine trees. Dad was standing up inside the curved prow.

Over the years he's continued to visit my dreams, coming to me from who knows where — always tormented with his wounds, and always more diminished. I may have avenged his death, but in doing so I certainly didn't free him.

This time, though, he was tall and straight, and every bit as thick through the chest and belly as he ever was in life. He was dressed in a blinding white tunic, tailored leggings and a heavy leather vest. A helmet with gold-tipped horns. Next to him stood an enormous black dog. For what seemed a long time I just watched him, his face dappled with tree-filtered light. I waited for him to lift his eyes and notice me. Maybe he'd wave me down to water's edge to join him. I wanted to see him up close, to see his head and face, which I could tell, even at this distance, were whole again. I wanted to talk with him, listen to his voice. I wanted to stare into his eyes, the left one of which had never, in all its years of use, settled its gaze squarely on me.

Then a breeze came up, rattling the leaves and snapping taut the sheet of his sail, and he looked up at me and laughed, gold fillings shining in his teeth.

He raised an arm in farewell.

His boat moved out upon the water.

Acknowledgments

This book has been long in coming, and the debts have piled high.

For gifts of money and time, I'm grateful to the Copernicus Society of America for a James Michener Award, and to the Minnesota State Arts Board, the Jerome Foundation, and the Lake Region Arts Council. For crucial, early encouragement, I'd like to thank my teachers at the Iowa Writers' Workshop, especially Jack Leggett, Susan Dodd, and Bob Shacochis. For their ongoing support, thanks to everyone at Minnesota State University Moorhead — colleagues, friends, administrators, and students past and present.

It's one thing to write a book but quite another to find a place for it. My thanks therefore to Devin McIntyre, my brilliant agent and navigator; to Mary Evans; to my editor, Helen Atsma, for her passion and clarity; and to everyone at Little, Brown and Company for their generous welcome and their professionalism: Michael Pietsch, Oliver Haslegrave, Marie Salter, Terry Adams, and Tracy Williams.

The world my parents gave me was one in which dreaming was acceptable — even encouraged — and my brothers and sister wandered through it with me. I thank them all. And I thank Leif for raising the bar.

Finally, for their love and perspective, I thank my beautiful family: Hope, whose instincts and inner compass have inspired me; Nick, whose unwavering faith has buoyed me up; and most of all Kathy, whose love and honest support, day in and day out, have meant everything. She alone understands the meaning and the cost.

About the Author

Lin Enger teaches writing in the MFA program at Minnesota State University Moorhead. A graduate of the Iowa Writers' Workshop, he lives in Minnesota with his wife and two children.